ABOUT THE AUTHOR

The only child of parents who worked at a top security psychiatric hospital, FRANCES VICK grew up receiving disquieting notes and presents from the inmates. Expelled from school, she spent the next few years on the dole, augmenting her income by providing security and crewing for gigs, and being a medical experiment guinea pig. Later jobs included working in a theatre in Manhattan, teaching English in Japanese Junior High Schools, and being a life model in Italy, before coming back to London and working with young offenders and refugees. Chinaski is her first novel.

www.francesvick.co.uk

Photograph by Anne Naisbitt

CHINASKI

Plus Support
AT
Paradiso
Friday 12th March 1993
Doors 7.30pm
Tickets 7.00 Advance   00163

FRANCES VICK

Cillian Press |

First published in Great Britain in 2014
by Cillian Press Limited. 83 Ducie Street, Manchester M1 2JQ
www.cillianpress.co.uk

British Library Cataloguing in Publication Data.
A catalogue record for this book is available from the British Library.

Paperback ISBN: 978-1-909776-08-1
eBook ISBN: 978-1-909776-09-8

Set Of Stage Light In A Theater Photo © Jolin - Dreamstime.com
Author Photograph © Anne Naisbitt
Chinaski Ticket Painting © Siân Hislop
www.sianhislop.co.uk

Published by Cillian Press
Manchester - United Kingdom - 2014
www.cillianpress.co.uk

For M, J and T

4th August 1993

The old lady has been outside all morning, wandering around the roses and adding fresh cat food to the welded remains in the bowls around the door. Eventually she heaves herself up the back stairs, through the kitchen and back to the front room where the TV is kept on at high volume. She rarely leaves this room, and sleeps in her chair. She hasn't entered the big bedroom since her husband's funeral seven years before. She will not enter the spare bedroom until the second funeral two weeks later, and then only in response to the confusing urgency of a journalist she thinks she might have known as a boy. He asks questions she doesn't understand while someone else takes photographs.

In the spare room there is no sound at all except for the insect ticking of a wrist watch. The watch is wrapped around the moulded wood handle of the bedside cabinet, next to a bottle of pills. It will tick for another two days, stopping only an hour before the young man's body is found.

* * *

Carl Howell died at a quarter to two on a sunny afternoon three days before the plumber broke the door down. He wore jeans and a t-shirt with future tour dates printed on the back. He had one Converse trainer on and the other was lying at the foot of the bed. Once his heart stopped, blood began to pool and stagnate. His body cooled. The side of his face, his right arm, the flung out fingers, changed from pink to red to purple to blue, and each hour his skin temperature dropped until it matched the temperature of the room. One eye stayed open, its dark pupil fixed. Inside his body, in the pockets and folds of the intestines, the chest, the bowels, he was still warm. Things were still alive in here – bacteria, enzymes, things that ferment and bubble and push up through the body, eroding it from the inside. By early evening, rigor mortis had set in and the blue patches on his body began to join up. Two days later, when the ambulance was called, the stiffness had left and he had just begun to soften and swell. A blackish stain spread slowly from the marbled veins. The ambulance crew took one look and called the police.

The older officer edged his way into the spare bedroom, and glanced at the body on the bed. His younger colleague was in the living room, negotiating with the old lady to turn the TV down. She rocked a little on the edge of her chair, her fingers scratching her knees spasmodically, and didn't respond. If the younger officer had looked he might have noticed that she was weeping. Instead he backed into the kitchen to use his radio to call the duty coroner, leaving her to the older man.

Turning off the TV, bringing round a footstool so he could face the old lady, he took both her hands and squeezed them slightly while looking at his knees. Once he sensed her raising her head, he looked into her eyes and smiled. She smiled too, squeezed back.

"Can I ask your name?" he asked quietly.

"My name is May," she answered. "My name is May Howell." She spoke carefully, like a girl, speaking a language only learned in the classroom.

"Can I call you May? I am a policeman. Can you tell me who the boy is on the bed?"

May started, her eyes widened and one tear slipped down her cheek. "He's Carl. He's my grandson. He's not been well. I told him to lie down."

"May, Carl is dead."

"I know that." She smiled proudly, as if she had answered a difficult question correctly.

"Do you know how he died? Do you know how long he's been there?"

May's eyelids drooped and her hands fell slack away from his fingers. "You should ask his friends. They'll know. They know more about him than I do."

"Does he have parents? We need to contact them."

May was tired now. She gestured to the drawer on the telephone stand. "Miriam's his mother. In the book. Bob's in there too. Bob Howell."

He nodded his thanks. "Can I get you a cup of tea, May?"

A grateful, girlish flutter: "Oh, yes! Three sugars!"

But she wasn't interested in the tea by the time he came back. He put the TV back on with the volume low. Then the forensic team arrived with the coroner and everyone forgot about her again.

It was a dizzying afternoon for May, hunched by the TV in the darkening room. First came the plumber, then the Nice Policeman, then more people, who spoke to the Nice Policeman. Then there were questions, some of which she almost understood, some she couldn't hear. At one point someone tried to turn the TV off but instead increased the volume, and May blinked at their angry reactions in the light of the screen. She discovered that she didn't want them to mention Carl's name, it hurt her. It made the tears come again, and she gestured anxiously at the spare bedroom door. She wanted to say, he's in there. He's sleeping. Be quiet or he'll wake up, but found she couldn't form understandable words. Then the Nice Policeman offered his arm, and helped her down the front stairs to a waiting ambulance, where a sweet-faced girl gave her a blanket and let her lie down. And then she was speeding away, so quickly it almost made her giggle, I have butterflies! she thought, and fell asleep again, warm, contented.

In the bedroom, professionals padded around the body, now examined by the coroner and headed for the morgue. The watch and the bottle were collected, the shoes bagged, the vomit scraped. Bags were put over the head and the hands. And eventually the body was lifted onto a lightweight plastic bag with a zipper running from bottom to top. Some hair caught in the top, and the coroner had to yank the zipper down to free it. Two detectives caught hold of the handles, and heaved the body onto a waiting stretcher. They moved carefully down the steep front steps towards the waiting van, straight into the path of Carl's parents, estranged for years, now suddenly reunited.

* * *

It was Bob Howell who called to tell Peter what had happened, about the plumber who had called the police. The old lady hadn't noticed, but she'd left a bathroom tap running and it had damaged the neighbour's ceiling so the landlord had sent him over to deal with it. She also hadn't noticed the smell seeping out from under the bedroom door; but the plumber did, forcing his way in, over her bewildered objections.

"They don't know how long he'd been there," said Bob. "They don't know how it happened. You know the ones to call up and tell, you know his friends. I've already told that nice couple who gave him his start, but the rest..."

So Peter called Chris Harris' pager, and when Chris called back he was in what sounded like a building site; men bellowed in the background, and Peter could hear a drill being turned on and off, on and off.

"I'm with that piece of shit band, Gag," said Chris. "They're doing some TV show in a button factory. That same one you guys did – remember? They made you all sell broken biscuits on that market?"

That memory irritated Peter: a Sunday morning music show aimed at teenagers and older viewers who didn't yet think of themselves as too old. A pert girl and her funnier male co-host interviewed up-and-coming indie bands and established acts more resigned to their own absurdity – all scripted insults and facetious quizzes. Sometimes they would go on location to a nearby kebab shop and make celebrities carve meat, or busk on the street to see if any passers-by noticed them. Or they'd take them paintballing and cut the footage to the theme from Platoon. It was a very popular show and Peter looked on it with an unexamined but pure loathing. Carl had said he liked it. Said it was a laugh.

He started lamely, "Look, I really think you should go somewhere a bit quieter and maybe sit down. It's about Carl."

"Wait wait, there's someone at the...door...just let me get rid of them... OK. OK."

"Carl died."

There was a long pause and Peter heard the drill again. Why would you need a drill in a button factory? he wondered. Maybe it wasn't a drill, maybe it was a button pressing machine, or something that makes the holes. He imagined the cramped factory floor, the intrusive camera crew, the sound people and the assistants, the runners. He imagined the factory workers amused, maybe starstruck; the sour monkey face of the funnier co-presenter. And he thought about the band, clumsily sorting buttons on the moving belts, wondering what good this was doing them, cursing their manager while putting on a brave face for the cameras. What everyone needed was a proper job really, a sense of self worth... when he had worked in the bike factory that summer...

He heard Chris light a cigarette, inhale and say, shakily, "Does the label know yet?"

"Yes, I think so. I think the police told them." Peter twisted the telephone cord around his wrist, waiting for Chris to make it better, to give him a plan.

"Don't talk to anyone. The press. I'll handle it. I'll be out of here in an hour, you'll be able to get me in the office by 4." And he put the phone down. Only much later did Peter realise that Chris hadn't asked how Carl had died.

The last call Peter made that afternoon was to Lydia, Carl's ex-girlfriend. By this time he was so depleted that he even considered asking her to make the rest of the calls – however inappropriate it might be. Lydia would be a lot better at it, he reasoned. She would make a point of being in charge, she wouldn't even try to respond to all the intrusive questions. Why was he there in the first place? How long had he been there? Where was the body now? Was there a note? Who'd told the label? Can I help you by telling the label? Eventually, each time someone offered to tell the label, Peter learned to count the seconds between telling them that they already knew, and the disappointed 'OK' on the other end. It was, he had to admit, pretty much the same disappointment he'd experienced when he'd asked Bob the same question a few hours ago. He'd been dreading calling her; not because he'd have to deal with the shock – he'd already made a dozen calls that morning – but because he just didn't like Lydia. Nobody liked her anymore.

But telling Lydia was the hardest, because she took it in an un-Lydia-like way. There was no music playing in the background when he called. Carl had once told him that she would press play on the stereo as soon as the phone rang, or there was a knock at the door, to give the impression that she always listened to music when she was alone. Today her voice was muffled and timbreless in the absolute silence of her flat. When Peter told her the news she said nothing, but he could hear her breathing shallowly, rapidly, like an animal. Expecting questions, hysteria, the obligatory offer to call the record company, instead he heard only her rasping breath, and then, "I'm not...I can't talk. I'm sorry."

He tried to sound like he cared about how she felt, while waiting for the sobs, bracing himself for Lydia's large, stormy emotions. "I'm sorry Lydia. I know that you still cared a lot for him, and..." and what? Lie? Say something like, 'I know he felt the same way'? No, that wouldn't do. But if a lie won't work, then what will? And he felt sudden panic – what can I say to this woman who isn't the woman I was expecting? How to handle this quiet stranger? And then he heard her bottomed-out voice say, "Thank you. I hope I can get to the funeral." Then the click of the receiver being replaced. That was the call that finished him. It was exhausting to feel so much pity mixed with such contempt.

Lydia

After she had put the phone down, Lydia sat perfectly still, breathing noisily. Her chest felt crushed, weighted. It was one of the few times in her life that she didn't feel as if she was being watched and assessed. She didn't suck her belly in, or practise smiling to disguise her crooked eye tooth. She didn't worry about her breath, roll a cigarette, pour a drink or pull her hair over her cheeks to hide what she thought was a double chin. She didn't notice how her bitten-down fingernails throbbed, how cold her feet were or how long she'd been staring at the floor. She didn't think of getting dressed. Once or twice the phone rang but she didn't answer it. "Carl's dead," Peter had said, and life had simply stopped for a while, and the room pulled in around her, like a cool, heavy shroud.

It was a long time later, dark, when she took the pills. Fifteen Prothiaden, all she had left, with a cold cup of tea. When the headache came on, she lay down on the sofa under the satin eiderdown her mother had always wrapped around her when she was off sick from school. Later, when she tried to run to the toilet, she stumbled against the door frame, banged her ankle, and was sick on the floor. That's where her mother found her an hour later, wedged up against the door, her head between her knees, limp fingers trailing in vomit.

They took her to the hospital, the same paramedics who had been called when Carl's body had been found. They took her to the same hospital where his body was waiting in the mortuary. She found this out later, and took it as a sign.

The practised hands of the paramedics opened her eyes and shone lights. They called her name and asked what she'd taken, looked for the empty bottle. As she was picked up by the shoulders and ankles her robe fell open and the large breasts that she hated so much fell under her armpits, her too-tight underwear barely held together by its popped elastic. Her mother sobbed and tried to pull the robe back over her, tried to tie the belt around her waist, but one of the paramedics spoke to her sharply and heaved Lydia out of the door.

In the ambulance they spoke to her, asked her mother to speak to her. They stuck something in her arm and rolled her to the side, placing her unresisting chin in a cardboard bowl, hoping to catch vomit.

"Darling? Darling?" said her mother, "Darling, I'm fastening your robe. I'm just going to fasten your robe now, don't worry."

Lydia was choking when they reached the hospital and the paramedic hurriedly shoved some fingers down her throat, "Passageway's blocked." They put her onto a gurney and rushed her into a curtained corner. More practised hands fed a thin tube up her nose. Her mother winced, and waited outside the curtain, clenching her hands together, bunching up the rings and trying not to listen to the sound of the suction.

Some time later, after they'd rinsed out her stomach a few times, pulled out the tube and dealt with the bleeding, they let her mother back in. Lydia was lying on her side with the robe clumsily wrapped around her; her mother tied it over one hip in a firm double knot. Dried blood stained Lydia's right nostril, her face was swollen and there was a carpet burn on her chin from being dragged up off the floor. She cried when she saw her mother, and they held each other awkwardly. Her mother, mindful of her silk shirt, rearranged the sweater tied around her shoulders and moved Lydia's head onto it.

"There's my darling. There's my darling. Who's my darling?"

"I am," a clogged choke.

Mother took her firmly by the chin. "What a silly thing to do darling! How did you make such a mistake?"

Lydia looked at her with dull eyes, "I didn't make a mistake."

"Oh yes you did." Her mother tugged on her chin to make Lydia nod with each syllable. When she tried to look down, her mother pushed firmly up again until their eyes met. "You must have done, darling. You must have been very, very tired."

"Carl died."

"I know, darling, I know. That's why I rearranged my afternoon so I could come and see you. I thought you might be in a funk about it."

Lydia began to cry again. Her mother drew her in and positioned her face onto the sweater. Lydia allowed herself to be pushed into her warm, Chanel-scented shoulder; the amber necklace digging into her cheek; Mother's voice telling her that she was just tired and needed looking after; Mother telling her what a silly mistake she'd made; Mother saying, "You'll bounce back, you always do."

She was to be kept on the ward until she'd spoken to a psychiatrist, and then overnight for observation. In a bed in the corner of a hot ward, she wanted to draw the curtains but the nurse who was changing the drip said no.

"You have to be in plain view. By rights you shouldn't even be in the corner, you should be second on the right or left so we can see you as soon as we come in to make sure you haven't tried anything, but we haven't enough space." She gestured at a large family clustered around an unconscious woman on the bed alongside, and an old woman doubled over on the edge of the bed opposite. "You'll be away soon if the psychiatrist lets you."

Lydia closed her swollen eyes and turned her head to the wall. Her throat and stomach were raw and her face throbbed. Why say all of that? Why did everyone have to know what she'd done and how she'd failed? She began to cry again, trying to be as quiet as possible about it, trying not to move. She was still pretending to sleep when the psychiatrist arrived.

"Miss Hunt, I'm Doctor Adler with the mental health team. Before we can let you go home I have to ask you some questions, and you really must be as honest as you can. Your family won't be given any information that you don't want to share with them. Wait – you are over 18 aren't you?"

"I'm 26."

"Brilliant, brilliant. OK, well this shouldn't take too long. Is it OK to call you Catherine?"

"I prefer to be called Lydia."

"Ok, Lydia. Can I begin by asking you why you did this?"

Lydia swallowed painfully and drank some water. "My boyfriend, my ex-boyfriend died."

"Boyfriend or ex-boyfriend?"

"Uh. It's a bit complicated. Ex-boyfriend, but we were still quite involved. We were still..." What? Still meant to be together? She was scared to express what she meant in case it came across as pitiful; some sad little obsession of her own. She didn't want this doctor to jump to the wrong conclusions, she couldn't trust that he'd have a sensitive and subtle enough mind to appreciate the situation. So she just said, "We were about to get back together."

Dr Adler nodded and tapped a pencil against the list on his pad. "So he died..."

"Yes." She felt herself beginning to cry.

"How did he die? Was it recent?"

"I don't know how he died. They didn't tell me. I don't know when it was. But it must have been recently, in the last few days."

"But you were close?" He frowned.

"Yes! Yes! We were very close. But certain people didn't want us to be together."

"Did you take the pills as soon as you heard?"

"No, I took them a few hours later, I think. I don't remember how long afterwards."

He made a quick tick on his list. "So in those few hours, were you thinking about harming yourself?

"No. I don't remember what I was thinking about. I don't think I was thinking of anything."

Tick.

"And did you call anyone to tell them what you were intending to do, or had done?"

"No."

Tick.

"Did you write a note?"

"No."

Tick.

"Do you live alone, or with friends?"

"I used to. I live alone now."

"Are you working?"

"I'm a self employed promoter. And events organiser."

Painfully, Lydia imagined the picture he was sketching of her – the cast off girlfriend, living friendless, alone. Possibly with a cat. A girl past her prime with nothing but a dead ex-boyfriend and a prescription for antidepressants to call her own. Some feeble stirrings of pride made her sit a little more upright against the stiff pillows. "It was a shock. I had a shock. But I honestly didn't plan this. I mean, if I had I would have taken more pills and locked my door wouldn't I? I wouldn't have planned to have my mother find me like that. I would have put some clothes on."

The psychiatrist looked at her politely, intently, waiting for more. Lydia was unequipped to deal with silence; she couldn't help seeing it as a blank page to fill with information about herself. Even when it was the worst thing to do in a situation, even when she dimly realised that others might find her irritating or dull, she would plunge on, explaining herself, declaiming. Most people, on meeting her for the first time, assumed that she was on speed.

"I live alone, because I enjoy living alone and because I keep different hours to normal people. I mean my work is different to normal work and I need space to entertain friends in the music industry, and so I can't very well live in a shitty shared house. I mean the assumption is always that a woman must either live with friends, which is fine when you're a student, but after that, they have to have a husband or a boyfriend to live with them, to legitimise them. Which is bullshit. Really. So, I make no apologies for that. And this whole thing," she gestured at the ward, "is really just a mistake. I oughtn't to be here –"

"But you are here. You took an overdose of antidepressant medication."

"Yes, but –"

"Are you telling me that it was an accidental overdose? Because I find that very difficult to believe. Do you have a history of self harm?" His pencil hovered over the tick box.

Lydia gave him the look she'd learned from her mother – a sudden straightening of the back; pursed lips and sucked in cheeks; widened eyes, astonished with just a hint of hurt. "I don't know what you mean."

The psychiatrist sighed. "You have six fresh horizontal cuts on your left forearm that look like they've been done with a razor blade. There's a couple of burns on your right wrist and a series of half-healed smaller cuts on your thighs. I'll bet there's more, but they're the ones the emergency staff noted. Judging by what they got out of your stomach, you haven't eaten for a while either."

Lydia lost the look and sagged.

"Look, I'm not here to catch you out, I'm here to assess risk. I need you to be honest enough with me so I can get you the help you need and let you go. Because I don't want to see you back here anytime soon." He drew something on his pad – a frowny face, it looked like. "Would it help if I asked questions? OK? We've established that you have a history of self harm –" he raised his hand over Lydia's feeble objection, "What I'd like to know now is if you've ever tried anything like this before?"

Lydia shook her head.

"And you say this was unpremeditated? OK, and it was because your boyfriend, ex-boyfriend, I should say, died. Had you been seeing him long?"

Lydia found the question difficult to take in. Had she been seeing him long? Had or have? The past was still so present for her. If Carl was dead then that left her stranded. She swallowed dryly. How long? Five years since they met; three since they broke up; eighteen months since they slept together; a year since that terrible time she saw him with the girl; the same since they last spoke. But times, dates, meant nothing, it was all arbitrary, because they were timelessly connected in a way that no-one could possibly understand. She thought of the time they'd cut their arms and mingled the blood in a giggling ceremony that became solemn – years ago now. They'd vowed that no matter what happened – whoever they were with in the future, wherever they were in the world – if either one got a phone call from the other, they'd drop everything and meet. They had swapped rings too. She had worn hers on her ring finger until he told her not to, while he kept his on a string around his neck, close to his heart. Nothing could keep them apart. He'd said that, she was certain. Or if not those exact words, then others that were equally precious. "We'd been seeing each other on and off for about five years," she said finally.

"Was it a supportive relationship? Was it something that you relied on?"

Was it a supportive relationship? No, probably not, viewed from the outside. Was it something she relied on? Oh Christ, more than anything! Years ago she had shifted all her ideas about her future, her sense of identity, onto Project Carl. It became her role to overcome his past, whip up his confidence, promote his ambitions, shape his future. Everything, everything was rooted in him, and since he stopped speaking to her, she'd learned to survive on miniscule nourishment. Someone mentioning him, reading old letters, looking at photos, could buoy her up for days. Who was there in the world who could fathom what this meant for her? Peter. Peter would. But he hated her now too, she felt it.

"Had you had contact with your ex-boyfriend immediately prior to his death?" the psychiatrist prompted.

"Yes," she lied.

A few weeks ago she had run into Peter at a record fair. Chinaski had just come back from Reading, and she'd heard that there was a chance of them touring with Nirvana. She longed to pump Peter for information, but he probably wouldn't be able to tell her anything, and anyway, he could be so negative about things. And Carl really valued enthusiasm. Lydia wondered how long Peter could stay in the band, after all the tension in the studio she'd heard about and after what she'd seen even earlier, on tour. Peter could be so amenable one minute, and then so mulish the next...so difficult to work with, and just at the time when the band really needed to focus their energy and get behind Carl.

When she saw him coming her way she smiled, but he mustn't have seen her, because he carried on past her stall, myopically studying the sleeve notes on an album. She called out to him. He could barely look her in the face. Probably he still had a bit of a crush on her; he had a few years ago. Carl used to tease him about it, and Peter had been distant with her ever since. She sparkled at him to help him get the courage to speak.

"So what's this then?" he indicated her stall. "You selling your stuff?"

"Yes. It's all going! I'll replace most of them with CDs though."

"You can't get much on CD. Some of this stuff is irreplaceable I bet." He drew out a few albums – Slint, Bitch Magnet; things she'd bought but hadn't really listened to. "You won't be able to get this stuff again. Did you keep them on tape at least?"

"Oh," she was breezy, "everything's going to be on CD soon, and I can wait." Peter muttered something that she didn't catch. There was an awkward pause. "How are things? Carl?"

Peter looked at the ground. "It's fine. He's fine."

"Really?" The great thing about Peter was that he was a terrible liar – very easy to catch out. You could break him with persistence. "Is he really fine? Because I heard..." she trailed off, waited for him to take the bait.

"He's been a bit moody. Down. I think he's tired more than anything."

"I suppose you've had a lot to organise..." Peter was trying hard not to respond, she could see him struggling. "I mean I imagine you have a tour to set up? And the album must be mixed by now, no?"

Peter shuddered; inexplicably she'd lost him.

"Well, we're always busy, you know." An embarrassed pause. "I've got to go now, actually, rehearsal."

And as he turned to go Lydia said, too loud, "We'll have a drink sometime. Is your number the same?" and she thought he nodded as he walked away, but couldn't be sure.

That evening, Lydia sat alone at home with a beer, when Chinaski's video for "Shattered", the one that was making them massive, came on the TV. She quickly stuck a video in and pressed record, hands shaking. It was the first time she'd seen it.

A simple idea on paper, it had been tricky to shoot. Filmed in a warehouse set up to look like a club, it was an ambitious idea, involving professional trampoliners, crash mats, wires and stunt men in dreadlocked wigs. Two extras were injured, and one was sick on the fake PA system. There was a thin gauze partition between the stage and the pit to allow for a decent matt shot; twice an overenthusiastic fan got too close, and tore it. From the opening bars the audience started jumping to the music and their jumps became increasingly, improbably, high. Small groups leaped, and on their descent, other, larger groups jumped even higher, until the whole crowd was jumping, higher and higher, their descent animated by slow-motion shows of rage, ecstasy or possibly vertigo. In the meantime the band stayed static, locked in by gravity, until, by the chorus, the sheer weight of the audience's enthusiasm, their gravitational pull, forced the band to jump in turn. The stage showed little swells, as if it had turned to half set gelatin, as Carl, John, and Peter, complete with drum kit, also bounced, rose in the air in response to the crowd. By the second chorus they were leaping so high that they had formed ladders of limbs, on one another's shoulders, leaning perilously forward towards the stage. The band, too, were drawn to the crowd surging upwards and forwards. By the end of the chorus it seemed as if they would meet, touch, but then, at the last second, both audience and band were propelled apart by some unseen and malicious force. The ladder of fans broke and kids fell on their friends, boots in faces, hands outstretched. The band were slammed against the back of the stage in slow motion, drumsticks flying, hair in their faces, legs extended. And this happened again and again, faster and faster, until the end of the song; the audience struggling to get to the band, and the band being sucked in towards them, before being spat out against their own huge name on the backdrop.

* * *

Peter had found miming difficult, as had John, but Carl had had no trouble at all. He'd gone through take after take, being pulled backwards on wires that eventually left welts under his arms and around his midriff, with no complaints.

Carl had told Lydia about it. Well, not really. Not only Lydia. It was more like he was telling a crowd of people in The Bristolian and she was there at the back. They'd said hi to each other, though, she was sure of that. It was the last time she'd seen him.

Lydia watched the video again and again while she finished her can and opened a new one. She watched Carl being pulled back and forth, thinking about what it meant, what the message for her might be, and at midnight she began calling him, dozens of times. Perhaps he didn't live there anymore. Still, you'd think someone would answer if only to tell her that he'd moved out, or was away. She'd heard that now there was a way of finding out who had called you, you just had to call another number or something. Perhaps he'd already done that, realised it was Lydia calling and was stubbornly not answering. Or perhaps he didn't even know that she was calling, perhaps he was being kept from her by some jealous girl who was monitoring the phone. She tried to leave a few minutes between calls to catch the girl out, but soon couldn't resist heaping them one after the other – as soon as one rang out to a dead tone, she'd call again. Getting more aggrieved, getting more angry, lighting a new cigarette off the butt of the last one. And then, success! The receiver was picked up. It clanked and rattled, and she heard a TV, faint in another room, and laughter. Maybe from the TV? Maybe not.

"Is Carl there?" Lydia's voice was hoarse from shouting and cigarettes. She heard the TV sound, a door closing. Someone was there, not talking, but there was another rattle and a creak – someone walking away? And then the receiver was placed on something. She heard a record needle hitting vinyl with a jump, and at the end, the needle stayed circling, a pointless whump, whump, whump. A few hours later when she picked up the phone to call Mother, the sound was still going. No-one had replaced the receiver at the other end, and Lydia's line was blocked. She listened to the womb-like sound of the record needle going nowhere, until she slept.

She had thought about hurting herself then, after the record incident, but she wasn't going to admit that to the psychiatrist now or she'd never get out of this hospital. But she had thought of it. Kept it in the back of her mind, as a possible escape route. As the record went round and round she allowed herself to consider the idea that Carl was cruel. Not misled, not duped or unaware, but actively malicious. Why had they even picked up the phone? Why put on a record and why that record in particular? Only Carl knew what the song meant. It was a message, and the message said Fuck You, because that record was the only one that Lydia hadn't been involved in in some way; their latest album, their first for DCG. When Chinaski had been signed to Deep Focus Carl had run everything past her – lyrics (which she'd advise on and rewrite if necessary), song structure, the minutiae of what had happened in rehearsal time. She'd been in the studio for the first album and the second single; she'd booked them on support slots and briefly been on their first European tour. She'd styled them. What had happened, that she'd been abandoned?

For a while now, she'd noticed people she'd known for years distancing themselves from her. Her status was eroding. She wasn't invited to as many parties, wasn't tapped for as many favours. Since moving into her flat more than a year ago she'd barely had any visitors – Carl once, her parents, few others. The sofa bed she'd bought to put up visiting bands and entourage spillovers had never been used and the stereo system Carl had advised her to get was more often than not turned off. The volume never really got over 4 even when it was on. She'd thought when she moved in that she'd have to charm the neighbours so they'd let her get away with parties, but as it turned out she needn't have bothered. All those gig posters she'd carefully pried off walls in dank European clubs, lovingly ironed and had framed, what had been the point if there was no-one to see them? It was as if a meeting had been convened, and it had been decided that she was not to be included, wasn't even to be noticed much anymore. As much as she had struggled with this idea, it had never crossed her mind that Carl might have something to do with it. Until tonight.

* * *

A year ago, the time of that terrible party, that was another time she'd thought of hurting herself. She had actually hurt herself by burning her wrist on the grill. There was still an ugly scar there. She usually hid it with bangles.

DCG had thrown a signing party for Chinaski. There was to be a free bar, and an open invitation to all people employed or associated with Deep Focus. Wearing an uncomfortable black dress that she remembered fitting her better, army boots and her newly un-dreadlocked hair in what she hoped were cute pigtails, she arrived too early to be unobtrusive. In the past, no matter how early she was or how late everyone else was, she would always look and generally feel happy on her own for a while. Plus there would always be someone she was acquainted with or not, to talk to. But that ability had deserted her lately, and she wasn't on her own turf. Friends from Deep Focus hadn't arrived yet, and Lydia felt the drinks she'd had at home turn on her. There wasn't anywhere to sit down. She didn't know where the toilets were so she couldn't hide in there until the room filled up, and she was too visible and exposed to just leave. She thought Peter had noticed her but he was at the bar talking to someone with his back to the room. There were some people taking pictures of a flurry of wise-eyed girls wearing clothes that were the fashion industry's idea of alternative. Still, thought Lydia, they look nice. And they fit. She tugged her dress down at the armpits and pulled up her tights so they'd flatten her stomach a bit more, took a deep breath and strode over to Peter, who was talking to – whatshisname? Chris Harris. The one who wrote the overwrought reviews and had been hanging around the band so much during the first tour. The one, she'd joked to Carl, who must be in love with him or something. Peter looked friendly enough, gave her a kiss, and a glass of actual champagne. Chris Harris lit her cigarette with a courtliness that made her relax a little.

"You remember Lydia? She was really so helpful to us at the start," Peter was babbling. "She was on the tour when we met you – in Germany, was it? She's been fucking brilliant really."

Lydia peered at him suspiciously. After all their bitching on that tour? After practically asking her to leave? And not even inviting her to the studio since? Then she saw the fleck of white below his left nostril. Oh well, if he was going to say nice things about her then who cared why? She'd keep an eye on him and follow him to the toilet to make sure he gave her a line.

Chris Harris crinkled his eyes and bared his stained teeth at her, "Yes. I remember. I think in, oh God, some horrible hole in Holland or somewhere," and he leered significantly.

Groningen. They'd been in Groningen when Chris first arrived – she still had the flyer at home waiting to be framed. Now she felt frightened, because of course he remembered her. He knew that she'd had to leave the tour. Why hadn't she, as soon as she'd seen him at the bar, offered some rueful reminiscences of her own – something to make him understand that the way she'd been then was just a weird aberration. She tried now, hoping it wasn't too late, "Oh God! God, yes! Yes, of course. Wow. Yeah. You were covering them on tour weren't you? Yes. I was so busy misreading maps that I probably didn't get to speak to you!" She allowed herself the artifice of asking his name, and just for dessert, finished with a "...and you work for...?"

Chris Harris said nothing. Then, with a twirl of his stained fingers, he produced a wrap of cocaine and began chopping out monstrous lines on the bar with the edge of his bank card, handed her a rolled up note and nodded.

Lydia was used to speed. Coke was – well, an establishment drug, an insider drug, and she had no way of judging how big the lines were. They were a hell of a lot longer than the lines of nutrasweet-cut speed she sometimes shared with friends, giggling in the toilets on student nights. Chris' practised, balls-out flourish took her aback, as did the fact that no-one noticed or seemed like they'd care if they did. The coke hit the back of her sinuses and dripped down her throat, making her gasp.

Chris gave her another glass of champagne and edged closer, nudging one sharp elbow into her waist, just where her tights dug in. "You do look lovely. I wouldn't worry about it."

How kind it was for him to have noticed her discomfort, and offer his time and cocaine to help her out of it! She allowed herself a vague fantasy – what would it be like to go out with a music journalist? Less to worry about in terms of other girls...more bands to know...potential for travel, and it would help her career a little. He must have a lot of contacts. Maybe she could get into the same thing; she'd been good at English at school...she began to sparkle at him, but his attention was on someone else. With his head cocked and a smile waiting, he oozed through the crowd towards Carl.

Carl was wearing a t-shirt she didn't recognise, and some carefully distressed biker boots. Everything else was the same though; similar, anyway. The pale skin with the hidden freckles; the blonde, vari lengthed hair – fine hair, but such a lot of it, and always tangled. The sleepless smudges under the eyes. The long limbs, 'scrawny sexy', some reviewer had said once. He was carrying a fake fur leopard print jacket and she thought that that pushed the whole outfit into the contrived. Until she realised that it wasn't his jacket. It belonged to a girl – a slim hipped, fine boned beauty – who took it, and his hand, with equal possession as they were ushered over to a table. Carl passed within two metres of Lydia, but she couldn't tell if he'd seen her or not. Her view was hidden by Chris Harris, who was whispering something to him. Carl nodded, gave his heart-stopping grin. The girl smiled too; everyone around him did, it was impossible not to. As he turned, he let his grin level into a tight smile as he briefly faced Lydia. And then, with Chris Harris at one elbow, and the beautiful girl holding the other hand, he was out of her sight again.

Lydia found Peter and bullied him into giving her another line.

Finally some familiar faces from Deep Focus arrived. They were sorry they were late, was she OK? Shit, they'd never seen so many industry types! That guy in the suit with a freshly pierced eyebrow? He had to be nearly 35. This whole thing's mental. Some of them – I remember them from gigs before they went over to the dark side. No, no, there's nothing *wrong* with signing, so long as you don't sign all your control away. Sonic Youth got it right. But Sonic Youth suck now. Well, there were a couple of good tracks...no, no, there were no good tracks. Since Nirvana there's been a free-for-all. Seriously, we could start a band now, right now, and we'd get picked up in a month. And we'd get dumped in a year. Well, yeah...it's a bubble. It's a market. You can't blame people for wanting to make a bit of money. Fucking 10 years touring in a van for nothing – someone wants to pay them. What's wrong with that? But we can't pay out however much – what was it, 150K? I heard more. I heard it was more like 250. Well, it's not like we'll really know. I bet the band don't even really know how much. They have a 30/70 split I heard. It'll all go to shit if they don't earn out the advance anyway.

Every now and then, Lydia glimpsed Carl through the crowd, and fought the temptation to follow him with alcohol and more lines cadged from Peter. She was the grown up one here. She had been invited and wanted to wish him well as a friend, but, you know, if he wants to ignore that, that's not my problem is it? The music was loud, and people had to lean in close to hear each other. Groups eddied together, split apart and drifted to others. Just like life, Lydia thought – people are allowed to move on with no reason or evil intent, but just the need for something new. And they always come back. That's the main thing to remember. There's wisdom in crowds, in the study of crowds. Someone must have done a study on this, some PhD. But even if they had it would be a dry, academic, rats-in-a-box, because you can't really know anything, or come to wisdom, without experiencing it, while being outside at the same time, doyouknowwhatImean? You have to be on the outside, but still be inside to experience whatever it is you're studying, because otherwise you'll never know. The truth I mean. That things have a purpose without us even really being aware of it and maybe to look for the reason is the worst thing, like a watched pot never boils, you see? Because if you think you know the answer then you'll short circuit the route that the answer has to take to you. You Have.To.Just.Let.It.Be. Things kind of go in an orbit, and you can't interrupt an orbit, or you get, like, asteroids happening. It's like if you love something then set it free, because it will come back.

The people around Lydia would nod, hedge and peel off, to be replaced by others, strangers now. And Lydia was having a wonderful time. She and her mutable group would approach an A&R guy they recognised and start talking about the gigs they had in common, really getting them onside, and then get coke out of them, or at least a cigarette. And if it didn't work, they'd just barrel along to the next one. They started the dancing, crazy versions of the tango. Oh it was funny! No-one knew what to do with them! All those industry types. All those vampires. Charging up to the bar with Peter – or not, he wasn't there, maybe he's left – with some other people then demanding Things On Fire, drinking Sambuca.

When the crowd began to thin out, Lydia was having such a good time that she stayed. Balancing her drink on her laddered tights, letting it fall, hilarious! Hearing Chris Harris with his pockets full of ash and his brick red face, laughing laughing laughing with someone impossibly well groomed. Some girl. That girl. Very polished. But not real, no history behind her. And how can you have a future with no history? A future with Carl? How? And Lydia was moving towards them like a proud ship, away from her new friends, and her vision was crystallising into Polaroid-like snapshots, like walking through a strobe. She pushed herself between Chris Harris and the girl and began to sparkle sparkle sparkle. But underneath the sparkle (only Lydia knew) was real contempt, hatred for this girl, this thin, beautiful girl who had never been to a fucking gig in her life, not a real one anyway. This girl, who'd never hauled a PA about, who'd never printed up flyers or demanded the door money. This girl who had arrived a few minutes (or maybe more than that, maybe an hour?) ago with Carl. She felt sorry for this girl. She really did. Because he will turn on you, he will leave you. Because of the orbits. Because if you love something then set them free. And she showed her the scar on her arm. And then Chris Harris got up and Lydia fell to the side, struggling to get up, and someone took the girl away and someone else asked Lydia to leave. Sometimes she'd hear Carl's voice very near but when she whirled round he was never there. Someone told her that he'd left but she knew that was surely a lie – he was just here – so she went looking for him, only to feel hands, many hands holding her elbows and her fingers. She was grabbed by the waist and pulled quickly – too quickly – backwards. She felt sick and the strobe vision came back again as freezing air hit her. She was by a taxi – the taxi driver didn't want to take her, but whoever she was with said that they'd make sure she wasn't sick. If she was sick then they'd pay for cleaning. The taxi was on a bill – it was all paid for. Just take her away. Chris Harris tugged a pigtail as he pushed her into the backseat, waving her off, his stained teeth bared in a grin, "Kisses!"

Deep Focus

Before that terrible evening, since they'd officially split up, they'd still slept with each other – at first fairly regularly. Then he stopped staying with her all night, and eventually began leaving as soon as they were finished. They would meet as part of the same crowd in pubs – usually The Bristolian. They'd drink a lot, each with their own circle of friends, separated. But with each drink, gradually, semi-consciously, they would draw closer to each other while still talking to other people, and after a few hours, they would be close enough to speak nonchalantly while being buffeted by the crowd around them. Then Lydia would go to the toilet, hoping that when she left, Carl would be hovering about outside. Sometimes her prayers were answered and they would share a few drunken, meaningful words, and back in the crowd they would stand a little closer to each other. If their arms touched the hairs on hers would bristle. Her neck shivered when she felt his breath near her. They would go to the bar at the same time, casually but on purpose, and risk a significant glance. Lydia would leave right then, Carl would generally make his way to the other bar so he could leave without anyone noticing; and Lydia would be waiting around the corner outside, shivering with excitement and cold.

There was something almost satisfying about this complicity, it almost passed in her mind for real intimacy, and she never, ever, even in her darkest moments, thought that this was anything but temporary. It could only be a glitch that they'd laugh about in later years. All that sneaking around was stupid, but wasn't it sexy? Weren't they mad to think that they could survive without each other?

While he slept, Lydia tried not to; difficult, given the amount she'd had to drink by the time this elaborate dance had finished. But it was her only chance to look at him without upsetting him. His long torso was smooth and his belly was flat, and she would press her body into the small of his back and bury her face between his shoulder blades, stroking her top lip on the invisible soft down. She could kiss the back of his neck and nuzzle her nose against his ear. His face, slightly pugnacious even in sleep, his jaw faintly taut, was a marvel to her. When she saw the fluttering of his eyelids and knew he was dreaming, she wondered desperately what he was dreaming of, and would trace the line of his eyebrows to calm him. She could help him, ease him, without him even knowing it. She could indulge herself like this when he was asleep. No-one had ever loved him more. They couldn't have.

She never understood why they'd broken up. There hadn't been a definitive moment. She never knew what she'd done. She only knew that the people she'd known for years now, whose band she'd nurtured, didn't want her around anymore. Carl didn't want her around anymore.

It had begun to change during their first trip to Europe. Hastily scraped together by Deep Focus, to capitalise on the relative success of their first album, it was a real chore of a tour. Huge swathes of country had to be covered, and more dates were tacked on at the end, and edged into days when they really needed to travel. Support bands were mostly arranged hours before the gig, with club promoters putting up anything – tribute acts, their nephew's death metal bands, punk semi legends that everyone thought were dead and who everyone was embarrassed to see relegated to support slots. Still, Chinaski had a lucky break about halfway through, when they were offered support with The Jesus Lizard in Holland for four nights. And that's when Chris Harris first descended on them.

Previously so sure of her ownership of the band, of Carl, she felt herself being pushed out by this man who was better at talking to men. She didn't know the language, didn't understand the customs, and it had been frightening, disquieting, riding in the van with friends that were suddenly strangers. There were no girls working at the venues, except for a few intimidating ones with Einstürzende Neubauten tattoos and painful looking piercings, who manned the bars and were married to the club owners. She was horribly aware of the unsettling prickliness that would surface once Chris had drunk most of the rider, his pointed stares, his sarcastic diplomacy. He was very friendly with The Jesus Lizard, and when he arrived, she'd assumed that he was only writing about them, but as it turned out, it was Chinaski he was interested in, and Carl in particular. Lydia would find them together in the van, shrouded in smoke, smothering laughter when she slid the door open.

She'd tried to master her fear by pretending to be confident, but so often came across as shrill and strident instead. By Germany she was alternately sulking or trying to involve herself too much, dimly realising that both strategies were doomed, but unable to stop herself. She would work up courage for the day by starting to drink in the morning but then annoy everyone in the van by needing to stop all the time for the toilet. Relegated to map reading, she often took them the wrong way, insisting that she was right even when she was pretty sure she'd been wrong miles ago. And then she'd drink some more to cover the shame and embarrassment, and then have to make them stop the van again and annoy everyone even more.

Chris Harris rode with them, smoking his shitty cigarettes, grinning his dirty grin and sharing his stories that made the band snigger like children. Once, when Lydia had them heading over the border, he asked to stop at a garage, and came back with beer and the news that they had driven 150km in the wrong direction.

"I really don't think we should blame poor Lydia though," he said as he shared out the drinks, "she's doing her best."

Lydia, hating him, still took a beer.

The next day Carl and Chris opted to travel with The Jesus Lizard for a while. With them both gone, the atmosphere deteriorated into mutinous silence punctuated with comments that Lydia didn't fully understand but couldn't ignore. And then, finally, there was that business with the door, and Peter getting hurt. She knew she hadn't done it, and even if she had, she hadn't meant to. Carl had been the one lunging to open it anyway, she was sure, she was almost positive. Carl had opened the door and it had hit Peter in the face, and naturally, everyone blamed her. If she hadn't been drinking all day, she would have been more sure of the facts, more able to put up a defence. As it stood, they had all gathered about Peter and his smashed up face, throwing nasty looks her way, and it was so unfair, just unbearable. She gave up then, called up Mother, asked for some money to be sent, and took the first in a long series of trains home the next day.

For a while after she left Carl had called her every day. That fact was apology enough. He was lonely, he said. He missed her, he was homesick. She received a few short letters written on the back of setlists, a live tape, a Polaroid of his face and on the back in marker pen, 'All work and no play makes Carl a sad boy'. He told her about David Yow kicking holes in the ceiling with the heels of his cowboy boots; about a club in Berlin that served coffee instead of beer, and the spoons had little holes drilled through them to stop junkies cooking up with them. She heard about Peter shaving his head in a toilet in Hamburg, and how their driver abandoned them somewhere in the South of France. She heard about Chris Harris daring them to buy dwarf porn in some specialist shop he knew in Pigalle. She heard about some crazy girl who showed up to every gig and fingered herself distractedly throughout their set. He'd mentioned some major label interest Chris Harris had told him about. And always, always when he called, he sounded tired. There were parties – Chris was always organising parties. He didn't have time to be alone, to relax, to rest. But she wasn't to worry, he'd be home soon, and then they'd be together.

And then, suddenly, nothing. The calls stopped. There were no more postcards. She had to rely on press and gossip for news about him. She read a couple of live reviews and even called one of the venues to see if they knew where Carl was, but her French wasn't good enough to make herself understood. When Freida at Deep Focus told her that they were coming back, she ate nothing but apples for two days so she'd be thin, but the welcome home party was a disappointment. Carl wasn't there – he'd stayed with Chris Harris in France. Peter and John were tired and flat. They didn't meet her eyes. It was all so confusing.

To give herself a good chance of hearing any news, she began to hang around Deep Focus Records again. Freida and Ian, the owners, had gone from producing a fanzine of the same name, to putting out flexi discs of their friends' bands, to starting a label, sometime in the 80s, and soon had a sizable and appreciative following. Now, in the aftermath of Nirvana making the leap from also-rans to mega stars, Deep Focus was simultaneously attracting international attention in terms of its signed bands, and losing money like a leaking hose. Local talent, that would previously have automatically signed to them, now bypassed them, instead signing with a major (or a major's vanity indie label). A few other bands – old friends some of them – had been tempted away by large album advances and more comfortable tours with big names. And since Freida and Ian famously disapproved of formal contracts, they didn't have the wherewithal to check what promised to be an exodus.

The Deep Focus offices – an old two story building in what used to be the manufacturing heart of the city – was still a place of pilgrimage for visiting bands and fans though. She had even met Carl there, years ago, when he had a job screen printing posters and t-shirts in the basement. Lydia remembered seeing him around at a distance, hauling out the bins or leaving with hundreds of flyers to be posted on walls around the city. He could turn his hand to anything: fixing the photocopier, tuning guitars, driving to the airport to collect visiting bands (did he even have a driving licence? How old was he anyway?), breaking down drum kits, making deliveries to record shops. And always with the same quiet efficiency, and the same sunny and unassuming smile. Lydia hadn't really taken much notice of him at first.

But now it seemed that Carl was propping up the label. The unexpected but immediate success of 'Alloyed' brought them out of the red for the first time in two years, but Freida and Ian didn't seem to know where to go next. Now, they had Chinaski's EP on their hands, which was doing very well, despite woeful promotion, but no plans to follow it up with an album. Lydia was hazy on the details, but felt sure that a follow-up album was in the order of things, and in Carl's absence she felt it only right that she do some of his work. First to be dealt with was Peter; it was Peter she was really pissed off with. What kind of a person abandons his best friend in Paris? When he's exhausted, and needs support? And now Peter was back and doing nothing for the band at all. If Carl was here, he'd be making things happen. It would serve Deep Focus right if they signed to a major. Lydia didn't believe that major labels hoovered up original bands only to ruin them by bad marketing and neglect; there was no nobility in impoverished indie-dom. Look what happened to Nirvana: a nice, catchy, crisply produced album that went platinum. What wasn't to like about that? Carl (for it was really always Carl in her mind, not a band that he was a member of) could easily have the same thing if he wasn't being held back by the shortsightedness of Deep Focus, and by his sentimental attachment to Peter, a powerful, but unimaginative drummer with appalling dress sense. All those rugby shirts. She became more and more indignant on Carl's behalf, and eventually requested a meeting with Freida and Ian to discuss the situation.

Freida and Ian were rarely in the same room. There was always so much to do that they attacked the tasks separately; studio time to be booked, t-shirts to be ordered, printed, posted. The frequent rows between band members had to be refereed, drummers mollified, guitarists stood up to, singers scraped off bar floors. The building was a focal point for journalists, aspiring bands, casual dealers, wide eyed youths, and Freida and Ian were always on hand, always cheerful and always exhausted. Today they were sitting behind their shared desk, swinging on swivel chairs and eating doughnuts. Jam had dripped onto a few of the t-shirts they were inspecting, and Ian was scraping it off with the edge of a cassette cover.

"Lyds! Sit down, sit down." He pulled over a swivel chair with his foot, and sat down on the edge of the desk. Freida began piling up the t-shirts and putting them back in the box, humming to herself. "You sounded ever so serious on the answer machine, we were a bit worried, weren't we Fred?"

Lydia felt that familiar irritation she always experienced with her parents when their mood was in opposition to hers. "Well, it's not me that I'm worried about Ian, it's you two."

This didn't have as much effect as she assumed it would. Freida still kept up that maddening humming, Ian just looked at her politely.

"On the tour –"

"Yeah, how did that go? We were a bit worried to hear that you'd left halfway through. But then I suppose being trapped in a van that size with a bunch of lads isn't that comfortable, so I can't say I blame you. But..." Ian paused delicately, "it did leave us in a bit of a pickle with the t-shirts. I mean, you weren't there to sell them and so we lost out on some merchandise money. If, whatsisname – darling, what's his name?"

"Chris Harris," came Freida's voice from behind the t-shirt pile.

"Yeah. If Chris Harris hadn't stood in we would've been, well, not fucked, but – well, yes, fucked. But, as it happened, Chris whatsisname, him, being there for longer, actually worked to our favour. Look –"

He pushed a magazine at Lydia. A four page spread, with a huge headline: 'Chinaski Syndrome'. Live pictures of Carl, his backlit hair fanning out like a halo, hands from the crowd grabbing and plucking at him; strobed shots of stagedivers; a few phrases in bold print '...golden fissures of pure sound...a landmark in brutal beauty...rapturous meltdown of rock...squeezing your heart like a loved up boa constrictor...' She handed it back to Ian with a grimace.

"Yeah, I know I know, it's all a bit...over the top, but it's done them and us a lot of good. Anyway, it's all finished with now. So no harm's been done really. How are you?"

36

Lydia summoned up some indignation. "I left the tour, Ian, because it was a shambles. Really. The support bands were all over the place. One of them was an experimental *jazz* trio for god's sake. The venues were really substandard, very small, and sometimes there wasn't even anywhere for the band to stay – I mean we'd have to stay in the van, or at the club manager's house or something. Or actually at the *venue*. And then I saw how The Jesus Lizard were travelling – I mean it wasn't *amazing* or anything, but it was *better*. I mean, you have a very marketable commodity on your hands here; they're, potentially, a very very big band. Plus –" Unnerved by Ian's silence, his slight smile, she prepared to use her trump card, earlier than planned. "– plus, there's significant major interest in them. Did you know that? That's what I've heard, and if it's true, then you'll lose out. I really think you need to – well – consider your strategy. With the band I mean." She stopped breathlessly.

By now Freida was sitting on the desk next to Ian, both suddenly solemn. Ian frowned at his hands. "Lydia. How long have we been doing this? Me and Fred?"

"A long time. But –"

"A long time. Do you know how many tours we've arranged? Do you know that each and every one of those venues, that you found so objectionable, are steps on a well-worn path every band walks when they tour? Did you know that? No. Of course you didn't. I'll tell you. First you do them as a third support band, then as a second, and then, finally, as a headliner. Some of the larger venues – the ones they played with The Jesus Lizard – *you can only fill* if you've paid your dues with relentless touring over fucking *years*. Like The Jesus Lizard. That's how you earn your stripes. And, incidentally, that's how you also get a slightly better van and a chance at staying in hotels. Now, for Chinaski – a very new band – to have sold out some of these venues on the strength of one album and an EP no-one had heard much of yet, is phenomenal. So. If you think I don't know my business, then you're wrong. The band did very very well on this tour. The fact that you didn't think so proves your inexperience. Sit down now."

Lydia sat down.

"Carl begged me to let you on this tour and I agreed because it would keep him happy and help us out with the merchandise. But you didn't do your job, Lyds. You didn't stay with Carl and you didn't sell our stuff. Now I wasn't even going to mention any of this to you, but you decided to come in here and tell me – us – our job. And I can't let you get away with that."

Lydia stood up again, trying not to let her tears spill over. She still had one piece of ammunition. "If you've been managing it all so well, how come you'll be losing them to a major?"

"That's what we wanted to happen, you silly girl!"

Here Freida stepped in. "Lyds, here, dry your eyes. You shouldn't get so emotional about things. Look, we were approached by DCG a few months ago about buying out the contract. We decided to hold out until this tour was over, and the EP found its feet. The publicity from Chris Harris has really helped our position. Really really helped us. We spoke to Carl and the rest of them a few days ago, and everything should be handed over within a month. So, really it's all worked out for the best."

"You'll lose their future though. They're going to be huge."

"Well, we've thought about that," Ian said. "We own the back catalogue. We own the rights to the demos that the new album's likely to be based on. So we'll get a percentage of any future royalties. This is what I've been telling you Lyds, we've been in the business a long time, and we know what we're doing."

"We assumed you knew," said Freida quietly. "We thought Carl would have told you."

She hadn't known. And Carl had been back for days. She hadn't known that either.

Freida signalled to Ian to leave and gently closed the door behind him. Pulling up a chair she sat in front of Lydia and gently squeezed her hands.

"Lydia, what's happened between you and Carl?" Lydia shook her head helplessly. "I'm asking because things seemed to have changed so much since the album, and since this tour. You were so happy together, and it made Ian and me so – well, relieved really, that Carl had someone to care for him, someone with their head screwed on, who we trusted. But something's changed now, I can feel it. Ian's right, we were happy about major interest, and we still are, for the band as well as for us. But I can't help thinking as if it's the end of an era or something, And you two having problems, well, it's just heartbreaking. I know that it can be hard for a woman to be really included in band type scenarios. Believe me. I've done my time touring, and it's harder for girls. It's so macho, very exclusive. I did worry about you a great deal. Ian was upset about the t-shirts, but I think he was also upset that you left the tour – felt as if you had no choice. It meant that there was no-one there to deal with Carl, and you know what he can get like without guidance. It all goes to his head. Have you seen him at all since he came back? No? Well, it's almost like he's not the same person. Or more like the person he was when we first met him when he was a boy. You remember the pilfering that used to go on with the t-shirts? And the petty cash? That was him. You didn't know? Oh yes, that was him. But he was so young. And coming from that background...that horrible father. We thought that keeping him with us, keeping a close eye on him, would help. And it did, didn't it? If he feels safe, if he feels trusted and, well, supervised almost, he's at his best. But when you left the tour we lost track of him. Peter was upset because Carl was late or drunk – and you know he can't drink. He shouldn't. And Chris Harris – I mean he's done us a favour with the publicity – but I don't trust him. I don't feel he's the best person to be around Carl, do you? Ian doesn't agree, but I think he almost wants to get rid of the responsibility, for Carl I mean. Oh I know that sounds awful, and he probably doesn't even know it himself, but I think he's had enough. So, in a way, you were my last hope." She smiled wanly.

"I'm sorry...I just felt so...excluded. It was just so awful."

"I understand even if Ian doesn't. But he will. I'll talk to him. I think that maybe no-one could have kept an eye on Carl that closely, and maybe we shouldn't do it anymore. It's too big a job for one person. He's an adult, after all. And maybe he won't grow up until we – me, Ian, and you too – cut the apron strings. Maybe this Chris Harris guy will take over now, not that I like that idea, but maybe it's not my business anymore. Maybe you have to take care of yourself now, Lyds. Finish your degree? You should take care of yourself."

"How? I love him. How?"

"I don't know darling, I do too."

And so the two women worried and fretted. Later, they found ways to meet and discuss their worries once neither of them saw Carl anymore. They worried themselves sick right up to when the body was found.

* * *

"Do you have close friends to talk to if you ever feel this depressed again?"

Dr Adler wanted to wrap this up, Lydia realised with relief. He wants me to go home. And she thought, not of her flat, but her old bedroom at her parents' house. The thought of going home, of being a child again, was comforting.

"Yes," she answered firmly, "yes, I have friends I can talk to. But nothing like this will happen again, I'm sure."

He pushed his notes together with his index fingers, "You have too much to live for Lydia, to do something like this again. I'm sure you know that. We'll keep you in for the night just to see how your system's clearing, but you'll be discharged first thing tomorrow."

That night she dreamed that she was five years younger and none of this had happened, and when she woke she felt happy; but quickly, reality pulled back its arm, knocked her flat again, and the tears came. She felt a tapping on her back and turned to see the large, gentle face of the father from the family next to her – surprisingly close. He spoke in an unfamiliar, guttural language, smiling. The whole family turned away from their unconscious relative and they too were smiling beautiful, kind smiles. Lydia felt her fist being opened, felt something placed in her palm and looked down – a nectarine.

The father leaned in close, "It good," he said and smiled, nodded. The rest of the family broadened their smiles, nodded, and Lydia nodded, smiled, and closed her eyes. When she opened them, the family had gone and she still held the nectarine.

When it was time to go home, the nurse found her sitting up gazing at her open hands.

"What's that?"

"It's a nectarine."

"You can't eat it you know. You can't eat anything until we say you can."

"I don't want to eat it."

The nurse eyed the nectarine with irritation, "Can you put it down please?"

Lydia put it carefully in the expensive leather nightcase her mother had brought. When she was discharged she was given careful instructions to see her doctor as soon as possible, eat only soup and drink only water. Instead, Mother gave her a Valium and a brandy on the daybed in the sitting room and they watched some version of Wuthering Heights on the TV together.

Lydia stayed at her parents' for days, not knowing if it was day or night, taking Mother's Valium and trying to keep quiet and still because movement, speech was shattering. She'd never felt anything like it before. The grief didn't come in gentle waves, but vast black tsunamis. After an hour of feeling nothing, the sudden choking slap of grief would beat the breath out of her. She found herself talking to herself, or pleading, and sometimes speech would fail altogether, leaving only heavy, whistling gasps. Sinking down into corners, she could briefly feel small, safe, and protected from the need of others to know that she was Coping Well, and the crushing weight of Being Fine. Sometimes it wasn't the first thing she thought of the second she woke up, and what a reprieve those first few seconds were. But then it all rolled back in a scummy flood, this grief, this horror, this fear. Because now she was alone, and no-one could understand the depth of that loneliness.

41

Now she had to change but wasn't equipped to change, wasn't entitled to change because change is a betrayal and she must stay strong and firm in her love. It's what Carl would have wanted.

Carl and Lydia. Lydia and Carl. It was meant to be. It felt right, because it *was* right. And she hadn't always been this way – needy, desperate. At the beginning, at the beginning, well, Lydia had been a force to be reckoned with.

Punk looking girls who knew about music were rare. There were some who flirted with temporary dreadlocks, carefully hair-sprayed in on a Friday night and brushed out on Sunday. A lot went the goth route – the easiest of subcultures to master, and the most open to disdain. There were older punk women, the old guard, with bleached rude-girl hair. They could be name checked and respected at a distance, but the idea of going out with one was frankly terrifying, and so Lydia stood out. She was tall, slim and straight-backed. She walked briskly, purposefully, looking you straight in the eyes. She spoke fractionally too loudly. She changed her hair a lot and was always just ahead of the curve. Before crimping stopped being generally accepted, she switched to dreadlocks, and when dreadlocks became more mainstream, she began to bleach and dye hers, piling them up into a giant, multi-coloured bee hive. In fact, Lydia was the first white person with dreadlocks who was allowed in the Rastafarian pubs – this at a time when none of her set knew any black people at all, and were terrified of this being discovered in case it meant they were an inadvertent racist. Lydia negotiated passage for her friends to come too, so long as they covered their dreadlocks with hats, hoods or scarves.

She was a fixture at Deep Focus, not drifting in and hanging around like so many others, but actively, vehemently present. With her degree on hold, she was already promoting gigs around the cheaper venues, or at the university where she could get a good rental rate. Bands on Deep Focus were automatically steered towards her to get a gig. Her influence didn't stretch much beyond the city yet, but she was only just 20. At some point, she knew, she'd move into band management as well as promotion. At some point she'd move away from here all together. Mother wanted her to go into PR – "You'd be putting your skills to good use darling; you'd make some money too" – but Lydia had a genuine love of music, a real passion for it. She wasn't especially discerning – in her record collection Bad Brains would be next to U2, Rush beside the Minutemen – but her enthusiasm was one of the things that made her so attractive, so unusual. It was easy, when she was younger, to recast that humourless self regard as admirable confidence and determination. People liked her because of the strength she exuded, and the favours she could grant, but no-one ever truly found Lydia lovable; they found her admirable, and for a time she didn't notice the difference.

One morning, arriving at Deep Focus to collect some flyers, she found the building locked. A van door slid open and slammed, and Carl came trotting round the corner, with a huge set of keys. He avoided her eyes and smiled mutely at the ground when she tried to make small talk. His hands, turning the keys, shook. They walked through the dark building together, putting on the lights and checking the answering machines. Carl's tangled hair fell into his eyes while he was struggling to pull out the box she needed from an overfilled cupboard, and, with the sort of peremptory gesture that was typical of her, she smoothed it away so she could see him more clearly. She saw startled blue eyes ringed with sleepless smudges and eyelashes like fine, dark spokes. She saw a blush spreading across taught cheekbones, and bright teeth glinting in a nervous smile. She saw his straight brows, the shredded, red mouth, and he was the most beautiful thing.

"Where do you live?" she had asked, and smiling, he'd thrown his arms wide, meaning Here, I live here. He was like a boy who had been left to bring himself up far from civilisation, in the woods maybe...a faun-like beautiful boy. Such a beautiful boy. That blonde hair like a tangled halo, that pale, flawless skin. His skinniness was beginning to merge into sinew after a few years now of loading vans, carrying

44

equipment, earning calluses, the odd scar, the marks of a life led. She saw the sudden shaking, worse in the morning, or later after no sleep. The long, finely shaped fingers, with one flaw, a crushed and twisted tip to the left thumb – explained sometimes as an accident, sometimes as his own fault and once as a result of his dad slamming it in the door. On purpose? Surely not. And Carl gave a shrug, a nod and a smile that could have been interpreted any way you wanted.

They were together in the empty building for two hours. Lydia talked, and Carl stared at her face without saying much of anything. Sometimes Lydia would ask him a question and he would respond, but haltingly, as if he wasn't used to using his voice. How old was he? A smile. Where was he from? A lot of places, but here for the last three years. Before that? A smile at the floor and a shrug. It didn't matter. He wasn't going to say. How did he know Freida and Ian? From gigs. He had a friend who had been here for a long time. He'd introduced them. What do you want to do? What do you want to be? And then a look without a smile, a direct look from a face that seemed older, grimmer, and for a moment she thought he wasn't going to answer. But then she heard him say something that she remembered later as, "Needed." They sat on Freida and Ian's scarred desk and gradually lapsed into silence, holding hands, and Lydia felt – complete. A weird feeling, like she'd come home. Like she'd been missing something and had never known it until it came back. Carl's warm hand in hers, the dented thumb awkwardly stroking her knuckles, the quiet soft rasp of his voice, it all felt – it all was – right. And she thought, I am for you, I will help you, and we will be together.

In her memory of that year, it always seemed to be summer, or cosy delightful winter. She spent more and more time at Deep Focus, becoming closer to Freida and Ian, who drew her into their Committee for the Preservation of Carl. He became the focus of so many well meaning interventions, late phone calls and hasty, worried conferences, and was particularly close to Freida. They could often be seen huddled conspiratorially by the photocopier or sitting on the back stairs sharing a beer. Sometimes Carl would be murmuring something that made Freida laugh, and sometimes it would be Freida who was whispering something urgent to Carl, her lips angled to the back of his ear because Carl rarely looked anyone in the face. He would stare at the floor, making it hard to work out if he was listening or not. He slept either in Freida and Ian's van when it was warm, or on a mattress in the basement when it wasn't. He had his pick of leftover t-shirts, which he always wore with the same jeans that had ripped and ripped again so that Freida would have to patch them weekly – eventually Lydia took over this chore. He never seemed to notice what he was wearing, if he was tired, if he was hungry. He had to be reminded to clean his teeth, to take his medication, the physical things didn't seem to impinge on him at all – he lived entirely for Deep Focus, and in his unobtrusive, persistent way, he became indispensable. Freida needed him as a confidant; Ian as a gofer, a driver, an acolyte; Lydia, increasingly, as her foundation.

When someone converts to a new religion they achieve – however briefly – a kind of ecstatic calm, and being with Carl had this effect on Lydia. She seemed quieter and more considered, though in fact she was merely preoccupied. Sometimes, when she arrived at the offices, Carl would already be up having coffee with Freida. They felt like a family; they'd sit on the back steps, smoke and chat, listen to demos and eat toast. Then Carl would wander off to do his chores, and Lydia and Freida would get down to the serious business of fine tuning their care strategy.

"Carl needs to take his medication in the morning," Freida told her. "He really shouldn't drink – oh a beer or two won't do him any harm, but he can't take more, so he needs reminding of that. Once in a while his mum will call. Take a message and say that he'll call her back when he can – don't ever just pass the phone to him. We did that once, and it was...oh, it was just awful."

"And his father?"

"He doesn't know he's here. Him and the mum aren't in contact so he won't find out that way, but sometimes Carl will get the idea that he wants to call his dad. Watch out for that. If it happens it happens when he's had too much to drink or he's tired. He gets twitchy when he's tired, you'll have to look out for that too. I don't think he has the dad's number but just in case, try to get him on another topic until the mood passes."

"Is dad so bad?" Lydia was used to a soft, indulgent father.

"He's pretty bad," Freida twisted her face, "I've never met him of course, but the things Carl's told me have been...bad. Quite abusive. He's ex-army you know. A drunk. Wanted Carl to be just like him – lots of shouting, punishments. Didn't like Carl being ill – well, not ill, but, you know. Took it personally. I don't think they've seen each other in years, but whenever we've spoken about him you can tell that he's still scared of him."

"Are there any other brothers or sisters?"

"A half sister I think. Older. A lot older by about 15 years or something. He sometimes talks about her, but I'd tread carefully with that too. That all involves Miriam, his mum, and she's – tricky to handle. Look, you're not going to get all of it from Carl, he just won't open up, but it's only fair that you know some of this stuff. It will make it easier for you. Once Miriam knows that you're with Carl she'll get in contact with you. She'll be very nice at first – she *is* nice, or can be...I don't know, but she has a bad effect on Carl. She'll try to get you on side and then use you to get close to Carl – she needs someone to drink with and to get money from. I mean Carl doesn't have any money, but he always makes sure that when she asks for cash he can give it to her. I don't – but that's all over with now, you don't need to know that."

Freida trailed off confusingly. She lit a cigarette and continued, "I hate saying this Lydia, but there's a chance he'll try to get money out of you, and that's not his fault, it's all about Miriam. He lived with her when his parents split up, until he was 12 or something. And then something happened – I don't know what – and he had to go and live with his awful dad instead. Whatever it was that happened – well – Carl feels bad about it. Guilty. And so when his mum pops up being nice he leaps all over it and doesn't notice when she stops being nice and starts being manipulative. It's tragic really. He'll do anything for her. Like a kind of

47

penance. I do think, I really *do* think that she loves him. But her needs override his if you know what I mean. She's not *caring*. She's not a caring person. And he so needs someone to care for him. The epilepsy – Miriam doesn't believe he has it, so if he's with her she'll actively encourage him not to take the medication. It's hard enough to get him to take it in the first place, without seeming, you know, like his keeper or something. He forgets. Lyds, you have to be prepared to work very hard to protect him against all this – all this stuff. It's a big job, but then he's still so young and you're so capable that I really really can't think of anyone else who could do it."

And so the job of shielding Carl Howell from a harsh world passed from one woman to another.

Miriam hovered on the edges for months. Sometime Lydia caught the end of phone conversations, and sometimes came across letters written in an ambling scrawl across novelty note paper. "...you no that your the best thing that ever happened to me and I couldn't do without you. I'm so proud of you and your career and the life you've made. Even when you was a baby I new you was going to be important..." And at the end of each note there would be either a pitiful admonishment for not sending money, or dignified thanks *for* sending money. Carl got some kind of salary from Deep Focus, but it couldn't be much. When she asked him why Miriam needed money, the answer was always opaque: Miriam didn't need it, it was for Aunty Rosa. Aunty Rosa? Her sister, sister-in-law? Miriam needed the money to pay off fines; lend to a friend in trouble; pay off an old lady's gas bill. What fines? What friend? What old lady? But Carl would only offer a thin smile and look down at his shaking hands until the questions stopped.

They finally met by accident, at Deep Focus. Carl was in the van with a woman wrapped in cardigans and cigarette smoke. Lydia knocked, and Carl opened the door to let her in, but made no move to introduce her to the woman who was busy digging around in her handbag, pulling out tissues, till receipts, and broken lighters. Her fingernails, Lydia noticed, were beautifully shaped and well cared for, an odd conclusion to the squat, twisted fingers, now pushing a fresh cigarette into a smeared mouth. "You're looking at my hands," the woman exhaled, "I had the most beautiful hands. People said they were like a model's hands. And in fact, I was a hand model. And a croupier. You need good hands if you're a croupier. But all that dealing – hard work it is, dealing – ruined them. Arthritis." She offered her hand to Lydia with queenly graciousness, "I'm Carl's mum. His proud mummy!"

Lydia saw Carl shift and frown. Lydia gently shook Miriam's hand and got a hearty squeeze back.

"I've heard all about you, and let me tell you it's all good. It's *all* good. And I want to thank you for looking after my boy, because he does need looking after. And God knows I haven't been able to do it. They wouldn't let me do it. I've been put on the sidelines. And it's a terrible place to be, on the sidelines, watching your only child – well your only son and sons are special aren't they? – be turned against you..." – A tiny groan from Carl – "...Yes! Yes! Turned against you. Because addiction is a terrible thing, Lydia, it's a disease. And although I'm rid of it now I try to help others – others to..." she trailed off confusedly.

"And where do you live?" Lydia's voice sounded impossibly upper class to her own ears.

"I've got my own house now. They give you that if you're in need. And I am, what with this," Miriam thumped at her chest, "and these," she rapidly wiggled her fingers. "You'll have to come for a visit. There's quite a few of Carl's old friends, aunties and the like, who'd be happy to meet you, especially if you bring the prodigal with you. You'll have to drop in." Carl had ducked his head as low as he could and his hair covered his face. Lydia gently touched his knee and he took her hand, squeezing it spasmodically.

Miriam was still talking, her voice climbing the class ladder and getting louder at each rung, "And, son, I'd like to thank you for the loan of £30." She thrust a handful of notes at him, "Here it is back, like I promised you, because when I make a promise I keep it. Only there's a fiver or so missing because I had to keep some back to put in

49

your contribution to Aunty Kathleen's party."

Lydia glanced at Carl, who looked blank. "Party?" she asked.

"Oh Carl, you can be so...naughty, forgetful. He does it on purpose I swear. It's his Aunty Kathleen's party on the 5th. We've got it all set up, all the family will be there. All the old crowd. Got the big room at the Fox till midnight" – Carl still looked blank – "YOU KNOW THIS!" shouted Miriam with sudden violence, and then, just as suddenly, gentle, "You *know* this my darling, because we *spoke* about it last *week*. And you said you'd come along with the lovely Lydia so we could all make her acquaintance" – and Carl smiled – "There. I told you he knew. Sometimes that boy...he does it for attention. You know. God love him."

Miriam began to make a series of heaving shuffles sideways, "I'll have to keep a tenner," she reached out for the notes still in Carl's hand and took one, "because now there's the two of you coming." One last shuffle and she was at the door, fiddling with it, and swearing under her breath until Carl opened it for her.

In the silence that followed Lydia tried hard not to ask questions, knowing how counterproductive that would be. You got more out of Carl if you let him say what he wanted in his own time. "She seems nice," she allowed herself eventually, and Carl, sighing, tapped her hand indicating that they should go inside.

Over the next two weeks, Carl went through a series of brave advances and sudden, spooked, retreats. There were days when he would answer questions about his family – his mother's side of the family – easily and with humour, even, at times, with affection. One afternoon he showed Lydia a photo of a small boy, a younger Miriam and a frowning man standing next to a caravan on a desolate beach.

Lydia gazed at the boy's blurred urchin face, "It's you! Weirdly you haven't changed. Oh my God, you haven't! And is this your dad?" And as Carl's smile became hazy, she knew that she'd said the wrong thing. She didn't get any more information that day.

Sometimes he wanted to go to the party. Sometimes he was adamant he wouldn't go. Sometimes he affected to have forgotten about it. The phone calls from Miriam increased, as did the little notes. Carl borrowed some money from Lydia, swore to pay it back, and did, early. She assumed that it was for Miriam, but didn't ask. She thought about telling Freida about it, but decided not to. Freida would worry, she'd try to talk to Carl, give him advice, and Carl hated that. No. This was between Carl and Lydia. And if she could help him help his mum, well, that was a good thing, surely. Miriam was almost like a child herself. The whole scenario made Lydia feel mature and bountiful, and she enjoyed the frisson of immersing herself in the exoticism of the working class. She had begun to really look forward to the party.

That evening, Lydia dressed with unusual care. Piling her dreadlocks on top of her head, pencilling her eyebrows, she selected the tights with the most holes, the t-shirts with the most artful rips, all to intimidate and impress Carl's relatives, making them see how much he had moved beyond them. She anticipated the girlish admiration of his little cousins. She'd let them touch her hair, tell them that girls could dress any way they wanted and still be attractive. Lydia would be someone they'd remember, an exotic influence. Lydia's excitement transferred itself to Carl, who allowed himself to be slightly styled – a smaller t-shirt; the more artfully patched jeans. And then it was time to go.

Standing together at the bus stop, she realised that she rarely saw Carl outside of Deep Focus or her bedroom, and it was a novelty being together on a Saturday night, with normal people – dating couples, gangs of girls and half drunk office workers. She enjoyed the journey too, until the familiar landmarks disappeared, passengers from the centre got off and were replaced with a different type of person – very young mothers with too many kids; loud and unpredictable groups of men. Victorian buildings in various stages of disrepair slid past the scarred windows, followed by estate after estate, settled in their concrete nests, like decaying fortresses. While Carl lapsed into Zen-like silence, Lydia thought, this is where he's from, these are his people.

The Fox was a low, sprawling prefab of a pub, purpose built for the estate. Like many housing schemes conceived in the 60s, it had all the amenities that upper class architects assumed to be essential to the urban poor: a pub, a bookmaker's, a post office, a chip shop. They walked through the dank underpass that led from the bus stop to the estate, and Lydia took a deep breath as Carl led her through shadowy high rises, to the pub at the centre, and into a big room with a lot of clashing patterns on the walls and carpets. Terraces of men watched football on screens dotted about the cornices. The barman pointed them towards a bouquet of drooping balloons tied to the back door near the toilets.

In the back room, Miriam had really gone to town. Shoals of balloons clung to the picture rails. The tables, covered in wipe clean sheets, were obliquely set in clusters of three. Streamers and banners hung from the ceiling, most of which said 'Happy Birthday' but some were printed with 'Happy Anniversary' and 'Merry Xmas'. Miriam had gone for effect rather than accuracy. A fat DJ played snatches of earsplitting party tunes, trying to get the levels right. There was no-one else there.

Carl and Lydia retreated to the bar, and Lydia began to drink quickly and nervously, on edge, waiting for someone uncouth to start taking the piss out of her. Looking at Carl's calm profile, she wished he'd speak to her; she didn't feel confident enough to speak herself, in case her voice carried and her accent gave her away. Eventually however, these feelings receded, and instead she became upset that no-one appeared to have noticed her at all, so she slowed down on the drinking and tentatively turned to look around the room.

It was half time. The regimented rows of men broke up a little. She could see a few overdressed women amongst them, and a couple of dark, sultry teenagers who were adjusting their tops to show their bras and backcombing their hair in the tinted mirrors on the back wall. A blowsy woman in a tight blue dress came by and pinched their cheeks. A middle aged man wearing an orthopaedic shoe made an impossibly long order at the bar, and when he'd finished, nodded to Carl. Carl shook his hand, didn't introduce him to Lydia, and helped carry the trays of drinks over to the teenagers and the woman in the blue dress. It was a weird situation. They were all, presumably, related, but hardly a word was spoken. There wasn't a tense atmosphere, just one of bored companionship, as if they spent all their time together, and there was nothing more to be said.

53

The teenage girls – Carl's cousins – whispered, giggled and spent a lot of time going to the toilets to put on more makeup. The man with the orthopaedic shoe gazed into his pint, while the woman in blue pulled at her tight dress and kept up a monotone mutter aimed at the back of his head: Kathleen bought some shoes and wore them and took them back to the shop, Jeanette won on the scratchcards, her baby father was out of prison but the boyfriend was back in. More and more relations and friends gathered in the same corner, morosely waiting for the party to begin. No-one, after Carl's vague introductions, asked Lydia anything, or asked Carl anything, they just maintained their grim faced vigil, staring at the balloons on the back doors.

In Lydia's family, relations were properly delineated. There were no second-cousins-once-removed, no uncle's baby mothers, no aunts younger than yourself. When family members saw each other, at Christmas or New Year, it was in someone's home. Large, comfortable cars driven by large comfortable uncles splayed the gravel on the drive; kisses were exchanged in the hallway; guests were ushered in with smiles and drinks were enjoyed by the fire, or in the tasteful conservatory. Children were jocularly assessed as growing up just like Dad, or Mother, ambitions and hobbies were inquired about. But here, there was none of that. Lydia struggled to see any resemblance between Carl and these dissatisfied, lumpy people with suspicious eyes and aggressive attacks of humour. To see Carl next to them, so slight, so sensitive, so vulnerable, it made her hurt. This, then, was what he grew up with. She looked around this mean, low ceilinged room and vowed to help him up and away from here.

When the back doors opened and everyone filed in, though, people loosened up a little. True, the banter was crude, and there was no getting-to-know-you politeness, but the novelty of being taken as she was without having to resort to explanation was actually a relief. Lydia was used to explaining to patient, perplexed relatives just why she wasn't finishing her degree this year, why she had to have her hair like that, what she hoped to achieve. Listening to other people's peculiar narratives and knowing that hers wouldn't be the most peculiar, and wouldn't even be asked for, was relieving. There was also something attractive about the self sufficiency of the young cousins too – shamelessly drinking their MD2020s in full view of their mum, letting their skirts ride up to show their knickers. At Lydia's family gatherings Mother had always cajoled her into sober trousers and a loose t-shirt ("You don't have the legs for short skirts, sweet. And a looser peasant style top is much more flattering if you have larger boobs. Oh, don't get all haughty about it, it's true, and it's best to dress for your shape. You'll thank me for this later.")

As time went on, the party turned into a twisted version of a formal dance from a Jane Austen novel. Dowagers and young mothers sat at the edges in gossiping clusters, while the dancefloor and bar were left to the young singletons. Sugar-ridden children pulled at the banners, eventually ripping one down. A chain of women attached themselves to Carl, rubbed his head, tried to push up his chin, tried to make him meet their eyes, tried to cajole him onto the dancefloor, but Carl always refused, smiling, hunching his shoulders. The cousins, Roisin and Maraid, eventually succeeded, dancing and twirling around him like sluttish fairies.

Lydia found herself sitting between two women, one large, one small, both drunk, both discussing Miriam.

"...waste of money and where did she get it from?"

"It's nice, it's a nice thing to do. And poor Kathleen."

"Poor Kathleen my arse. Poor Kathleen should have paid for this herself, she gets enough from the social. Plus there's the kiddy money. That's why Miriam's doing this, all this. Kathleen's the golden girl with the social, taking in them kids and Miriam thinks she can do the same if she gets Kathleen onside. They wouldn't let Miriam foster, never never." The large woman's slack face quivered. "Never never. After what she did to her own? Never. I'd call up. I'd tell them a thing or two about her."

"Cora you wouldn't do that."

"I bloody well would, who had the boy afterwards? Me. Who had to look after him, after all that?"

"Bob. Bob took him." The small woman intoned with closed eyes.

"Before Bob it was me! They couldn't find Bob, so they got me. Two weeks and the boy couldn't leave the house! Had to eat at night he was so scared. Slept all day. I tell you. After that it was Bob. Bob didn't see the state of him first though. They should've locked her up."

"Didn't they? I thought they did?"

"He was too old, if he'd been a kiddy it'd have been different. He said it wasn't her fault. Said he just wanted to live with Bob. Scared. And Bob scrubbed up well, new suit, all that. She got off scot free I tell you that. She's got a nerve inviting me."

Lydia, included in the conversation via gestures and questions posed but not meant to be answered, hazarded a question:

"When did Carl leave home?"

"Not early enough. Not nearly early enough." Cora swelled indignantly at the recollection.

"When did they come back here?"

"When Bob left the forces. Five years?" the slight woman with half closed eyes murmured.

"Five years then. Or six. Yes. that would make him – eleven? Something like that. And they lived in – where?"

"Holmes Court."

"Holmes Court first. Yes. And then Bob got bad with the –" Cora mimed drinking, her little finger outstretched, "and then Miriam left with him, with Carl. And she moved in with me until the council got her her flat. A flat I helped her get, by the way. Lovely it was at the beginning. I even gave her one of my mother's nests of tables, never got that back. And she was there until after Carl got taken away, maybe still there. But I doubt it, after what she did the neighbours wouldn't stand for it."

Lydia's mouth was dry. "What did Miriam do to Carl?"

Cora let her eyes bulge melodramatically, nodded at her sidekick.

"She doesn't know – boy hasn't told her. Not surprised though, knowing what I know about him, God love him. Like blood from a stone. She went on holiday. She buggered off to God knows where with someone. For a few months."

"Two months it was," said the soft voice of the sidekick.

"Two months is long. For a kiddy. Not a kiddy but young."

"And who looked after Carl?" Lydia asked.

"She's asking who looked after him? Who? No-one. No-one. Nobody knew. Summertime, so the school didn't know, neighbours were away. No-one knew until they found him going through the bins next door. He was hungry. She didn't leave him any money, nothing. Leccy got cut off. Couldn't find Bob, too ashamed to find his family. God love him. They brought him to me, then Kathleen's. He would have stayed with me, but I'd booked Tenerife."

"And then what happened?"

"She's asking what happened. He hasn't told you anything, eh? He must be getting worse. Do you know he gets fits? Well, at least you know that then. He went to Bob's, to his dad's. Bob convinced them he'd stopped drinking, maybe he has."

"Says he goes to meetings," said the soft voice in the shadows.

"He goes to meetings. If he's stopped drinking fair play to him, fair enough. But I still say the boy would've been better off with me. I wouldn't have minded. Better off with me than with Kathleen and those slut daughters. Well, they are, look at them!"

"You're not his blood though, Cora."

"And neither are you! No-one is here apart from Miriam, and that's a curse if you ask me." Turning to Lydia: "To answer your question sweetheart, Bob took him away. Got him into school over there, and that's the last we heard until now."

"You're not related to him?" Lydia's head swam.

"Who Bob? Oh, Carl. No. But I feel like I am. Miriam is my late husband's first sister in law."

"And," whispered the woman in the shadows, "he's my step nephew. I was married to Bob's brother, Mick. Not Kathleen's Mick, the other Mick."

"And Kathleen? Is she his aunt?"

"Oh no. Kathleen...is she your cousin, Cora?"

"Second cousin."

Lydia closed her eyes and opened them a few times to try to clear her head. She looked for Carl on the dancefloor. Roisin and Maraid had wrapped him up in a Happy Anniversary banner and were grinding their crotches against his legs. He wore an expression of endearing helplessness. These girls were children – his (almost) cousins – they were just playing with him; but Lydia felt like taking them to the toilets to scrub their sluttish faces raw. She saw him accepting their fluttery kisses, she saw him allowing himself to be dragged off into a dark corner. He was laughing.

Cora whistled through her teeth, "Look at that, you want to watch that, they'll eat him alive if you're not careful."

Lydia was about to go and help him but their mother, Kathleen, got there first. She slapped Maraid on the behind and sent them both to the bar and wrapped herself around Carl. When Lydia got up, a soft voice behind her said:

"You should watch her too. Watch all of them with him. You need to keep an eye on him. They all love him."

Suddenly Lydia realised how drunk she was. The short trip over the dancefloor was like walking up dozens of shallow stairs and she had to touch stray chairs and shoulders for support. Kathleen, also drunk, was holding on to Carl's shoulders and nodding vehemently with each sentence:

"...happy you're here, haven't seen you in so long, we all miss you...part of the family. Love you..." and when Lydia swayed into view, Kathleen's narrative stream forked to include her: "...happy you've got someone now...got to sit down, sit down with me." She dragged up some chairs and set them in the middle of the dancefloor. The little cousins came back with a tray of drinks, setting it on the floor, away from Kathleen's swaying stiletto.

Kathleen stared first at Lydia, and then, warmly, at Carl. She gathered their hands between her own dry palms and squeezed them before dropping them in favour of her glass.

"I just wanted to say how happy I am that Carl has got someone to look after him, because he needs it and God knows we haven't done a good job at it. No!" – She held up her hand, warding off an assumed contradiction – "No, we haven't. If I'd had a boy I think he'd be like

Carl. People always said we looked alike, didn't they girls? When he was staying with us? If I'd been blessed with a son, he'd have been like Carl. Because you are like a son to me. I couldn't feel closer to you if you were my own son." Maraid rolled her eyes, sneaked a cigarette from Kathleen's packet, and took Lydia's lighter. "And you're good for him, I can tell. Miriam might have a problem with you, but I don't. Why should I? We don't own the boy."

"Miriam has a problem with me?" Lydia was hurt.

"Oh," Kathleen whirled her cigarette, "bugger her. Yes, she has a problem because she wants the boy to herself. After everything she's done she wants him to herself. If she had her way he'd be living with her and giving her his pay packet every week so she could piss it up the wall. She thinks you're too upper class for him too, she told me. Says you think you're above her. And I told her, we're all above you, Miriam! Over her head it went though. I'm more open minded. I've lived abroad. I'm not prejudiced. My partner's half caste, isn't he Ros?" Roisin nodded, yawned. "What I mean is, there's love for him here, but it's –" Kathleen frowned, trying to find the right phrase, "– it's fucked up is what it is. There's too much history. He needs a clean slate. We all do, don't we, sometimes? You're that clean slate, my love."

Lydia noticed Kathleen's urgent dry hand high on Carl's thigh; the giggling of the girls. She saw Carl's face completely absent of expression. She saw Miriam waving at them from the DJ booth. The drinks churned in her stomach.

Miriam had got hold of the microphone and the room shifted gear into silence.

"I want to thank all of you for coming tonight. I especially want to thank my big, beautiful son for coming all the way across town to see his Aunty Kathleen. He doesn't manage to see much of us, but when he does it's always a treat. A real treat. So, thank you Carl." Fond stares from the women, drunken cheers. "And, I'd like us all to wish our lovely Kathleen a happy birthday." A few people began to sing but Miriam carried on talking, "And, Kathleen, I know we've had our differences in the past, but you know that I love you, and so, with that in mind, I'd like to sing a special song now, with the help of the birthday girl." The guests geared up for Happy Birthday again, but were drowned out by the opening strains of 'I've got you Babe'. Kathleen was coaxed up to take the Sonny part, Miriam was Cher.

And then something strange happened. Kathleen, drunk and laughingly awkward, peering at the printed lyrics, was an average, normal, off key singer. She enjoyed herself, but would be happy to sit down again and have a drink. Miriam, however, was transformed. She became taller, almost willowy. Her ugly hands threw practised, nuanced gestures towards the ceiling, towards the crowd; full of pathos, filled with drama. Her strong, bold voice held the notes with confidence and relinquished them with good grace. She became, in three minutes, a star.

The applause was long and hearty. Miriam took it all in, signalled to the DJ, and settled in to sing another number.

Kathleen, giggling her way back to her seat, patted Lydia's knee, "I knew she'd do it! Bless her! She can never resist. Oh, but she's good though, you've got to admit it."

"Is she a singer then?" asked Lydia, dazed.

"Oh well, she was. Club singer, you know. What was the name of that band she sang with Carl? That cover band? What were they called? Leather and Lace! That was it. They did the circuit for a good few years when Carl was young, when they came back here."

The room was hushed and attentive now. Even the children sat quietly in the corners, and on their parents' knees, gazing at Miriam backlit against the DJ booth. Her ringed fingers reached up, up past the cracked ceiling tiles, towards the imagined stars. Her dewy eyes confessed, beseeched, submitted; her voice swooped and darted around the melody, and, just when it seemed to be heading out of control, returned to earth. Her feet, in sensible low heels, never shifted, it was all in the torso, in the arms, in the eyes and that wide gash of a mouth; the sound of an angry talent pouring out painfully in a run down pub at the edge of town.

Lydia looked at Carl and he looked just like everyone else. His hands hovered over his thighs, as if he wanted to reach out but was stopping himself. In the half light, with his mouth slightly open and his wide eyes, he looked startlingly like Miriam, or rather she looked like a ruined version of him. As Miriam reached out to touch an imaginary lover, Carl's fingers twitched, his eyes watered, his lips parted. The whole room breathed with Miriam, and as the last notes lingered and departed, the crowd sighed as one.

When midnight came, they had trouble getting Miriam away from the microphone. She and Kathleen stayed hugging and swaying with one another in the emptying room with the DJ packing up around them and Kathleen's kids tiredly ripping down the rest of the banners and balloons. Carl and Lydia had missed the last bus back into the city and had to get a taxi. Carl's hand lay limply in hers as he dozed, and she looked out of the window as they headed back towards more familiar streets, trying to put together what she'd heard and learned that night. It didn't make sense to leave your defenceless child alone. It didn't make sense to throw a party for someone you knew hated you, and then invite a whole crowd of other people you know hate you too. But then it also didn't make sense to love someone you hated, and there had been love there, between Kathleen and Miriam, between Carl and his family. There was an affection towards Carl and a vivid, intense yearning to do right by him. Carl was the damaged core of so much devoted activity.

The next morning Carl lay heavily asleep while Lydia took painkillers and made coffee, and showered. He stayed asleep despite the volume of Lydia's flatmates. His breathing was ragged and loud and when he didn't respond to strokes, prods, shouting and eventually shaking, Lydia began to panic and was about to call an ambulance. Then he'd opened his eyes, stopped making that terrible noise. He'd taken his medication, a double dose he thought, too late the night before on a belly full of beer. He tried to laugh it off, but it took him a good hour to calm Lydia down.

So, apparently, Carl was in a band – she'd never heard anything about it. Normally anyone in Deep Focus's orbit who even thought about starting a band would raise the idea of recording with the label first, just to hedge their bets; but even Freida hadn't known. Carl, ubiquitous and obliging, was nevertheless secretive. Sometimes he would disappear for a day, coming back with a new and jarring item of clothing – once an ancient Bowie t-shirt, once a fur trapper's hat. One day Lydia saw him driving the Deep Focus van through the city centre with two obviously drunk, obviously homeless people lolling on the front seats. Since he always arrived at the offices alone and never mentioned any friends, it was easy for Lydia to assume that he had just washed up on her shore, his past wiped clean. But this wasn't true.

Carl had mentioned his band casually to Ian, who told Lydia. "I asked if he'd be able to help me sort those t-shirts this evening, and he said he had a rehearsal. I said rehearsal of what, and he said it was his band. He said it like that, His band. Did you know about this?" – Lydia offered a non committal shift of posture – "Because I'd happily find some time at the rehearsal space for him, I told him but I'm not sure he heard me. Can you let him know?"

Asking Carl anything always made Lydia nervous, because it forced her to remember that there were still private pieces of him that were beyond her reach, pieces that belonged to an unknown past. He could also be prickly and, worse, distant if he felt cornered. So it was a surprise when he not only admitted to being in a band (and Ian was right, he referred to it as his band, only his band), but offered to introduce her to the rest of them and let her watch the rehearsal.

They arrived in an affluent suburb in the west of the city. Mock Tudor mansions sat side by side, a respectful distance between them, each with their own tasteful barrier against the outside world – wrought iron fencing, privets, and faux rustic walls. They stopped outside the last house on the left – this one slightly smaller than its neighbours, but still as large as the comfortable home in which Lydia had been raised, in an equally affluent eastern suburb.

Carl led her round the side of the house, down an iron staircase to a basement that was an adolescent boy's dream. A collage of posters, flyers, headlines ripped from newspapers, marker pen banter covered the main wall. A drum set was against the back flanked with two guitars on stands. An old sofa sagged below the small window facing a mute TV, and nestled in its springs was a gnome-like man with tattoos on his face. Lydia recognised him as one of the homeless people she'd seen in the van with Carl that time. The man tapped the ash from his roll up shakily into an empty beer can and nodded at her impassively.

Carl was full of nervous energy. He didn't make introductions, acting as if she must already know the man on the sofa – who later identified himself as Dom, offering her a solemn handshake. Carl made her tea and forgot to take the bag out of the cup; he put some music on – a tinny, badly produced demo on a cheap cassette. He rolled new cigarettes before finishing the one he already had lit, and Lydia began to feel uncomfortable. Had he taken his pills? Should she stop him opening another beer? No-one had spoken for a while now and the silence was only broken by Dom sniggering at something on the silenced TV. Lydia, uncharacteristically unsure of herself, was wondering what to do when a large boy in a rugby top and the beginnings of a beard walked heavily down the stairs into the room. He carried a record bag, and when he saw Carl and Lydia he grinned happily, shyly.

"Mate!" to Carl. And, "I think I know you from school – Catherine?"

Lydia, trying to ignore Carl's startled look, answered, "It *was* Catherine, but I'm called Lydia nowadays."

Peter looked blank, then, smiling understanding, "Oh OK. Lydia's a great name!" and Lydia smiled back despite her disquiet.

She didn't remember this boy from school. He would have been a couple of years below her anyway. But it was slightly alarming that he remembered her because how she was at school ran counter to her carefully crafted image now. As Catherine Hunt, she had been a school prefect, a hockey player and was heavily involved in the theatre club. She associated only with the richest and most confident girls – the princesses with ponies, expensive orthodontics, well preserved mothers and high powered dads. This was a necessarily tiny elite and other girls in this prosperous and sought after school, those who didn't make the cut to join Lydia's set, tasted a disenfranchisement that they were never to experience in later life. Those girls, middle-class though they were, were not *upper* middle-class, and the pain of knowing that they were not quite good enough led some of them to rebel against the elite that rejected them. One autumn term for example, there had been a campaign against Lydia, almost an insurrection. Nasty rhymes were written in lipstick on the walls of the girls' toilets. Someone had viciously slashed at her sports bag. And then, on a poster appealing for volunteers to help out with the school Christmas play (which Lydia was directing), the H of her surname and all of Catherine apart from the C was carefully tippexed out. It was the only time in her life so far that Lydia had been hurt and confused. It crossed her mind that if this could happen here in school, where she was queen, then it could happen anywhere. She decided to mitigate the chance of her name being used as ammunition in the future by swapping her first name for her middle one.

There was a lot of waiting about. Carl withdrew to a corner, tuning the already tuned guitars, and his energy seemed to have deserted him. Peter kept disappearing up the stairs and then coming back with more and more equipment. Dom stayed pinned to the back pillows of the sofa, his eyes screwed shut now.

"We're auditioning bassists today," Peter told her. "Carl met some guy at Deep Focus, and we have someone coming over who saw the advert at DiscKings. I think there's someone else. Dom's here to help out. So are you going to give us your opinion? You know your stuff."

Peter seemed very interested in Lydia, almost in awe of her, and kept asking her questions. It was quite flattering. Yes, she'd been promoting for a couple of years now. Yes she knew Ian and Freida very well; when they need help, a second opinion on things, they know where to come.

"Well, you'll be very useful to us then – we really need to get things off the ground now. Me and Carl have been doing this for ages now, but we always have trouble with bassists."

"That's 'cause most bassists are cunts," intoned Dom from the sofa, his eyes still shut.

"Cunts," Peter agreed, blushing.

The first cunt arrived a minute later. Chubby, on the wrong side of twenty five, and squeezed into scuffed leather. Lydia had seen him around the Deep Focus office mostly sitting on the back steps smoking weed when he should have been working. He mimicked the bassline from War Pigs and his features screwed themselves up into a repellent orgasmic expression. The second one never showed up and third guy was a slight, taciturn youth in clogs that Carl had got talking to in a record shop. He played a reasonable, remorseless bass. Carl murmured to Dom, who nodded. It was decided that the new guy – John – would stay, listen to the first track of the demo and try to play along with Peter and Carl. The tinny demo was played and played again. Carl duplicated odd whiny scraps on his guitar, John made a good fist of copying the unimaginative basslines, while Peter pounded away at his drum kit with remarkable aggression. Then they would suddenly stop and huddle together, muttering to each other. Carl would peer at Dom for a yes or no. There were more yes's than no's, along with cryptic comments:

"A bit Crimson," was one; and, "if you don't pull it together it gets pushed out," was another.

Carl nodded sagely, his face a blank, and Peter turned to Lydia with pain in his eyes. Eventually, when they took a break, Dom went to buy some more beers, and Carl and John edged into a corner talking guitars, he tapped Lydia's elbow, "What do you think?"

Lydia hedged, "I'm still surprised that Carl has a band, I mean he hadn't told anyone."

"Yeah," Peter was rueful, "Carl's like that. But I was so keen on getting you down here, you've been around, you know about music. I really, really wanted to get your opinion. If it was up to Carl we'd never record anything, probably. Just rehearse the whole time like we've been doing since school. He has Dom come over because he trusts his opinion, but I never understand what he says. Do you? So I told him, 'Get your girlfriend down here, you're always saying she knows what she's talking about, let's get her opinion.' I mean I need to know if I should apply for university or not, if it's worth staying with the music."

Lydia was caught between being offended that it had been Peter who'd invited her and not Carl, and being flattered that Carl was proud of her.

"I think what you're doing is OK," she began carefully, "but I'd need to hear more. A better demo definitely. And I haven't heard the vocals, do you have a singer yet?"

"Oh that's Carl."

Lydia didn't have time to hide her surprise. She blurted, "Carl? But he doesn't even talk much...I really can't imagine...he's so shy."

"Oh, he changes when he's singing. Really. It's really surprising, to people who know him. If I'm honest, I think that's the thing we have going for us, the vocals."

"Why hasn't he sung today?"

"With you here? It took me a month to get him to invite you."

That stung, but she made a quick decision, "Let me ask Ian if you can use their space to do a decent demo, that'll give me a better idea of where you are. And Freida would like to hear too, I bet."

Without realising it, her voice had raised. Carl stood frozen with his mouth open. His hands shook a little and his head bobbed slightly one two three. For a second Lydia thought he was having a fit, then realised that he was nodding, he was happy, and that he was frightened.

On the way back in the van Lydia talked. She'd been dying to give her real opinion for hours, but the lugubrious presence of Dom, and John's obvious nerves, had prevented her. She managed to keep quiet until they'd dropped off Dom at an urgently described corner – "the one where Angie was then...that one...near the green door. That time. YOU know" – and as soon as the door slammed shut she began.

From what she'd heard they sounded too much like two other bands on Deep Focus. They had to work on that. Peter's clothes need urgent attention – nobody should wear rugby shirts. And those baggy jeans! Carl, too, would need to invest in a whole new wardrobe, and she'd help with that. If the new bassist could be dissuaded from staggering about like a drunk then that would be for the best. All eyes really ought to be on Carl. And she really had to hear his vocals so they could work on them together before talking to Freida and Ian. At this Carl smiled.

But Lydia never did hear him sing just to her. The next day she swung into Deep Focus, and finding nobody in, left a note on Ian's desk: 'It's close to home, but I have a potential new signing for you. Can I have studio space sometime next week? Trust me, this might work.' Then she went back to her parents' to do her laundry and stayed overnight. By the time she came back, she had a nearly formed script in her head about introducing Carl's band to the label. In the last two days she had convinced herself that Chinaski not only had potential, but great potential. True, she hadn't heard the vocals yet, but vocalists didn't have to be good singers, just charismatic images with lung power, and even lung power could be taught. She allowed herself a pleasing imaginative montage: listening to the vocals and sensing something – a glimmer of greatness; a strenuous series of vocal exercises; a comedic series of styling sessions – Carl (and she supposed Peter and John as well, though they weren't as appealing to imagine) stepping out of changing rooms wearing various outfits running from the fey to the ridiculous. The final outfit (somewhat fuzzy in her mind) perfectly complementing his beauty, his otherness. And finally, the stage performance – or rather the backstage aftermath; the awe, the surprise – mousy little Carl coming good, and Lydia gathering praise, congratulations, envy.

After a while, waiting in the office by herself though, she became restless. She got up to find people, and almost ran into Freida in the doorway, along with Ian, Peter and the studio engineer, Mason, all looking excited. Ian was gleeful, holding Mason's elbow and demanding, "Who knew? Who fucking knew?" while the usually impassive Mason allowed himself to raise an eyebrow, crack a grin. And trailing at the back, his hair in his eyes, smiling a dazed smile at everything and nothing, was Carl.

They all tumbled into the office. Carl was wearing clothes she hadn't seen before – nothing outlandish or peculiar, but new, almost self consciously new. Normally he'd wear an oversized t-shirt, more like a robe, its sleeves reaching to his elbows with the ever patched jeans gone baggy at the crotch. Today, someone had given him (because he surely wouldn't have thought about doing it himself) a t-shirt that fitted his chest and clung slightly to his biceps. His jeans were slim, clinging, with artful holes at the knees. He had washed his hair and it looked lighter for it. It almost looked bleached. Lydia felt a wave of jealousy – something she'd never, ever in her life felt before. She hated the person who'd given him these clothes, whoever it was who'd arranged this without her, excluding her. She hated the person who'd taken her beautiful montage and re-edited it to make themselves the star.

Carl got ill after that, and she'd had to take him away. He needed her so much. For days in her room she'd coached him, encouraged him, fed him his pills and begged him to call Freida and Ian. "It's what you've dreamed of," she told him. "It's what you need. Don't you want to see what you can become?" And finally, finally, he'd gone back to the studio but wouldn't be parted from her, couldn't function without her. He owed it all to her, really. He owed everything to her.

Peter

After calling Lydia, Peter drifted around the city; a sentimental journey. First past the shop where Carl bought single cigarettes after school. He remembered standing guard outside here one drunken night, waiting for Carl to finish forcing the back window; he'd come back with bloodied knuckles and two dented cans of Stella.

For a while he sat next to the canal – on the bench where he and Carl had sat every Monday, pooling their money until they had enough for a much discussed and coveted record. They had agreed that any purchase should always be kept at Peter's house, because it would be safer there. Peter, of course, had a generous enough allowance from his parents that he could have bought an album a week on his own if he'd wanted to. But he'd kept this from Carl, telling himself that he didn't want him to feel poor and different, but of course, deep down, it was Peter who didn't want to feel different. Carl was always, effortlessly, cooler; and if playing poverty allowed some of that to rub off on Peter, well, there was no harm in that. Later on, when Carl had disappeared from school, and no-one seemed to know where he was (although there were rumours), Peter would listen to their shared record collection alone. He never knew until later where his best friend had gone for those two years, and to this day he didn't know why Carl hadn't let him know, hadn't stayed in touch. It made him angry at the time, hurt. He still felt hurt, when he thought about it.

The whole school knew Carl's backstory within days of him appearing at assembly that Monday morning. An army kid, six or seven schools, divorced parents, living with his nan. In this staunchly dull, middle-class school, any sniff of difference was intoxicating, and Carl, with his tangled long hair, his open, flower-like face, the obviously second hand uniform, well, he was famous right from the start, in large part because he really didn't seem to care about or notice other people. There were no finger holds on him; bullies had no traction. He didn't even need to speak to anyone at break time. Girls, even those who never normally spoke to each other, formed dense packs of distanced lust. Boys, even the hard ones who lived on the estate next to the park, gravitated towards him and held a respectful orbit, sometimes nonchalantly moving forward, asking a question, nodding to him in the lunch queue.

Carl had free school lunches. Normally this would make a kid a pariah. Even the poorest kids hid their shame by bringing in a lunch box, but Carl didn't seem to care or notice, and so he got away with it. In the second week Peter had come across Carl and Darren King smoking in the toilets. Smoking Darren's cigarettes. Darren-King-Of-The-Psychos. The only kid in school who was universally deemed a 'problem child'. Darren, whose violent whim could annihilate a kid's chance of ever feeling safe again. Carl, a practised smoker with the orange finger to prove it, was just taking his cigarettes, not asking, not saying thanks, and Darren was smiling at him with something like anxious hunger in his face.

After that, Peter began to notice more weird things about the new kid. His homework was one. He'd hand in reams of it, or nothing at all. They were in English class together, and whenever menopausal Ms Clancey asked Carl to read from the text, he would refuse in a blurry mutter that would have antagonised her if anyone else did it, but not Carl. Instead she would pass on the duty to Peter, who sat just behind. Similarly Carl didn't get into trouble when he had obviously not done the homework.

Sometimes Peter would linger, hoping to leave at the same time as Carl, maybe speak to him, but he never succeeded. Carl was always the last to leave, always spending time at the end haltingly answering questions in his indistinct way, listening quietly to Ms Clancey and drawing from his bag sheaves of paper. Or nothing at all.

Perhaps Peter noticed and concentrated on the new boy because his own way of life had recently been derailed. At the start of the year, he began to get headaches, migraines really. His vision crumbled into black at the corners, his lids weakened and trembled, and the pain would start. At their worst, the headaches lasted a day or more, and came with shakes and weakness, rolling in like a tornado, gathering nausea along the way. His father took him to every specialist he could find. His mother worried that he'd inherited her weak eyesight, and took him to specialists of her own, but they all came to the same conclusion: the headaches were severe, and inconvenient, but not serious or disabling enough to be worrying, and he would probably grow out of them. In the meantime sports were out, TV was to be kept to a minimum, and he had to carry his medication around with him all the time – a red pill at the first rumblings of pain; a yellow pill if and when it got worse. After three weeks off school he came back ten pounds lighter. He couldn't rejoin the rugby team and his parents had made a special request that he be allowed to stay indoors during breaks in case strong sunlight and jostling boys brought on an attack. In the space of two months, he went from popular athlete, to the kind of boy girls feel sorry for.

His parents felt guilty. They worried. He was their only child. They had nurtured the idea of him during the dark days of failed fertility treatments, and so far nothing had happened to cloud their sunny relationship. Somewhere along the line – perhaps even before he existed – they had convinced themselves that he was a physical boy, given to boisterousness and hi-jinks, and he played along with them, because he didn't really know himself what his tastes were and wanted to make them happy. If Dad wanted a rugby player, Mum wanted a smart brained lawyer, well, so be it. Peter loved his parents, was aware of how much they'd invested in him, and had no desire to disappoint them. So when they presented him with the somewhat bizarre present of an electric guitar, he happily accepted this, too, as something he had always wanted. It was, Dad explained, to help him get over the loss of rugby. It was also, Mum intimated, something to take out his aggression on. Obviously he had some latent anger, maybe even at them, for not being able to prevent the headaches, for not having perfect eyesight, for all of the half articulated assumed failures parents wall themselves in by. None of the doctors had said anything about loud noise being detrimental, and really, it would be good for him to learn an instrument. A loud-boy-violent instrument; the sort a rugby player might have. They even sound-proofed the basement.

Throughout the school year, the headaches lessened, settling into a predictable pattern: stress becomes pain. Peter had never before thought of himself as an anxious person, and truth be told he didn't really now, but the headaches said otherwise. Surprise tests in science summoned shakes and sickness; sitting too close to Lisa Pike, the girl he'd been placidly obsessed with since the first year, was now impossible. His vision would fissure and he'd rise unsteadily to drag himself to the nurse's room, spending the next few hours in isolated, painful misery. It was a surprise that one day he had company there.

One afternoon, in manageable pain, but with his medication at the ready, he pushed the nurse's door and ran into an unsettling scene that he didn't fully understand. A body shook on the bed, and the nurse's well-muscled shoulders strained against her tabard, pressing something down, hard. Without looking round or letting go, she shouted over her shoulder:

"Help me hold his arm down or he'll fall off the side!" – and when Peter hesitated – "Hold him down I said!"

Coming to the edge of the bed he saw the boy in his English class, in his art class, the boy who had the free meals, the new boy who everybody, Peter included, wanted to know. And Carl was shaking, wide eyed and pale under the panicked grip of the school nurse, saying something that she hadn't heard, but Peter thought he understood.

"I think he's OK."

"He's not OK, he's fitting, he's having a fit. Help me hold him down before he hurts himself."

It wasn't in Peter's nature to contradict an adult, but looking at the terrified eyes and now still limbs of the boy on the bed, he felt that he had no choice.

"Really, look at him. I think it, whatever it was, is over. I think he's OK now. Look at him."

Carl nodded vigorously, still scared, and the nurse took her hands off his shoulders and sat up straight. She pushed sweaty clumps of hair away from her temples, and wiped her hands on her tabard while Carl gained more control over his face, brushed his hair in his eyes and lay still.

"Did you bite your tongue? No? Dizzy? OK. You can't be too careful. Do you take medication? What? Valporal? Do you have it with you? Well did you take it this morning? Why not, if you're supposed to?" She was walking around now, trying to mask her embarrassment at assuming a grand mal from a minor seizure. She hoped Migraine Boy wouldn't talk about it, but Migraine Boy looked too sick to do anything. She got him lying down on the other bed, let him take his pain relief and left both boys together.

That moment, the moment when they were left alone, was, Peter recognised later, the most significant of his life so far. In the ten years since, Peter would be asked, and ask himself many, many times, what they had talked about that afternoon. Both of them lying in the small room on narrow beds, close enough to touch, close enough to hear each other breathing. Both of them now apart from the crowd, singled out by weirdness, by illness; the fascinating and the fascinated, both already content with their roles.

They compared notes on teachers, and Carl surprised Peter by saying some scathing things about Ms Clancey. They agreed that she needed a good fuck and Peter hoped his blush didn't show. They talked about books they liked. Peter was reading Kerouac and talked a little too long about On the Road, losing Carl's attention. Carl was more of a Clive

73

Barker fan, and he promised to lend Peter Books of Blood once he'd finished it. He never did, to Peter's secret relief.

Blowing cigarette smoke out of the window, Carl talked about music, which he seemed to know a lot about. There were, he explained, two types of performer. You had the worker type, and then you had the showman. The showman was someone like Iggy Pop, John Lydon, David Bowie. The worker type wasn't expanded on, because Carl wasn't interested. But the showman, that lit him up. The showman's job was to draw people in and push them away at the same time, because music should upset people, it should make people angry, but keep them wanting more. Peter remembered later that, even at the time, he'd thought that these phrases seemed oddly adult, rehearsed. A fourteen year old offering a sober but confused analysis of old rock stars – it was incongruous. But Carl seemed so certain, and Peter, his knowledge of music confined entirely to what his dad played in the car, was happy to agree with him. When he mentioned that he was learning the guitar though, Carl's face assumed a peculiar expression and Peter gathered that he'd somehow said the wrong thing. The silence grew, lengthened, conversational gambits were ignored. Peter felt bereft. And so when it was pointed out to him that, no, he wasn't a guitarist. No. He was a drummer, well, he felt so happy that they were talking again that he agreed. Yes, of course, that made much more sense. Of course he was really a drummer, he was that type. Carl played the guitar.

And so it was that Carl decided that Peter liked music, just as his parents had decided that he liked rugby. Carl urged music on him in various subtle and not so subtle ways. He introduced him to Darren King as his friend the drummer; he'd sidle up to him at lunchtime with a secretive air and a record bag under his arm, and Peter, prodded to take a look inside, learned how to make the appropriate response, the one that Carl wanted. It was in Peter's blood to acquiesce to what other people wanted him to enjoy, and so he learned. He learned to feel genuinely excited about coloured vinyl. He learned to listen to John Peel from 10 every week night, one finger poised over the pause button on his tape recorder, ready for anything that sounded promising. They began to arrive at school dark under the eyes and eager to compare notes and swap tapes. If it happened that they had recorded the same things, a feeling of deep kinship would come over them both, and they would nod almost shyly at each other, aware of how similar they were becoming, how far they were moving beyond their classmates.

Sometimes though, Carl was too tired and said that he hadn't been able to listen the previous night. Sometimes he looked as if he'd slept in his clothes, smelt unwashed, and he would hide his swollen eyes behind his tangled hair. In class, his heavy head would droop and he'd be asleep in moments. Peter assumed it was the epilepsy. They hadn't spoken about that since the fortuitous but peculiar day they'd met, and the subject was understood to be off limits; only once had Peter awkwardly suggested that Carl go to the nurse's room to rest, and Carl had shunned him, very obviously, for a week.

One time Carl disappeared from school without explanation. After the third day, Ms Clancey took Peter aside and showed him a note, dirty in the folds, the letters clumsy and hesitant, like someone writing with broken fingers: 'Please excuse Carl from school this week,' it said, 'he has felt ill and poorly all week so I let him stay home. Yrs sincerely Mr Howell.'

"I need to ask you Peter," she was blinking anxiously behind her glasses, "if you have seen Carl or spoken to him this week? Perhaps on the telephone?" It was typical of Ms Clancey to say telephone rather than phone. Everything had to be nicely and perfectly enunciated, proper and upright. "It's unusual to receive an absence note after three days, and I haven't been able to speak to Carl's father myself..."

She was irritatingly unhappy. Peter didn't enjoy adults stepping out of role, becoming subservient to children, being needy. So Carl's dad had sent in a note that she found suspicious, why did she have to involve him? Why not take matters into her own hands, like an adult should, and just go over there herself? Ms Clancey's eyelashes trembled with tears, her voice began to shake as she said, "I've noticed that you boys have become quite *close*, I just wonder if there's something he's been keeping from me, from the school, I should say. Something that we can help him with. Carl is a very special case, and I'd never forgive myself if something, well, unfortunate, had happened..."

And Peter understood that she, too, had fallen into respectful worship of the boy, and she was imagining terrible scenarios, to the point that she'd even lowered herself enough to beg a teenager for information. Irritation fought with sympathy and sympathy won. He laid a paternal hand on her quivering shoulder,

"Carl's OK, I'm sure. If you like I can go over and check up on him."

Ms Clancey's gratitude was embarrassing, and when her tears dried up, Peter felt that the world was settling back into its proper balance. In reality though, close though he and Carl were, he had no idea where he lived, or who he lived with. With his nan, supposedly; that was the consensus in school. So why was the note signed Mr Howell? Peter knew that Carl's parents weren't together, but he had no other information. Brothers? Sisters? Peter didn't even know if he had a pet. Spending the evening imagining ways to keep Ms Clancey at bay until he found Carl, he slept uneasily, and woke up worried, only to find Carl shuffling about at the bus stop outside school, apparently waiting for him. He didn't explain his absence but Peter shamefacedly accepted Ms Clancey's thanks for his help anyway.

Carl was rarely seen without his record bag; sometimes it was so full he could barely carry it. After school he would scurry away on his own using a short cut to the city centre, a slip road by the canal that all the school kids avoided. He never told Peter where he went, and, by now, he knew better than to ask: it was wiser to wait until Carl decided to include you. One day Peter's patience was rewarded and they walked together, not only from the school gate to the corner, not only to the shop at the top of the main road, but finally down by the canal, past grimly smelling alcoves and trashy corners. Peter stayed a few paces behind Carl, away from the edge. An escaped lunatic had killed seven people in twenty minutes along the canal – just knifing them and dumping their bodies in the water. Everybody in school knew it. Maybe Carl didn't, he wasn't from here after all, perhaps that's why he wasn't scared to walk this way alone. But when Peter told him the story, Carl just laughed and gave him the bag to look in.

In it there were a dozen or so records: Elvis, The Beatles, The Kinks. The kind of stuff old people listened to, but not Carl's usual stuff at all. He was, he explained, taking it all to DiscKings to sell. Peter should come too.

Peter had never been there, never dared. DiscKings was an institution, established first as a market stall in the Seventies, it now had two branches in the city, one for new and second hand records, and one much smaller outlet selling CDs. The largest shop was two floors of music, posters and memorabilia, punks and posers. Old sofas and a few frayed wicker chairs were scattered about, next to tables of Melody Makers, NMEs, and (ironically) Smash Hits magazines. You were even allowed to smoke at DiscKings, so long as it wasn't over the stacks themselves, and you could listen to records on headphones in special booths, for hours if you wanted, and smoke there too. While students staffed the CD shop, the record shops were manned by people who knew their music; no-one younger than 25, and most of them with a history of band membership. It wasn't unheard of for them to refuse to sell a record to someone they thought wouldn't appreciate it, or was buying for the wrong reasons. Their criteria for accepting used records were stringent – pristine covers and original dust covers. If you knew one of them by name, that was quite a coup. If you knew one of them by their nickname, and had managed to have a conversation for longer than the time it took to complete your transaction with them, well, you were practically part of the family, and might, if the gods allowed, work there yourself one day.

Threading through alleys, crossing the corner of the graveyard, dipping through the police station car park, they arrived at the door of DiscKings far sooner than Peter would have thought possible. In the short time Carl had lived in the area (he was hazy about where he'd lived before), he'd mastered its geography and figured out all the little wormholes that could get you where you wanted to be.

Taking the bag from Peter, Carl pushed open the heavy glass door, all covered with stickers and flyers, and hesitated. It was the only time he'd paused since leaving school, maybe he didn't know this place after all, perhaps he, too, was intimidated. His body shrank, his shoulders hunched. He chewed his lips and smiled shyly, brushing the hair into his eyes before walking, almost knock-kneed, to the cash register, carrying his heavy record bag tight against his chest. His voice had altered too: usually it rang with authority, he was someone who made sure that you listened to him. At DiscKings he was practically inaudible and the tattooed sales assistant behind the desk had to lean down to hear him. The murmured conversation went on for some time before they both began to laugh, a boom from the assistant, and an unfamiliar titter from Carl. The records were handed over, examined, frowned at and an offer was made. Carl, with the same quiet simper, held out for more money, brushing the hair slightly out of his blue eyes and offering a fearful smile. The assistant hesitated, and agreed. Carl ducked his head, counted his money and wandered back to Peter. The whole thing had taken less than five minutes. Carl had his money and Carl's dad had half a record collection left.

Once outside, Carl straightened up, lost the simper, and led the way to the nearest off licence. They spent the rest of the afternoon in the park, drinking cheap cans of lager and smoking. Carl spent a lot of time trying to teach Peter how to blow smoke rings, before giving up and leading the way to the City Hall steps. He had friends to meet.

By five or six o'clock each day, the tourists and office workers who normally sat on the steps consulting their guidebooks or eating lunch were replaced by the all-day drinkers, the punks, the homeless. As soon as dusk threatened, a lurching, stumbling exodus began, out of the pubs, squats and parks. By the time Carl arrived with Peter, the top tier steps were full, and they had to hang around at the bottom with the goths and the wannabes. After only a few minutes though, Carl's name was called from above, and space was made at the top table of the dispossessed between an aged skinhead and a dishevelled woman with the tremors.

Everyone knew Carl. Peter was introduced to Angie, a glazed eyed punk in her thirties; Cookie, the skinhead; and Dom, the owner of five or six visible teeth and a collection of facial tattoos, who was the obvious leader. Later, Carl told Peter that Dom lived in a flat in the archway over the entrance to the cemetery and lived off Temazepam and speed. He cast astrology charts for everyone he knew, hinting darkly that he knew the date of your death. All this might have been true, but Carl knew how to spin a tale. Dom leaned in paternally and shook Peter's hand, "Friend of the boy's? Good. Needs them. Good."

Carl gave Dom half of the money he'd got for the records. Dom nodded thanks, tucked it into his shorts pocket and said something else indistinct that made Carl smile. Then they all sat quietly together, drinking and smoking until it was almost dark. Eventually the guilt at worrying his parents got too much for Peter, and he prepared, shamefacedly, to leave. Carl showed no signs of moving, in fact Dom had just sent Angie to buy more lager, and so Peter said his goodbyes to the uninterested group, called his father from a phone box and apologised all the way home for worrying him.

* * *

Peter had finished a couple of beers before it began to get cold by the canal. Remembering the old story about the psycho killing the seven people, he felt frightened, like a child, in the gathering dusk. Getting up quickly, he decided to walk to the flat Carl had lived in when they first met. It seemed fitting. He'd died there, after all.

The house looked even more peculiar now than it had then. It was a strangely disjointed building, the bottom and the top were mismatched pairs. The downstairs flat was obviously well cared for. Its well-tended front garden led smoothly to a welcome mat; the windows were clean. But the top flat ruined the effect. Rotten window frames pulled back from the glass like diseased gums, and the net curtains were smudged black at the bottom. The front bedroom curtains were closed and roughly folded on the sill at the bottom, the window was partially open. That was the room he'd died in, Peter realised, with a shiver. Some bunches of flowers lay by the side door and he read the cards. 'You were our sunshine. Take care my angel. Aunty Kathleen' – 'See you in Heaven babe! xx' – 'We passed upon the stair, we spoke of where and when, Although I wasn't there, I was his friend. D.'

There were older offerings too: notes mostly, and he could make out some words, 'Love – miss – can't believe,' but the writing was too faded now to read. It had rained earlier.

Crouching down, half drunk, Peter had a sudden urge to pick up all the flowers and take them back to his flat, back to somewhere safe. This estate, this whole area, was too harsh to host such poignancy. He imagined local youths pissing on the flowers, drunks stealing some to take home to their abused girlfriends. And then he had to smile at himself, even laugh, because he hadn't changed, not in all these years. This place still intimidated him, he was still an outsider, there was still that gulf between Carl and him, and now it would never be bridged.

One Friday, Peter had contrived to walk with Carl after school, pretending to be so immersed in their conversation that he didn't realise he was walking the wrong way until they were halfway to Carl's door. Either Carl didn't notice or had let him get away with it, because the third time it happened, Carl actually invited him in.

Peter knew that his own parents were prosperous of course. He knew that the suburb he lived in wrote its own narrative: doctors and barristers lived there with their happy, intact families; gardens were bountiful but understated, tasteful. Bikes were unquestioningly taken into the garage at night, and meals were eaten as a family, with a salad on the side, and a glass of wine for the adults. He knew that how he lived wasn't necessarily how others did too. He watched the news and had opinions on why people rioted; he'd seen housing estates when he'd accidentally taken the wrong bus home, and he'd grieved for the people that had to live there. His mother called him quite the little socialist.

As they got closer and closer to Carl's house, Peter tried to swallow the knot of anxiety in his throat, telling himself he was a snob. It wasn't helped by Carl turning the subject to the routine muggings, theft and arson that were rife around here. When he pointed out an evil looking block of flats where a gang of rapists lived together, sharing tips on kidnapping and putting the finishing touches to their torture dungeon, Peter finally understood that he was joking. He must have noticed what Peter was trying desperately to conceal, and wanted to torment him. Punish him. Peter felt ashamed. By the time they reached Carl's door they hadn't spoken for a while. Carl looked preoccupied – probably he was regretting inviting him over, and Peter was uncomfortable, afraid that he'd offended his friend by simply being of a different class.

Carl dug a key out of his pocket and opened the side door to the flat above. The first thing Peter noticed was the smell of air fresheners, and lurking below that, the dense musk of cigarettes. In the living room there was a vinyl sofa, its cracked arms taped over with black electrical tape. Dainty, dated glassware filled a teak cabinet. An incongruously large china dalmatian, stuck onto a piece of red perspex with mustard coloured glue, stood in the centre of the mantelpiece, alongside two plaster figures of the Virgin Mary, gazing at the ceiling with doe-eyed suffering. These were flanked by school photos of Carl, posed before beige or sky blue backgrounds, in a variety of school uniforms: Carl with gaps in his teeth, with startlingly short hair; with a yellow mark under his eye that looked like a stain on the photograph, but was actually the remains of a black eye. Peter sat down on the sofa, uncomfortable beneath the collective attention of Mary and the child Carl. The flat was quiet as death.

When people visited Peter's house, they were taken around on a tour, shown where the toilets were, asked to help themselves to anything in the kitchen. When he was younger, Peter would take friends to his room to play with Lego and Transformers. Now he was older he would take them to the converted basement – almost his own wing of the house – and they could play on the Sega Megadrive or mess about on his new drum kit. But Carl made no attempt to get off the sofa, speak to him, or even look in his direction. Peter must have really pissed him off.

Eventually there was the scrape of a key in the door and Carl disappeared, while Peter hovered at the living room door. There was a murmured, indistinct conversation, and Peter heard a man apologising for something, heard him tripping on the top stair, and come forward to the living room. When he saw Peter, he extended his hand and pumped his arm with surprising force. When he opened his mouth to smile, a rolling mist of alcohol enveloped them both. "This man is drunk," thought Peter as the arm pumping stopped and the man staggered a little as he let go. Carl had disappeared, leaving Peter with this drunken stranger, who now introduced himself as Bob, and when Peter looked blank, as Carl's dad.

"I thought Carl lived with his nan?"

Bob supported himself against the wall, "She's poorly. She's in the hospital." In the front bedroom Carl had turned the music on loud, so loud that Peter couldn't make out what band it was. Bob stayed swaying in front of him, and so Peter did what would be done in his own home, and offered to take Bob's coat, showed him into the living room and asked him if he wanted tea or coffee. He knew from films that drunks needed strong black coffee, but in the kitchen all he found were cans of braising steak, chicken soup and rice pudding. He finally found some Nescafe and some dusty china, put two teaspoons of powdered coffee in, and then, hesitating, another two.

The music pounded on in the front bedroom. Peter brought Bob the coffee and, not knowing what else to do, sat beside him on the sofa and watched him drink it. There wasn't much of Carl in his face. Bob was short, thick in the trunk and bandy-legged, pugnacious looking. His skin was leathery and brown and his hands were squat and powerful looking. The neat suit and trilby made him look like an extra from a Depression-era movie. His hands shook as he drank his coffee, the cup clattered against the saucer. He breathed noisily through his mouth.

"You're his friend then, from school?" Peter nodded. "Ah." Bob sighed and closed his eyes. "Oh I'm in for it now, then." The music stopped next door and then began again. Carl must have just turned the record over. "Oh yes, I'll get it in the neck now." He opened one eye, saw that Peter was still there, closed it again, and settled back.

Peter felt he had to say something. "Do you live here as well?"

"No. Just while Mum's in the hospital. Keep an eye on him. I've got my own place," he gestured vaguely to the right, "down the way there. House. He lives there too, meant to, but he likes his old nan."

The music became relentlessly loud and Peter couldn't help but feel that it was a signal to him, pulling him in, chastising him for being with Bob. He was just edging off the sofa when Bob suddenly sprang up, knocking a picture off the wall as he lurched through the door towards

Carl's room. He'd locked the door, and Bob was bellowing for him to open up and turn that fucking noise off. Carl answered by kicking his side of the door and cranking up the volume even more. After a few seconds Bob had worn himself out shouting and came back to the living room. Ignoring Peter now, he turned on the TV and put it on full volume. For a while the two cacophonies warred with each other until a series of loud thumps on the floor from the flat below made Carl turn the music down. After a few more thumps, Bob noticed, turned the TV down and Peter took his chance to leave the living room.

Carl made Peter wait until his timid knocks got a bit bolder, and when he opened the door Peter could tell that he had been crying. His hair was smoothed back from his face and there were little red blotches around his eyes. With the music still quite loud, Peter couldn't make out what he was saying, but came in anyway, and they sat on the bed together, looking down at their knees. Carl rearranged the hair around his face, making sure it spilled into his eyes, and they listened to one whole side of an album before they spoke and even then it was only about what record to put on next. Some of the records in the pile were unfamiliar to Peter, and he slightly exaggerated his ignorance, knowing that feeling superior would help Carl calm down. Once or twice he even made him laugh, and they almost forgot the man in the front room, the grandmother in the hospital, the estate outside. When Peter's stomach groaned, Carl told him about the best chip shop in the world, just around the corner, and Peter knew that this was his signal to leave.

Passing the front room, they saw Bob asleep in the armchair, with the TV still on. On the way down the stairs Carl brushed his hair in his eyes again and Peter didn't look at him until they were nearly at the corner. He bought them both chips, and Carl walked him to the bus stop, even resuscitating some of the horror stories about the estate, for laughs now, and they parted with a promise to swap tapes on Monday as usual. As the bus pulled off, Peter looked out of the back window at the receding figure of his best friend, hunched in his thin school blazer, sitting at the bus stop, throwing chips down the drain. Was he crying?

Peter couldn't tell.

When he got off at his stop, he put his hand in his pocket and found a note written on a page ripped from a school jotter: 'If things get bad can I rely on you? Can I stay at your house sometimes if I need to? If yes, don't answer this note. Your friend Carl.'

Later, months and years later, Peter knew the drill. If Carl asked you for a favour, then the favour should be bestowed, or not, with no further discussion. Most importantly, the actual asking of it should never ever be alluded to. But Peter hadn't learned this yet, and so he went home that evening, countering his parents' anxiety at his being late with the note and a breathless account of the afternoon. They wanted questions answered. Why was Carl staying at his grandmother's? Was his father living there permanently? Why didn't he see his mother? Were social services involved? Peter's mother sat on a great many committees, surely there was something to do for this poor child? They weren't that keen on having him stay, however. Peter worked on them for a few days, and then, filled with a sense of achievement, slightly stretched the truth and told Carl that he could stay whenever he wanted. Carl received the news in silence and was distant with him for a few days, then abruptly began showing up at the bus stop every Friday after school and staying at Peter's house at the weekends.

In a way it would have been easier for Peter's parents if Carl had had an identifiably bad effect on their son. They had steeled themselves for slammed doors, raided fridges and open contempt, but Peter was nothing but his own sunny self. The only overt influence his new friend had had on him was actually positive: disappointed that Peter had let the guitar go, they were impressed by his diligence in drumming. They admitted to themselves that the time spent with Carl hadn't affected Peter's school work, his disposition, his confidence; but they couldn't bring themselves to welcome Carl into their home as genuinely as they would have another friend. Anxiously they asked each other if it was his class that was the problem. His background? Oh God, had they really become those sort of people? No. No. After all, they had decided to

85

place their son in a state school precisely for that reason – for him to live in the real world, with real people. It was a skill that Peter's parents were proud of having painstakingly taught themselves, and they wanted their son to mix with all sorts of kids effortlessly and not have to learn how to do it later, as they had done. Naturally the majority of his peers were from the same background – there were a lot of children of lawyers, a few of doctors, and an MP's daughter, but there was a very visible minority of other types too. Of course neither Peter's mum or dad knew what it was that these other parents did, but whatever it was, it was real. It was representative.

But Carl. They never learned to feel comfortable with him. They found him uncanny, fey, monosyllabic. A neglected boy, a poor boy, a boy to be pitied for sure, but they couldn't like him. And Carl, as if knowing what he was up against from the start, never tried to win them round.

At the dinner table he would fold up salad leaves with his bitten fingers and shove them onto the prongs of his fork; cucumber would skitter around his plate and land on his knees. Rice and spaghetti foxed him. Peter's mother couldn't restrain herself from teaching him how to eat properly, but what began as a light-hearted lesson ended abruptly when Carl just sat there like a puppet with its strings cut, refusing to cooperate. He forgot, or didn't care about, saying please and thank you. He would dry the dishes in silence, his bruised looking mouth clamped shut, dodging questions, hiding from conversation. Peter's parents joked that he was mute, but at night they heard his unfamiliar voice drifting out from the open window in the basement room and he never seemed to stop talking. They'd turn to each other with raised eyebrows, and say, "You see, he can talk," but secretly they were perplexed, hurt. They gave this boy a home a great deal of the time, they gave him food, they gave him the gift of Peter, and what did they have to show for it?

Before Carl imposed himself on the family, the Friday Night Feast was an event: three courses and Peter would be allowed a glass of wine. His dad would talk frankly and hilariously about his job in the city; his mum would talk frankly but sorrowfully about her various charities. The conversation would turn on its well-oiled axis towards the virtues of education, the duty of the more privileged towards the less fortunate. Mum would bring out the dessert and dad would always put on a mock northern accent and call it 'pudding'. Peter was always given the biggest piece and his appetite was always favourably commented on. In fact, Peter associated eating too much with praise, and continued making himself uncomfortable at meal times until, much later, a journalist at Melody Maker referred to him as 'the obligatory fat drummer'. Then he went on a diet.

Once Carl began staking out his claim on Peter, though, the Friday Night Feast was curtailed to a modest one course in front of the TV, the participants cut from three to two. Peter had usually eaten by the time his parents came home, and was often already in the basement, either to meet Carl or to wait for him. Carl soon stopped taking the school bus with Peter and began arriving later in the evening, bypassing the front door and slipping down to the basement room via the stairs outside. If Peter wasn't there, he would sit on the sill smoking until he arrived. Animals liked Carl, and he liked them too, in a distracted, careless way. Neighbourhood cats and the odd dog would trot over to keep him company while he waited and in the morning Peter's mum would sweep up the cigarette butts and polish the greasy paw prints off the windows, her mouth set in a thin hard line.

And so one ritual was replaced by another. Peter would race upstairs and change out of his school uniform, putting on the combats and shredded t-shirts that his mother despised. He'd go through the stuff he'd taped off the radio during the week and make a master tape of all the best tracks, to share with Carl later. Then he'd stand in front of the fridge eating until he sensed Carl was on his way, and bolt down the basement stairs to prepare.

In his passively insistent way, Carl had made it known that he liked fresh air, so Peter made sure that the windows were open despite what the weather was. Carl preferred to sit facing the door, so Peter would clear any debris off the sofa and plump the cushions. Carl didn't like strong light, so Peter had brought down one of the standard lamps from the dining room. If he was kept waiting for a long time, he would be thrown back into the same worried helplessness that he'd felt when Carl disappeared from school for that week; that confusing realisation that he didn't know his best friend well enough to know where he was, what he was thinking, if he was ok. He felt the same later on, after Carl disappeared from school altogether. It was strange that he didn't have the same feeling at the end, when Carl disappeared for the final time, when nobody thought to look for him at his nan's.

In Peter's memory, those evenings in the basement had an elegiac quality. It was always dusk, it was always just cooling. Carl kept his guitar there and together they taught themselves their instruments, grimacing through mistakes, swearing through misunderstandings, grinning through sudden breakthroughs – two boys in a darkening room learning a skill that seemed to them eternally elusive and addictive. They poured all their dedication into learning, mastering, their instruments. The genuine delight one would take in the other's progress, the approbation of your best friend, that happy, close communion made this the happiest time of Peter's life. And then it ended.

One day Carl wasn't at school. There wasn't anything unusual about that, but the day stretched into a week, and the week into two. Peter avoided Ms Clancey in the hallways and shrugged his way through questions from friends. Darren King trailed him like a threatening puppy and girls plagued him with their worry. Peter's old friends, the preppy, rugby types he'd hung around with before Carl, stayed at a distance, uncertain about approaching him and letting him back into their set. They, too, were consumed with worry and curiosity about Carl; he was made to worry people, and everyone caught the fever. By the end of the second week, Peter was drowning in their anxiety, was anxious himself, but angry too, because for all their closeness, Carl had disappeared and hadn't bothered to tell him where to or why. He had treated him with contempt, just as he did the others under his spell – the Darren Kings, the Ms Clanceys, the giggling 5th years, all of them. Once, after school, Peter had swallowed his pride enough to go round to Carl's nan's flat, but there was no answer when he rang the bell. A neighbour told him that the old lady was still in hospital and nobody had seen Bob. Peter took the bus back to the centre and drifted towards DiscKings, flicking through their 50p singles and keeping one eye on the door in case Carl came in, but he didn't.

After a long time, Carl began to recede in people's thoughts. Peter pulled up his marks in science and thought about applying for medicine at university. In English, he put up with Ms Clancy's pointed remarks about the value of friendship in group discussions on Of Mice and Men, and avoided her hurt glances. He drew closer to his old rugby friends. One of them was taking classical guitar lessons and Peter tried to get him to listen to John Peel, but it didn't take. He kept up with the drums, going to lessons one evening a week. Eventually things got better, things became nearly normal. People stopped mentioning Carl, the graffiti in the girls' toilets faded and something like the Friday Night Feast began again at home.

One winter evening, Peter stayed in the city centre after his drum lesson to do some Christmas shopping. Unlit lights were slung around the main streets and the square; a minor soap star was due to turn them on in a few days. Peter ducked in and out of shops, vaguely looking for presents for his parents, but mostly keeping out of the wind that gathered itself up in corners and tumbled down the streets, not too cold yet, but with the edge of winter. The punks on the City Hall steps huddled together like birds on a telephone wire, drifting off in little groups when the temperature dipped. Peter heard an indistinct bark that sounded like his name, turned, and saw a man in shorts and a leather jacket waving at him, grinning.

Peter hadn't seen Dom since meeting him that time a year ago, and was surprised to be remembered. When he wandered over to the steps to sit next to him, Peter took the proffered can of lager and furtively wiped the opening on his sleeve. Dom seemed delighted to see him, chuckling and nudging closer. They sat together for a while before Peter hesitantly mentioned Carl, and Dom seemed delighted by that too. One eye dropped slowly into a wink. He shuffled closer.

"He's doing well. Doing well. Good."

"Where is he?"

"With me. With others. Around. You know." Dom spat phlegm on the step below. "He's been learning."

"Learning what? He left school. Before the exams."

"Our boy," Dom grew solemn, "our boy is a special boy. He's a one, that boy. I've always said it and it's in his chart. That boy is meant for special things. Destiny. I've seen it. He's been learning."

"His destiny?"

Dom nodded and grinned. Spitty lager dribbled down his chin. Peter shifted on the cold steps and frowned, trying to understand.

"What's your religion? What's your faith?" Dom asked.

"I... I don't have one."

"Ach!" Dom threw out a wavering arm, "Not God, not that. No. What do you worship?" Peter was confused. Dom pushed his face close. "Some of us worship people, others. The Supermen. The stars. Some of us have to be the worshipped. Yeah? So those people, *those* people, well they have to worship the fact of worship, don't they? They have to make themselves the worshipped. To complete the circle."

Peter tried not to smile. "And you think you're one of the worshipped?"

Dom was pitying, exasperated. "Not me. I do what I'm told, I do what I'm designed to do. Him. The boy. He's the one."

"Carl? You think he's a Superman?"

"He's a special one. You know it."

Now he smiled. "Come on. He's only 16. He's just normal."

"You need to think on, boy. You need to learn, get yourself out of your box." And he pulled the can of lager back. There was silence for a while until Peter got up and said, "If you see him can you give him a message? Can you tell him that everyone's been really worried about him and it would have been nice if he'd, you know, said something about going? Left a note or something..."

"I understand," said Dom. "You had your feelings hurt." Peter nodded, ashamed that he had tears in his eyes – "But some things are more important. He had to go, because he had to go. Jesus went into the desert, right? Bowie went to the Buddhist place, right? What happens? *You transform*, that's what happens. And you can't do that in the light of day. You can't do that in a fucking *school*."

"But you can do it in your squat or council flat or wherever you live, right?"

Dom held out his hands, shrugged. "It's a desert, like any other. It's hidden. It's safe."

"And what about his parents? What do they think about him staying with you and...people...? They must be worried –"

"Angie! Angie! He's saying about Miriam being worried! About Bob!" – Dom nudged a medicated woman, with a rude girl haircut and a bandage on her wrist – "Angie's the boy's sister," said Dom, turning back to Peter.

"Half sister," Angie corrected, sinking back into the shadows and putting her head on her knees.

"Says they're worried! Miriam, and Bob! Nah. Nah. He may have been born to them, may have been. But he's no more theirs than Jesus was to his folks."

"You've been telling him a lot of shit." Peter was shaking.

Dom took offence. He got up, bracing himself against a pillar, and snarled, "Better than your lot. More use than the shit he's got from you and yours. Teaching the boy to eat fucking avocado and I don't know what else. Teaching him to be a little prince in your little fucking castle. Trying to train the difference out of the boy," – his voice strained up to a falsetto – "Write on the lines, explain what you mean, wear your fucking uniform, don't run in the corridor and kindly direct yourself to the nearest gas chamber."

"Did you tell him to leave school?"

"I don't tell the boy nothing. Never have. Have I encouraged his independence? Yes. Yes I fucking have. Give the boy a leg up, let him know what he's got going for him."

"By telling him he's this special, I don't know, leader or something?"

Dom swung his face so close that Peter could smell his breath. "That's what your dad's done for you, no? Told you you're special? Told you that if you worked hard you'd get your heart's desire? No? Well that's what I've done. That's all I've done. Been a dad to the boy. But his sights are set higher than yours, very much higher, because he's more special than you. And all of them. You know it."

When Peter walked away, Dom kept shouting.

Peter stopped feeling angry with Carl from that day, laying the blame for his leaving school with Dom. In fact, knowing that Carl had been holed up in some grim bedsit being told he was the new messiah, made Peter feel better altogether. Carl hadn't left school for any other reason than his own ego, he hadn't been in trouble, he hadn't fallen out with Peter, he hadn't been hurt; he was just too busy being flattered by a man with obvious mental health problems. It felt good to feel superior to Carl, suddenly, and Peter found he was more interested in school, in his old peers and in the prospect of university. His parents were less worried about him, his teachers predicted impressive exam results, and everyone agreed that he was back to the person he was before Carl arrived.

* * *

While Peter had been sitting down amongst the flowers outside the flat, a few kids had passed and passed again on their bikes. Once, a young girl, laying flowers of her own, had tried to make conversation with him, but he didn't want to talk to her or anyone. He didn't want to be noticed, but realised that he was only going to get more attention the longer he stayed, so he dragged himself up and walked into the city. Hopefully he could be anonymous in a crowd; he might go to DiscKings. Hanging about in record shops always soothed him, and people were too self-consciously cool there to try to talk to him about what had happened.

* * *

The summer he left school, the summer before he was due to go to university, Peter got a job at a bike factory. Early every morning, his father would drive him down to a grimy edge of the city and drop him off a few streets away from the entrance. Sometimes Peter would walk the rest of the way with Darren King, who had been working there since leaving school two years before. They would talk about Carl – it was the only thing they had in common – and part at the iron gates, Darren heading to the factory floor and Peter making his way to the administration building. He liked the job, liked the older ladies who had been working there for years, liked that they were impressed by him going to university in a few months. He knew that he was different, exotic almost, compared to the majority of people who worked there, and he knew that he would find it a lot more difficult to be accepted on the factory floor, but as it stood he was proud of himself. His father had originally offered to pull some strings and get him work experience at his firm, but Peter had decided against it. It felt good to be independent, and the job at the factory also had the advantage of being paid work; for the first time he had money.

He'd got into the habit of going to DiscKings on Friday after work, and with his new pay packet could afford to consider new releases instead of the bargain bucket singles and EPs. He'd grown tall over the last year, and his confidence had grown with it. He didn't slink about record shops, hugging the walls with his eyes on the ground anymore; now he knew what he liked and what he was looking for. Every now and again he looked at the bulletin board and toyed with the idea of answering adverts for a drummer, but then he talked himself out of it because, after all, he was going to university soon, and there was no point. The sales staff still intimidated him a little, but he was getting better at pretending otherwise. The other week he'd had a long discussion with one of them about whether Big Black would be the same kind of band without the drum machine, and both had agreed to differ, but, Peter fancied, with mutual respect.

This Friday, he planned to spend half an hour or so at the shop to kill time before heading to a nearby pub, The Bristolian, to meet some friends. The streets were filled with semi-naked people with freshly sun-burnt skin and bellies full of warm beer. Girls puttered about in heels, on the arms of pugnacious men in football tops. Shops had had their doors open all day and the music spilled out onto the streets, puddling together into a pool of cheerful summer noise. The ubiquitous, spirit-of-77 punks were out in force on the City Hall steps, their ranks swollen by teenage pretenders on day release from the suburbs, and Peter thought he saw Dom Marshall on his perch at the top, but didn't move closer to make sure.

Inside DiscKings it was mercifully cool. Electric fans were turned up to the max; the adverts on the bulletin board fluttered and rattled.

Peter flicked through albums, pausing and passing, eventually deciding to skim through a few in the booth. He waited at the counter, but the assistant had his back turned and was talking animatedly to someone in the storage cupboard, and didn't notice him. The fans blew his hair around in wild whips – funny coloured, whitish, yellowish hair, neither long nor short, and Peter eyed it with irritation, getting bored of waiting. Just as he was about to put the records back and leave, the sales assistant turned round. And it was Carl.

The first thing Peter noticed was that Carl, too, had grown. He was taller than Peter now, still thin, but broad across the shoulders. The second thing he noticed was that Carl didn't seem to recognise him; he just stood there with an expression of blank condescension, just like all the other assistants at DiscKings. It was embarrassing. And then his face split open into a grin and he leaped over the cash desk. Peter felt himself being hugged, and hugged back.

Such things weren't done in DiscKings, and it was spoken about for years: how Carl Howell dropped his cool; how Peter Hamilton got his break and fell into his future. Over the years the tale of their separation became more dramatic, Peter heard Carl tell the story in interview after interview and it differed every time. Sometimes Carl had been expelled from school and was so bitter that he severed all contact with his old friends. Sometimes the school had threatened him to stay away from Peter. Once he hinted that he'd been in prison, once that he'd been abroad working although he'd never been out of the country until the first European tour – Peter went with him to get his passport. Each tale he told was a variation on the same theme though: sent away, banished from society, the boy Carl was forced to survive in a harsh world alone. But for his talent and his belief in himself – he would never have survived. Music, for Carl, was his life's work; his stint at DiscKings was his apprenticeship, and now he was ready to share himself with the world, taking Peter along for the ride.

In reality, he'd been holed up with Dom Marshall, watching old videos of Iggy Pop, Jim Morrison and the Sex Pistols; being told what a special person he was, what kind of a future he deserved, and what to expect as rightfully his. He'd been preparing. He'd been coached. The fey mannerisms, the pigeon toed walk, the hair in the eyes, all that stuff, Peter soon noticed, were on their way out now. He'd break out a version of it for girls and people he needed things from, but by and large Carl was now, well, almost cocky. He drank more too, Peter noticed later on. And his fits were still there, more frequent if anything. When he drank too much, he would become loud and his speech would fracture into little nonsensical pieces before the shaking began, before his eyes would become large and blank. Some people didn't notice. Others did but thought it disrespectful to admit it. It added to the mystique too: he was beautiful and damaged. He didn't have big, ugly off-putting fits, but small, sensitive, dainty ones. A girl could love a boy who fitted like that.

That Friday, Carl made Peter wait until the end of his shift by promising an explanation over drinks. There were interesting people for him to meet. Carl's people – and he referred to them as His People – would love him, he'd fit right in, they were all art types, musician types, writers, stuff like that. Peter's type of people. They knew all about him already. Peter, swept along, couldn't help but feel flattered that he appeared to be That Type Of Person himself. The friends at The Bristolian were quietly forgotten. He waited for Carl on one of the broken sofas, settling down to read an old NME. Some guy called Chris Harris had a long interview with Swans. Damn, he wrote well. It almost made Peter want to listen to Swans. Almost.

Carl's friends were older. Mostly in their twenties, a couple were maybe even thirty. Peter recognised a few from around town, from behind the counter at DiscKings or from gig venues. One was writing a book. "What about?" Peter had asked and the answer came back: "Magick. Crowley. Anton Le Vey. I need to get to Peru. That's the seat of magick now." Another, an eager, first year photography student called Sean, clicked, clicked, clicked away at everything. A tall guy with dreadlocks and an underbite pressed Peter to take a look at his hydroponics set up. The taciturn straight edger who'd been working at DiscKings the longest turned out to be a slightly camp carpenter called Anthony with a 'th' rather than a 't'.

They all seemed to hang around DiscKings most of the time, or at Deep Focus, the independent record label that Peter was in awe of. In the back of Melody Maker and NME, he often came across half page advertisements for Deep Focus events – all dayers with only Deep Focus signings, foreign bands as special guests. It was all impossibly exotic, and so close! In his city! But he hadn't been to anything like that and wouldn't have dreamed of finding the office just to hang out there, as all of Carl's friends seemed to do quite casually. It was a different world, with Carl at the centre. Peter's old deference crept back. Now that they were friends again, it was on the same terms as before. Carl wanted to start a band. Peter said, "Sure."

* * *

Now, five years later, Peter got as far as the door of DiscKings. He could see Anthony behind the sales desk, serving the obligatory blank look up to a nervous teenager. Time had added pounds and tattoos, but not friendliness. He knew that if he went in now, Anthony would drop the teenager like a hot brick and turn to Peter, oozing sympathy all over him. On the edge of the counter stood a cardboard advert for Chinaski's latest album, 'Smelling Roses, Hearing Flies'. On CD. Christ, everything was on CD nowadays, and Peter hated it. No gatefold sleeves, no secret message etched next to the label, tiny printed lyrics you had to squint to read. There was no satisfying heft to a CD – you could buy ten of them and carry them home easily. They were too easy…they were too *light* somehow. But that was the way it went. The last time he'd checked, Chinaski had sold nearly as many copies of the album on CD as vinyl. It was the future.

He backed away from the window and merged back in with the crowd on the street, eager to be with people, but not with anyone who would sympathise. He wanted empathy. He went to Deep Focus instead.

Their bassist problem continued all summer. Carl would meet someone, rave about them, introduce them to Peter, only to turn against them within weeks. It was always a different problem too: this one was too quiet; this one was too old. One nodded too much, while another had bad shoes. All this may have meant a great deal to Carl, or he may have just been saying it to avoid the band ever really getting off the ground. Peter had only deferred university for a year, he was due to move away in October, but whenever he raised this, Carl would become remote and Peter would have a lot of back peddling to do to get back in favour. He knew what Carl was doing, and he knew it was unfair. He also knew that if he had any sense he'd walk away from the band idea, go to university and maybe meet more dedicated musicians there. He told himself that Carl was lazy, and that he wasn't taking this seriously, that he was frightened of success, but deep down he felt, he *knew*, that that wasn't the whole story. Carl wasn't going to do this by halves. It did matter if someone had bad shoes, it did matter if someone was too old. Carl was playing the long game and all the ingredients had to be right from the start. So far he hadn't turned his criticism on Peter, although this, Peter knew, was only a matter of time. Already there had been raised eyebrows when Peter showed up wearing a tie-dyed t-shirt. Peter had taken the hint and never worn it again, but now Carl was eyeing his rugby tops with displeasure too.

Today they were auditioning three bassists, two of whom seemed hopeless just from Carl's descriptions. Dom had been in the basement for an hour already, and Carl showed up late with some girl and began doing all the things he normally did when he was pissed off about something – maintaining a heavy silence, grimly chain smoking, refusing eye contact. It was obviously going to be a waste of an afternoon. Peter took every opportunity to disappear upstairs and waited at the top of the steps, hoping to hear any conversation that might prove that the atmosphere was changing, before trudging downstairs with a pained smile.

The girl he'd brought looked faintly familiar. A real punk girl with multi coloured dreadlocks, torn up tights, the whole deal, and Peter was impressed despite not finding her very attractive. She looked quite extreme, not like the compliant and very young girls that Carl sometimes brought with him to rehearsal. She looked like she might have something to say for herself, she might even stand up to Carl. Then, when he heard her voice, he remembered her.

She'd been at his school – two years above, so she must be old by now, like 20, 21 or something. She'd been one of the Rich Bitch Jolly Hockey Sticks crowd. It was weird, looking at her now, and remembering her smug little face on awards day, it was hard to put the two images together. What was her name? Claire? No. Catherine. Oh, she says it's Lydia now. What? Oh. Oh yeah. And he remembered the whole Catherine 'the Cunt' Hunt scenario now, and the special assembly about verbal bullying. Oh well, let her call herself whatever she wants. She looks alright now, give her a chance. And so he busied himself making Lydia feel comfortable, asking her questions, making her tea, offering compliments, all activity designed to eat up the silence emanating from Carl.

The bassists were all late. They only really needed to see one of them – John, the one Carl had met at DiscKings. Peter suspected that the others were just window dressing to make Lydia see this as a serious event. She probably didn't know that they'd played with pretty much every bassist in the city and that Carl had driven them all away. Lydia was slightly ridiculous, with her self conscious steely glare and her notebook, as if she was somehow the judge. But then, maybe Carl had told her that to get her here. Maybe he cared about her opinion. There was a first time for everything. When John arrived, he was given the demo, told to play along with the basslines, and things quickly moved onto the chore of ignoring whatever weird shit Dom said, while appearing to agree with him.

By the dubious virtue of staying alive since 1977, he had become a scene fixture, respected, sometimes deferred to. There hadn't been many gigs by many bands in the city that he hadn't appeared at, first hunched at the bar, and then eventually, if the occasion warranted, unleashing his arthritic, disquieting pogo. There were a few people who claimed to remember him in his youth, or to have definite facts about him. He'd been a friend of David Bowie. He'd been in prison for murder. Or GBH. Or arson. He'd been a rent boy. He was psychic. He'd been in an asylum for ten years. The only facts Peter knew about Dom were those that Carl had told him, which was to say not much. Carl liked secrets and secretive people, and he took Dom along with him everywhere – like a toothless Jiminy Cricket.

As soon as he arrived, John had obviously picked up quickly that it was best not to question Dom's presence. He made every appearance of understanding what he said, and as a result now had Carl's full attention. But poor Lydia looked lost, and so Peter did what he always did with Carl's side-lined women, and tried to take her mind off it.

They talked about Deep Focus, about how long she'd been involved with them, about her career before that, about her ambitions. Lydia was one of those people who took it for granted that you wanted to know all about her, and Peter was used to that, used to not being asked any questions in return. He easily slipped into the role of eager acolyte; it made people comfortable and it meant he didn't have to think much. While she spoke he kept half an eye on Carl and John who seemed to be getting on well, John was letting himself be lectured and was making the appropriate responses. Who knew? Perhaps they'd have a bassist for longer than a few weeks. Then she asked who their vocalist was. Had Carl really told her so little? How long had they been seeing each other?

"Carl. That's Carl."

She said something absurd: "But he's so shy!" And Peter had to take time to calibrate his response. He said something about Carl changing on stage, about being charismatic, but she still looked sceptical, carried on with a lot of stuff about how unconfident Carl was, and how she'd spent so much time trying to boost his confidence.

"Perhaps," her voice was quite loud now, but it had a musing quality that made Peter think that she didn't mean to be overheard, "perhaps he's a little self conscious because I'm here. It may be that he doesn't want to, I don't know, let me down or something."

He hoped Carl wasn't hearing this; it was verging on impertinence – Carl didn't enjoy being told what he was like. Peter headed her off into talking about Deep Focus again.

"If you wanted to help us out, I mean, if it wouldn't put you out, maybe you could pass the demo on to Deep Focus? I mean, you have the contacts."

And naturally Lydia was jumping all over it. Not only would she do that, she'd ensure studio time for a better demo, she'd see to it personally. Her voice got even louder – now she wanted to be heard, Peter guessed – and John and Carl were forced to pay attention. She looked significantly at Carl and smiled, and Carl mustered a smile back. He's sick of this girl, thought Peter. He's sick of this girl already. And I don't blame him.

Throughout the rest of the evening, though, Peter's certainty wavered. Either Carl was a better actor than he thought, or in a weird way he really did like her. She was vehement, humourless, a bit pompous, and she made Peter tired, but there was a weird energy about her, she could get things done, you could feel it. She knew what she was talking about. That plummy voice might be at odds with the dreadlocks and the torn clothes, but she knew music, and she appeared to know the industry. She was protective of Carl, he noticed, and she had some power over him. When she told him to take his pills, he took his pills. When she questioned if he should have another beer, he put the can back. For all Carl played on it, there was something genuinely vulnerable about him.

When everyone left, and Peter was alone, he felt that something had been accomplished, that they were on their way.

A few days later Carl called him to say that he'd approached Deep

Focus, they loved the demo, and Mason had booked studio time for the next week. And Peter needed to sort out his clothes, no more rugby tops.

* * *

It had been a year or so since Peter had visited Deep Focus. Since Chinaski had signed to DCG, there hadn't been a lot of time to keep up with old acquaintances, and besides, going back to see Ian and Freida would have seemed...odd. Like visiting your foster parents, or your old English teacher. And anyway, they were Carl's people really. But today Peter wanted to be with Carl's people, not fans, not girlfriends, not hangers on. Ian and Freida were Carl's family; it seemed appropriate to be with them.

The converted mill looked the same, if a little sprucer. There weren't as many vans parked at the side and no-one was hanging around the entrance. Expecting the front door to be propped open with a box of flyers, Peter was surprised to see a new intercom system, and when he pressed the buzzer, a female voice asked his name.

Walking up the familiar stairs, with the owner of the unfamiliar voice, Peter at first hoped that she wouldn't ask how he was. After three flights of stairs worth of lack of sympathy though, he was aggrieved that she hadn't said anything to him at all. She was a pretty, open faced girl with smooth brown hair in a no nonsense pony tail. Too many girls were shaving their hair off nowadays, Peter thought. It was unattractive, off-putting. She was a little too self possessed though. It wouldn't kill her to admit she knew who he was. Compared to any bands she must know, bands stuck on Deep Focus, Peter was famous. He was a famous person in a famous band, whose famous best friend had just died. It made him feel like crying. "How is Ian, I suppose he's taken it hard?" he prompted eventually.

She made a tiny noise, a vocalised shrug, and steered him round some boxes of t-shirts blocking the corridor.

Peter prompted again, he couldn't help himself, "It's been a tough day..." No response. "A really tough day." Nothing. Really, this was horrible. "You've heard about it?"

The girl looked at him politely, giving nothing away.

"Carl Howell died. Carl, you know, from Chinaski. They found him dead yesterday. I mean, not they, the band. I'm in the band, I was his best friend." Nothing still, just the gaze, "I mean the ambulance people found him."

She murmured something about watching his step around a puddle of water on the floor.

Was she fucking retarded? Really, was there something wrong with her? Angry tears pricked Peter's eyes and when they came to Ian's door he didn't look at her or say goodbye. Bitch.

The office was in its usual turmoil. Coffee mugs tottered on pillars of CDs, t-shirts spilled out of boxes, ashtrays overflowed. Beer mats had been stuck under the short leg of the desk. The only thing different was a big new computer, pristine and incongruous. Ian creased his face at the instruction manual.

"Fred thinks it's time we used all this stuff. Computers. Says we can't be left behind." He tapped a key hopefully, and frowned. "I don't get them. You?"

Peter shook his head and took a seat. Was Ian going to pretend nothing had happened too? The room was silent. Peter stared at his knees and heard a sigh from Ian.

"How are you bearing up, Pete?" and Peter was so grateful that he was being cared about that he almost forgave the Pete thing. No-one called him Pete, except Ian. He wasn't a Pete. Never had been. As he opened his mouth to answer, the tears came at last. They'd been leaking all day, but he hadn't let go of it all, and now he found he couldn't stop. The tears poured down his face, slowed a little through the day's growth of beard, and dripped onto his t-shirt and knees. His meaty shoulders heaved with the effort of release. He gripped his forearms, his finger nails leaving little white half moon scars, rolling under the onslaught, until it exhausted itself, gradually, messily.

Ian was close to him, crouching down in front of him, with a box of tissues. Peter shuddered out the last of the tears and took one, along with the offered cigarette. They smoked in silence until Freida came in.

She had aged in the last year. Deep lines led from her nose to her chin and the frizzy red hair showed grey at the sides. She drifted into the room with none of her usual bustle and hilarity, and didn't comfort Peter, but stood near him frozen. Ian got up to put his arm around her and usher her into a chair, and then stood awkwardly, silent.

Freida tried to smile. "Poor Ian can't deal with me. But I can't seem to pull myself together. You know. His father came over, he was the one who called us. Then he came over because he said –" she choked a little, "he said we sounded kind and he wanted to thank us for what we did for his boy. He brought flowers and stayed for an hour. He did most of the comforting to tell the truth. I must have been dreadful to be with. He was very – kind. Very. Not what I expected."

"I never thought his dad was that bad. It was Miriam, she was the bad one," said Peter.

"Oh, Fred has a thing about bad fathers," Ian's tone was teasing, but he stopped when he saw Freida's grim face. "He said that the funeral is set after the post mortem."

"There's a post mortem? Like an autopsy?" Peter felt sick.

Ian nodded, kept his voice low, as if to keep it from Freida, as if she couldn't hear what he was saying right next to her. "There has to be. Unexplained death."

And Peter realised suddenly that he hadn't thought about that at all. Carl's dead, Bob had said, and that was all Peter had taken in. Carl's dead. Deal with that. There wasn't enough mental bandwidth to ask or absorb why. He didn't even remember if Bob had told him anything. Just where he was found. That was all Peter remembered. How weird, he thought, not to have asked. How strange of me. And he thought suddenly of Chris Harris. He hadn't asked either.

Ian was speaking, "...because he was so young they have to consider, you know, that he did it himself." Peter felt rather than saw Freida's stricken face.

"But he wouldn't have done that. He had no reason to, I mean, he was withdrawn, but he would, you know, shut down sometimes. It didn't mean anything, you know, serious."

Ian was silent and Peter pressed on, "I mean there was no note or anything. No? Nothing bad had happened. It was all good. Everything was going well."

Ian spread his hands and shrugged slightly, "We'll find out I suppose."

Freida was staring at Ian as if she hated him. "You're being casual. You're being *casual* about it."

"I'm not being *casual*. I'm just not falling apart, that's all. There's no point in falling apart –" Ian rocked uncomfortably on his heels and smiled his tic-like smile.

"I think about the poor boy lying in that room for days on end, and no-one bothering, no-one trying to find him...no-one caring –" Freida was crying now. "And I think *I* didn't try to find him! *I* didn't think to look either."

"Fred, you didn't even know he was missing. You hadn't seen him in nearly a year. Just, really, try to be logical about it."

"I can't be logical! It's shocking to be logical now, when he's dead, surely, Ian? There's nothing logical about him dying like that." Her voice was shrill now, and mascara no-one knew she wore puddled in the bags under her eyes, "You can say that because you didn't like him and you didn't care! Say what you like, because I know it's true, you didn't care about him the way I did, the way people ought to have done –" and she flurried away as Ian tried to hug her, hugging herself tight instead, rocking, gasping. It was the first argument they'd had in ten years.

"It's a tough day Pete. I....look I know it's been tough for you too, but I think Fred needs to be alone, or, you know, just with me." Ian wore the terrible, supplicating smile of a helpless man. And then the smile disappeared as the sharp end of a CD case hit him in the temple, and another on his shoulder.

Freida was shouting that she wanted him out of the office, that she didn't want to be with him, that she wanted to be with Peter and only

Peter, because at least he knew what she was talking about. She barged Ian out and bolted the door behind him with shaking hands. Turning back to Peter, with the mascara drying around her eyes and her red grizzled hair standing on end, she looked like a mad woman.

"Did you know where he was? Was he hiding from us?" Her eyes were unfocussed.

"I didn't know. I don't know."

"Why was he hiding away? Was he depressed? Could we have helped? Have you seen Lydia?"

It was one of Freida's conceits that everyone she liked, liked each other. Everyone played nicely together, was invited to each other's parties, as if they were in primary school, and she was the kindly head teacher.

"I called Lydia. I called a lot of people. To let them know. Someone had to –" Peter waited for sympathy, acknowledgment, but Freida was too distracted.

"I suppose Bob called you after he called us. Oh God, it must have been so hard for him! Calling up all these *people* he didn't know, giving them that terrible news. I can't imagine how difficult that would have been. Can you?"

"Yes."

Again, Freida didn't hear him. She began heaving folders out of drawers, knocking an ashtray over, spilling water as she slapped them onto the desk, one after the other.

"What are you looking for?"

"Photos. Pictures. Look! These!" A folder full of Chinaski, clippings and photos taken around the office and on tour, like a scrapbook kept by a proud mother. "There's everything in here, letters too. We can go through it and see –" She stumbled on her words.

"See what?"

"See. If. See if. There's something we missed. If there's something in *here* that tells us something, why –" and she sat down suddenly, broken and small on the swivel chair. Some of the pictures slid out onto her lap, and from there to the floor. Peter bent to pick them up.

Black and white shots that they'd rejected for the first album's inner sleeve, each of them self consciously posed, uncomfortable, and, oh, they all looked so impossibly young. Such soft babies. So anxious, so excited. Portentous shots in an industrial landscape. All army boots and combats and fish eye lenses. It was embarrassing. It was almost sweet. And there, in the corner of one photo, a woman's hand reaching out to smooth Carl's hair back from his forehead. Carl's forehead was creased with annoyance – at the wind? At Lydia's hand? Was he annoyed with her as early as that? And here, one of Chris Harris' articles:

NME

May 1990.

A MODEST PROPOSAL FROM CHRIS HARRIS

Loyal readers have noted my virtual obsession with Chinaski over the last few millennia. I am also cognisant of the fact that my hyperbole has its own gravitational pull – Planet Harris attracts haters and lovers indiscriminately (for what is an enemy but a friend you haven't taught to love you?) and misunderstanding has been swirling about my head like so much cosmic dust. My mailbag runneth over with your dirty little missives, most of which err on the side of concern. You say to me "Chris, why Chinaski?" You pull on my ragged coat tails and ask me to tell you why, why why?

Well, this is your lucky day. Strap yourself in and lend me your ears. When "Shattered" was released on Deep Focus, I said then that it was a work of rare genius. A superlative album, something of beauty with a cast iron fragility at its heart. If Iggy Pop, Kurt Cobain and Twiggy fashioned a perfect sex doll, it would be Carl Howell. I myself, in the early weeks of my burgeoning obsession, felt discomforted by the inescapable fact that the singer was – undoubtedly – a pretty boy. The face alone could launch a thousand releases (so to speak). A pretty boy with a voice of whispering gravel and the doe eyed charm of an animal in a trap. And then I began to pay attention to the music.

I can't think of a single band like them to come out of this country. I can't think of a live experience like it. Chinaski don't need the pyrotechnic gibberings of the Buttholes; the drunken aberrations of The Jesus Lizard, or the melancholic posturings of Nirvana.

Holy Christ and post modernist distance be damned, they are the finest live band I've ever seen. On ANY stage – be it the ponced up Paradiso or the murky Marquee – they have you stock still and breathing with them, they have you pounding your face and screaming with them. This is what rock music is meant to be about. It's what we've been waiting for. If the Majors have any wit, they'll snap them up. Oh! spare me your indie schlock horror. What did DCG do for Sonic Youth? It made you listen to them. They may work the same magic on Nirvana – who knows?

There may be some of you who just don't get it. That means – though it pains me to say so – we can never be friends. Chinaski are the Second Coming of Rock. You heard it here. You're welcome.

Freida squatted down with him and was scooping up the papers, arranging them on the desk. "Do you remember how excited we were about this?" She touched the article, "You remember? It felt like Chris was your guardian angel almost. And this – remember when you were all still here, all still friends?"

She was stroking a picture that a photographer friend of Carl's had taken. That time when he decided that they should have themselves documented. What was his name? Sam? No. Sean. Following them around for days, cropping up in corners with his unctuous smile, doing anything Carl told him to do. Peter remembered this picture now. It had been taken in The Bristolian, Lydia was aiming a mock punch at Carl while Carl grinned. Peter was told to just sit still, John to look mean. It was a stupid photo, naive, badly staged, but it made him smile.

"They were so sweet, Carl and Lydia. They *worked*. Don't you think? It *worked*. As soon as they split up, Carl began to drift away. It all went wrong for him. Did you speak to Lydia?"

Peter bristled. "Yes. I did. I called everyone."

Freida, still preoccupied, murmured, "Well. That must have been awful for you too," and immediately picked up the phone and dialled a number from memory. Peter heard it ringing on and on until she replaced the receiver.

"She must be out. Poor Lydia. She must have gone out to clear her head. We should call later. She must feel even worse than us. Yes! She must. She never gave up on him. Do you remember how scared he was? Nervous? Remember, at the beginning?"

At the beginning, after Carl had charged ahead and got studio time, things had stalled. Everyone had been so surprised that little Carl had a band, and that the band was good. Peter remembered Mason, the normally taciturn studio engineer, shouting through the intercom. "Fuck's sake!" he'd laughed. "Who knew?" And no-one had known, except for Carl, how good he was. He'd taken their tentative, slightly generic demo and turned it into something cripplingly arresting. That splintered, roaring voice he became famous for rolled out of him in waves, his guitar strings had snapped under the battering, and again and again he'd screamed, flailed and wailed, years of carefully compressed aggression hitting the walls and tumbling onto the spinning tapes in the booth.

But after that, as soon as he'd been practically carried back to the office, he'd withdrawn. Peter remembered him sitting down suddenly on the floor, amidst all the congratulations, all the excitement, closing his eyes and shaking. Lydia had taken him away, and no-one saw him for days, except her. They spent all their time together at that point. Carl and Lydia, Lydia and Carl.

For weeks there was no sign that he would come back to the studio or formalise things with the label. Peter, having put off university for a year against the wishes of his parents, was running out of excuses to put it off for another. If they had a deal, then maybe he had a chance of proving to them that deferring was worth it. If they didn't, and if Carl carried on like this, then the band would fold. He told Lydia as much, but he doubted if it got back to Carl. He was ill, she said. He couldn't come to the phone. He needed space. And so they all waited about like fools until Lydia let him out to play again.

But was that fair? How much of the truth had been poisoned by how much Peter disliked her now? There was something genuinely vulnerable about Carl, then, no matter how he played on it. There was something crazed and unnerving about his performance in the booth, something sick. It was like watching a man in a padded cell trying to escape from his own skin. Perhaps Carl had been right to withdraw, to question if this was what he wanted. Look where it got him, after all.

When Carl surfaced after a week or so, he was in good spirits, quiet but determined. He had them rehearsing in Peter's basement for ten days straight, and when he arrived at Deep Focus for the recording session he brought with him Dom Marshall, Sean, and Lydia – his support, his entourage. They ran through 15 tracks in 6 hours, and Carl kept his back to the band, keeping close to the wall. There hadn't been any drinking – once Dom had opened up a can and Carl had told him to leave. There was no slacking. There wasn't even much conversation. Peter had been so taken aback by Carl's sudden work ethic, that he'd done whatever he was told to do, making only half-hearted attempts to be part of the process. Sometimes Carl and Lydia had hushed but urgent conversations, outside in the corridor, and then Carl would come back in with a slightly different instruction to give; but that happened very rarely. The darkness in the studio, the stuffiness, the way only three people at a time had room to stand at the mixing desk, the broken clock; it was a timeless, hermetic space. And each time, when Peter left, bone tired, stinking of cigarettes, he was surprised to see that it was still daylight. He and John would walk to The Bristolian for a well needed drink, leaving Carl in deep conversation with Mason, barely noticing them leaving.

There were three more sessions over the next two weeks, all funded by Freida and Ian, who hung around the studio waiting for crumbs of information from Mason, or the odd gnomic pronouncement from Dom. Everyone at Deep Focus knew that something big was happening. Phones went unanswered, mail wasn't opened or posted and promotion of other bands was unofficially suspended. All eyes were on Chinaski, all hope was on Carl.

Carl was nervous. Carl wasn't happy. Suddenly skittish, he'd begged Mason to keep the tapes hidden from everyone until they were done just right. Mason objected that there were too many tracks and not enough tape – they'd have to record over some of their earlier stuff soon if they carried on like this, but Carl went to Freida and she gave him carte blanche. Tape after tape was filled, as his earlier confidence crumbled. He wasn't sure. He wasn't sure. There were two takes he liked but it's not quite right – is it cymbal spill? And he made Mason put a blanket on the kick drum. He taped coins to the cymbals; he tuned all the guitars to D and then back again. He fiddled around the edges of work, driving people from indulgence to anger, until Mason had had enough, mixed eleven tracks to his own taste and handed them to Ian without telling anyone. Carl was furious, but Ian was ecstatic.

Six months later they were on tour in Europe.

It was sudden, it was all so sudden, Peter would tell journalists later on. It's all been so quick. We've been so lucky, we've been so supported. The thought behind this, of course, was we don't deserve this, we haven't earned this, and eventually journalists got this impression as well, so Carl told him to stop saying it. But it was true. It *was* sudden, tremendously sudden. One minute he was fending off his parents about university, and the next he was in Maida Vale recording a Peel Session. It was ludicrous, especially when he looked around at all the other older, more seasoned bands he'd got to know and realised that Chinaski had already outstripped them, that he'd gone from being a middle-class school boy to one of the saviours of the scene in less than a year. He'd played the venues he only knew from peering at the gig listings at the back of Melody Maker. He'd appeared, briefly, in the video for their first single; just a flurry of arms and sweaty hair, really, Carl was in pretty much every frame, but still. He'd been on TV, sitting in front of exposed brick, trying to exude quiet menace, while Carl was asked about their plans for the future. He had a pretty, socially awkward, girlfriend who did media studies and made Fimo jewellery in her spare time. He had quietly burnt all his rugby shirts. And Carl was serene, calm, happy. He drifted about town like a little prince – no self doubt here. He deserved it all, he'd earned every minute of it.

* * *

On the day they had to leave to get the ferry, Peter had the shits. All night he'd been up and down to the toilet, and by eight he could only expel empty air and foul smelling water. Having no idea what to take with him on tour, he rolled up five t-shirts, a copy of Naked Lunch, his address book, a sleeping bag, a toothbrush and some Imodium. After a hesitation, he then cut the legs off his second pair of jeans to make slightly indecent shorts. Once he'd wedged himself between the equipment in the van, and they were setting off, he realised that he'd forgotten to pack any underwear. John, a touring veteran, having followed New Model Army since he'd been in school, told him where he'd gone wrong. On the floor of the ferry terminal, they shook out the contents of their kit bags to compare. All John had was a Swiss Army Knife, three t-shirts, guitar strings and a huge tin of spray-on deodorant to freshen up the crotch of his one pair of jeans. It was a miracle of economy. Carl threw Naked Lunch over the side of the ferry as soon as they began to move.

Once the land slipped away, and they were left lonely in the freezing mist, each of them began to feel shy of the others. Carl dealt with it by playing pranks – the Naked Lunch funeral at sea, pretending to undo the ropes keeping the lifeboats secure. Peter wanted to get John onto some touring anecdotes, so he could learn what he was in for, but John maintained an industrious silence, packing and re-packing his bag, avoiding eye contact. He'd never been abroad before. He was worried that they'd take his knife away at customs.

Eventually Peter went down into the bowels of the boat, to search out their van and talk to Dougie, their weathered and surly driver. Dougie was the only one who knew where they were meant to be driving once they hit land. They all had a hastily photocopied list of venues and dates, but no real understanding of where they all were or how long it would take to get there. Huge swathes of Europe had to be driven over, and Dougie was already tired and pissed off about it. He didn't like Carl, and he ignored John altogether. The only person he spoke to was Peter, and that was usually to make fun of him in some way, but Peter flattered himself that it was affectionate. Plus, Peter had been put forward by the other two to deal with him, so he had no choice really.

Dougie – like Dom – was an institution. Angry, taciturn and grimly amused by frailty, he was The Driver You Got On Tour, whether you wanted him or not. Dougie knew how to get to most of the minor venues in Europe, on that well trodden touring path all bands took at the beginning of their careers. He could probably find them blindfolded. This time, however, Deep Focus had thrown in a few new ones in Germany and France, and Dougie didn't like novelty, Germany, or France. He had refused to speak to Ian for a month and even Freida – the only woman he had any respect for – had trouble getting a word out of him. By way of revenge, he'd reserved the right to play only his own tapes in the van, and given that he only liked Celtic Frost, it was going to be a long couple of months. Peter's plan was to soften him up by keeping him in beer, expressing an interest in black metal, and, most importantly, keeping Carl away from him as much as possible. Dougie had once turned on him, and called him a gay little cunt. It was the only time he'd spoken to him or about him, and Carl, stung and scared, had wisely stayed away from him ever since. In the confines of a cramped Transit van though, that would prove impossible.

Peter approached the van, psyching himself up. Dougie might prefer him to the others, but he still didn't like him very much. He heard the muffled sound of Celtic Frost, and when he slid the door open, a rolling mist of weed tumbled out. Dougie was air drumming. It was as embarrassing as walking in on someone wanking. With eyes screwed shut in hideous ecstasy, jaws locked in a rictus, and his hands stiff at the wrist, he flailed away at the steering wheel. He probably looked better when he *was* having a wank. Backing away. Peter ducked by the side of the van, using the guitar solo as cover for closing the door. He waited until the track had finished, heard Dougie cough and light up, before making his re-entry. Christ it stank in there already. Dougie didn't believe in footwear, said it stopped the skin from breathing. He also didn't believe in washing hair, because everyone knew that hair cleans itself after a week or so, or in deodorant, because it was a con. The combined assault of feet, sweat, weed and scalp scurf was brutal, and they'd only just left home. At least he didn't have a policy against open windows, so at high speeds there might be a chance to fumigate the thing. But still. Christ. There was a beer can at his elbow. Was he pissed as well? Peter began to feel edgy about customs...and John had that fucking knife on him as well...

"You look troubled son," Dougie was expansive.

"That Celtic Frost?"

"It was. It was. You could learn from them, son. And where are, fucking what's their names, Mutt and Jeff?"

"Carl and John."

"Them? The guitar heroes?"

"Oh upstairs. In the bar I think."

"Best place for them. Might pass out. Then we won't get Blondie moaning about the Frost."

"Well, there are other bands. We've got a bag of tapes," Peter risked.

"Well," Dougie seemed amused, "you behave and I might let you. Keep Blondie on a leash and we'll see. Until his keeper comes."

"His what?"

"That posh bint. The one with the hair and the –" he shimmied his shoulders and widened his eyes –" fucking attitude. Her. Once she comes you'll be begging to sit up front with me."

"Lydia's coming?" Peter felt cold.

"So they said. Freida said to make her welcome. She's your tour manager, boy."

"She's our what? A tour...we don't need a tour manager!" Peter's voice shook. "What do we need a tour manager for? When's she coming?" Suddenly, two months with only Dougie's feet and Celtic Frost to worry about seemed like paradise.

"Dunno. Soon? Dunno. She's *his* manager, really. Blondie's. Not yours." Dougie stuck Rizlas together in his complicated way, with his tongue slightly protruding, "Double fucking trouble." He pulled the sticky buds apart and placed them fussily amongst the tobacco. "We're going to have to stock up on this shit in Amsterdam, boy, I tell you. Else I'll kill him and beat her to death with his corpse." He shooed Peter away, turned up Celtic Frost again and leaned back with his cap over his eyes, the smoke drifting up over the peak.

When Peter got to the bar on the second deck, he had trouble pinning Carl down on what he knew about Lydia coming and how long he'd known it. There were smirks, evasion, sudden fits of exasperation, hints of anger, but eventually Peter found out that Lydia was due to meet them in either Holland or Germany, in a week or two weeks, or sometime into the tour. Carl refused to see why Lydia's arrival should be a thing worth talking about, and that really got to Peter. It felt as if Carl was shoring himself up against him, protecting himself, hiring a body-guard. Also, why did Carl get to bring a girlfriend? Why couldn't Peter have brought his? In fairness, Peter didn't want to have his girlfriend on tour with him, but it was the principle of the thing.

Carl made it worse by insisting that Peter must have a crush on Lydia – that's why he was so *emotional* about it, and what started as a convenient joke intended to get Peter off his back, quickly became a van-powered meme. Everywhere they went that first week, Carl made sure to tell someone, the person he judged to have the biggest mouth, that Peter wanted to fuck his girlfriend. It became part of the fabric of things: Peter loves Lydia. Even John, at first in on the joke, assimilated it as truth after a while, once taking Peter aside to lecture him on the futility of jealousy. "It'll eat you up from the inside mate. You don't need it." Maddeningly, every petty disagreement they had, and every legitimate point Peter made, was shot down by Carl, mock offended, claiming that Peter was only saying this because he wanted to fuck his girlfriend. Worst of all, the contagion, if not the humour, had spread as far as the front seat of the van: Dougie didn't like him anymore. Celtic Frost grew louder and louder, and he didn't share his tobacco.

Despite this, the fact of actually touring, speeding down flat motorways, margined by fields of unfamiliar crops, through alien suburbs, to a waiting club, was glamorous, tremendously exciting. Wedged in around their equipment, sharing beers, sharing stories, peering out of the back window, watching the foreign road laid straight behind them, they shared a sense of purpose, destiny.

They all, at one time or another, nearly got knocked down crossing the road because they were looking the wrong way. Buildings seemed impossibly grand – five stories, some of them, with dark bars and dank venues below. Sometimes the club would be locked when they arrived, and they'd open the back of the van and perch on their equipment, wiggling toes and testing sore limbs, the excitement growing. The weather was warm, sultry, and Carl got into the habit of leaping out onto the street the moment the van stopped, and changing his t-shirt, his fish white belly showing, shrugging his shoulders into it as he walked, confidently, to the club.

Sometimes there would be only five or six curious people in the audience. Once there was nobody but the bar staff. But soon there were more, fifteen, twenty, even fifty kids who were actually waiting for them. Waiting! Peter signed an autograph, and managed to spell his name wrong. But always, already, they asked for Carl. They all wanted him; Peter and John didn't really count. A university student recorded an interview with them, posing all his questions to Carl. An earnest girl who ran a fanzine wanted to understand his religious faith, determined that he was either deeply religious, or a vehement atheist. One girl followed them around from the start, eventually turning up in Nijmegen with a shaved head and a Chinaski tattoo, fresh and swollen on one bony shoulder blade. Dougie said she looked like one of the Manson girls, and gave her misdirections to the next gig to get rid of her. Carl spent the next couple of days worried that she'd show up at a later date, a woman scorned, and stab him. That might well have been Dougie's plan, but as it was they never saw her again.

They never ran out of things to say to each other. Most of it was puerile; a lot of it involved complicated games of 'would you rather..?' – 'Would you rather fuck a midget or a dwarf?' was one that ran for two days. Even Dougie joined in on that one. Eventually, Dougie relented and allowed them to play some of their music on the tape deck. A day went by without the Peter Loves Lydia thing. Then another. Perhaps all it had been was a display of that nervous energy and giddiness that Carl was prone to. His jokes and his needling sometimes crossed the line into childish cruelty, but only when he was ill at ease or bored. A week or so into the tour he had visibly relaxed. His skin was losing its inner city pallor, and he stood straighter, looser. He met your eye. The bouts of feverishly talking about nothing were lessening, as were the not-too-funny practical jokes. A quiet Carl was a happy Carl. A lot of people mistook the quietness for shyness, or resentment, but Peter knew that that wasn't the truth. The truth was that Carl needed calm. He was a master at uncovering pent up rage during a performance, but he had to put a lid on it afterwards, or they'd all pay for it, because Carl, angry, wasn't a great person to be around.

For now, though, they all thrived on the routine. Each day different, each day exactly the same. The hangover. The cramped space in the van. Celtic Frost. The disappearing road in the back window. The roofs of unfamiliar buildings. The unintelligible conversations of people in the streets, of the fans, of the promoter. Each dressing room was a variation on a theme. A strip light. A stained sofa. A zinc topped table fixed to the floor. The walls were scrawled with graffiti from all the other bands that had been through there before, with dates going back ten years. Every night they tacked up the running order for the night on the back of the door, then did the soundcheck. Carl would gaffer tape the set list next to his guitar pedals. The t-shirt stall was set up, they'd have a beer or two backstage, keeping it quiet, contemplative. And then the gig.

Peter would always glance at Carl once they came off stage, noting his mood, seeing if he needed to keep things calm. Everyone was happier this way. A few moments alone, a valuable break, and then all the clamour from outside could enter without any danger. Carl didn't drink a lot after a gig, mostly giving his share of the rider to Dougie, which eventually eased the tensions between them. If they didn't have to get back in the van and start driving immediately, Peter and Carl would have time to talk. One beautiful night, lying on the flat roof of a club/youth centre/nursery in Northern Germany, they lay down together looking at the stars, sharing a joint and talking about how far they'd come, what was going to happen next, and how it was all predestined. With the intense nostalgia peculiar to the very young, they marvelled at what might have been if fate hadn't thrown them together. For years later, Peter looked back on this evening as the happiest of his life.

But as they made their way through Germany, and Lydia's arrival drew closer, Carl became more subdued. He looked tired. He complained of colds, of sties in his eyes, ulcers in his mouth. One morning, after an uncomfortable night sleeping on the floor in a cramped squat, Peter found him sitting with his back to the open fridge, shivering, feverish. He fed him some strange tasting European milk and some communal stew he found congealed in a pan and then asked Dougie to open the van windows to get some fresh air in. Together, they put Carl carefully in the back, wrapping him up in some towels taken from the one hotel they'd stayed in so far. Carl lay quite still, a wan mummy, with his eyes open. He didn't speak until they were discussing cancelling the next gig. Then he got up shakily and told them that the gig was still happening, he'd go on. He earned Dougie's respect that day. He was even allowed to sit in the front and chose the music.

It would be simple to say that everything changed with the arrival of Lydia, but Peter, despite disliking her now, couldn't in all honesty say that was true. At the beginning she had fitted in just fine, and Peter was relieved to have someone else there to keep an eye on Carl. Even Dougie was welcoming: now that he liked Carl, he was inclined to like Carl's girlfriend. She also claimed to speak a bit of German, which was vastly impressive and useful. She manned the t-shirt stall, and also brought along stickers with the eye catching Chinaski design on them – the C in a bold black circle. They sold well, and ended up on hundreds of guitars, flightcases, and car windows, spreading the word far better than a t-shirt. She put up with sleeping on floors, at venues, even in the van. Only her slightly too loud voice was grating, and her assumption that she was always right. Soon, though, she began to lose her grip, she began to wear out. Then it got bad.

She wasn't very good at playing the 'would you rather' game. She tried, but her effort took all the fun out of it, and so they stopped, and the long autobahn journeys began to drag. Lydia favoured more established party games, like Twenty Questions, the kind of games that she played with her family at Christmas time, but it was difficult to make a game like that smutty, although Dougie gave it his best shot, so it didn't really take. And then there was Carl and his illnesses. She and Dougie strongly disagreed about how Carl should be cared for if he felt ill. Dougie was very much in the 'fresh air cures all' camp, while Lydia was a firm advocate of wrapping up warm and lying in a darkened room.

"Good luck finding a darkened room," Dougie snorted, while Lydia countered that the gig ought to be cancelled, Carl needed to save his voice. Peter and John agreed privately that there was nothing wrong with Carl anyway. He had a cold? They all did. He was tired? He didn't have much reason to be considering he made sure he always got any spare bed in any house they stayed in.

They were hitting the part of the tour that Dougie had dreaded. Jammed in the middle of the schedule, at the last minute, were five dates supporting The Jesus Lizard. His mental map of Germany was delineated by the venues he'd driven to dozens of times, but these dates were in new venues, unfamiliar places, and all of his irascible prejudice against Germany began to seep out: it was a fucking shithole; the roads were too straight; the beer was piss. It was full of fucking goth pricks, weed was too hard to get and shit when you got it. He got lost on the first stretch of the autobahn, and had to resort to map reading, something that hurt his pride. Eventually, after drifting over to the other side of the road into the path of a lorry, he agreed to let someone else read the map. Lydia volunteered. And that was the beginning of the end for her.

Minutes flew like hours while they listened to her confidently point the way, only to change her mind a few moments later. Or worse, not change her mind for hours, even when it was obvious they were going in the wrong direction. The van swung in loops and curves around the German countryside, Celtic Frost and invective pouring from the driver's window. Lydia seemed to think it was hilarious, that was the worst thing. She'd just laugh, have another beer, and then insist that they turn off the road and find a service station so she could have a piss. Eventually, Dougie refused and told her she'd have to piss by the side of the road like a dog, but even that didn't stop her. The arrival of Chris Harris seemed heaven sent, and, to this day, Peter was still thankful to him.

Chris had been on some vague and epic assignment over the last few months, sending back missives from the front line, Chicago, Austin, Seattle, crafting a scene and riding the wave of it back home. Now he was travelling with The Jesus Lizard, and, just for a change of scenery, invited himself along with Chinaski for a while. Amongst the generally favourable reviews Chinaski had enjoyed in the last six months, Chris Harris' ecstatic, overblown pieces stood out. He'd made them Single of the Week, and the aggressive way he edged them into otherwise totally separate articles stirred up interest and controversy. By the time he was in Europe, NME had received so many letters about Chris Harris and his new obsession, that they had taken to publishing them separately in a little cordoned off section they called 'The Chinaski Syndrome' after one of his overwrought reviews. It was flattering, it was amazing really, that someone as talented as Chris would want to sit with a bunch of suburban near-teenagers in their shitty van, listening to Celtic Frost. He even got on with Dougie. And he was fun! He was really fun to be around. That time when he took over the bar in Berlin – everyone drank free and everyone seemed to love him for it! That time they took turns to stay standing on the top of the van, Dougie gradually speeding up, seeing who could last the longest. Peter had messed up his arm when he fell, but he didn't mind so much. Buying that Prussian march tape and driving slowly through Bavaria with the windows down and the music blaring. Persuading Dougie to pick up those girl hitchers and conning them into taking their clothes off –that was once Lydia had left, so they could actually have a good time again. He took them to the best tattooist in Berlin and they all ended up with the same Chinaski symbol on their upper arms, except Chris, who told them at the last minute that he didn't really approve of tattoos. John even tried to copy Chris' trick of opening a bottle with his teeth, and snapped his molars in half. He didn't realise the damage until the next day when he woke up with his tongue lacerated and a throat full of blood.

Chris was – to use the outdated expression – cool. Really, really cool, and they all fell over each other to impress him, to be his favourite. Peter remembered that now with some shame, but only a little. Chris had a way of making you feel so included, so valued, that when his attention shifted from you, it was as if the sun had gone out. Peter had been jealous – he could admit this to himself now – when Chris had taken Carl with him to travel with The Jesus Lizard those few days. Peter would have been incredibly intimidated to be with them himself, but he could have dined out on it for years. At the same time, he understood. It must have been painful for Carl to see the head-on collision between his messed up girlfriend, and his sleek new buddy.

The atmosphere in the van was wretched once Chris took Carl away. No-one else was speaking to Lydia any longer, and by now she had completely disintegrated. She couldn't read a map, understand jokes, buy food, find a laundrette, or adequately sell t-shirts anymore. Once or twice she shook off her torpor and tried to muscle in, negotiate with the promoters, or try to get them somewhere to stay, but it was an embarrassing thing to witness. People smirked, or just looked right through her. Girls heading for Carl didn't even glance at her anymore – she'd lost her girlfriend aura somewhere along the line. Not that Carl acted on anything – he couldn't, anyway, with Lydia standing next to him all the time like a zombie, dampening down the fun, making people weary.

And then, finally, she made that terrible scene. Carl was alone with her, without protection, otherwise there was no way it could have happened. Peter didn't know how long the argument had been going on, if it had all taken place in the tatty room backstage, or if it had been more protracted, more public and Carl had taken her there to keep it private. In any case they had been in that room for a long time. Sometimes he heard Lydia shrieking the way all women shriek when they're in the wrong and know it. Carl was restrained, or sounded it. Once there was the sound of something being hit, a solid welt of a noise, and then a whimper, and a low response of some kind, but it was impossible to tell who had made which sound. Nobody wanted to know really. It was all so low class and adolescent; embarrassing. It went against Carl's image, it went against their image as a band, and God knows what Chris Harris thought. The Jesus Lizard stayed away all day, forgoing their sound check, and their frowning silence when they all came back and saw the dressing room was still occupied made Peter cringe. In their eyes, Peter read their disappointment in him. It was his responsibility to sort this out. Carl couldn't do it. Carl needed his help and all he'd done was stand about all day watching the door and clucking his tongue like a pensioner waiting for the post office to open.

So Peter strode purposefully forward just in time to get the dressing room door in the face. He had time to see both of them before he fell, Lydia's mouth wide open in mid shriek and Carl slouched by the door, before the pain knocked him down and the blood pissed out of his eyebrow like a faulty tap.

He was knocked out for a minute, they told him, and the first thing he noticed when he came to was the thick coppery taste of blood in his mouth, the smell of it all around him. The right side of his face felt enormous and he touched it gingerly. It *was* enormous. His fingers came back sticky. Trying to get up, he fell back and someone caught his head and cradled it, asking for a cushion. Carl. Carl, white and sick looking, with blood on his hands, opening his mouth to speak, to ask something, to say something. Peter tried to smile at him reassuringly, but the nausea got the better of him and he was sick instead. Someone (Carl?) wiped his mouth for him. Someone heaved him up and propped him up on the sofa in the dressing room. Someone gave him brandy and someone else wiped his face, apologising in a foreign accent for the pain. Chris Harris was speaking in German, turning down the hospital idea, producing a professional looking medical kit and arranging fancy plasters about the small but deep cut that bisected Peter's right eyebrow. They gave him more brandy once it was done, and Chris accepted compliments on the neatness of the job. He showed a scar on his leg he claimed he had to stitch himself, and this led to a slightly hysterical group discussion on horrible accidents, near misses, scars and tales of the emergency room. John showed his broken teeth, Dougie dislocated his shoulder and snapped it back into place with a grunt, David Yow shared his scarred scalp. Someone knew someone who'd been shot with a nail gun. Everyone had gone to school with someone who'd been shot in the eye with an air gun.

Throughout this, Lydia was kept at bay by the bar manager, crying and braying, scrambling to get to Carl, to Peter. Through the heightened noise, little tendrils of posh girl whining would float their way – she hadn't done anything...she didn't even see him there...she was sure she wasn't the one who opened the door...she needed to explain. They all took turns to glance at Carl with sympathy whenever they heard Lydia's voice, and Carl would look carefully and deliberately at the ground. Poor sod. Poor bastard with this nut job girlfriend who didn't even acknowledge when she'd nearly killed someone. Trying to blame it on someone else, all the time. Always someone else's fault, never hers.

Pretty soon the combination of brandy and unnamed painkillers set Peter on a little cloud of contentment. It was decided that The Jesus Lizard would go on first, to give him time to recover, and in the end they made an event of it. The crowd at the door were told that Chinaski were headlining from now on, that their album had gone gold, that they were about to tour with Nirvana – all lies of course, but all harmless, all good natured. And people believed it, it felt like a significant gig, something they all ought to remember. David Yow introduced them as The Greatest Band Since Pearl Jam, which could have been read as insulting, but Carl seemed happy with the comparison. Chris Harris, from God knows where, had got hold of some paper rose petals, buckets and buckets of them, and he picked the prettiest girls from an admittedly motley bunch to throw them in Carl's path as he came on stage. The petals settled on

Carl's hair and shoulders like a halo of delicate butterflies. Some of them hit Peter in the face and stuck to his blood stained plaster.

The gig itself felt incredible. Maybe it was the pills and brandy, but Peter felt the tightness of the songs, the way that he, John and Carl, moved together smoothly. Each song, it seemed to him, had a perfection to it, a symmetry that looked all of a piece but was actually fitted together, constructed, intricately hinged. John's dogged, dull bass loosened up a little, and Peter followed him to the point that they both relaxed and the rhythm section breathed smoothly, swiftly, like some sleek animal. Carl's shattering, splintering guitar was the perfect counterpoint to that voice, that voice that begged, screamed and whispered at you to stop. Stop what you're doing and listen. Listen to me. And he was listened to, breathed with.

Chris Harris led the applause, hustled them into an encore, and they kept on playing and the kids obligingly went nuts, the t-shirts sold out, they had their pick of places to stay. The bootleg tape of that night went on to sell thousands. After Carl died, there was talk of releasing it officially, but DCG never got round to it. Peter and John chatted up the previously disdainful girls behind the bar, Dougie finally scored some decent weed, Carl stayed on the stage, rolling about in the confetti and drinking vodka with Chris Harris. Lydia could be faintly heard talking – crying – to someone on the pay phone in the corridor, and later on asking Alexander, the manager, in shaky German where the station was. He put her to bed somewhere before loping to the stage to join Chris and Carl. He nodded at Chris – everyone knew Chris it seemed – told the bar girls to bring over some lagers, and, carefully brushing away the dirty confetti, sat down on the stage next to Carl.

"Your girlfriend is sad," he sighed.

Peter edged over to Carl. It wouldn't be fair for the evening to be ruined by this, by Lydia, again. "She's drunk. She's just hammered," he said.

Alexander's face arranged itself in a series of downward points. "She is sad. She is drunk too, yes. But first sad, I think." He rolled a cigarette, lit it, and slowly peeled a thread of tobacco off his bottom lip. "Women get sad," – he inhaled, exhaled – "when they have no place."

The words hung heavily. Peter felt Carl shudder and Chris automatically handed him another beer. Peter touched the scab on his eyebrow, made it throb, and felt vindicated.

"She's OK. She's just made a fool of herself. She's embarrassed. She should be."

Chris Harris snickered and clapped Alexander on the shoulder. "Girls and tours, Al. Girls and tours shouldn't mix. Never. You know."

But Alexander's face remained grim and his eyes were soft and melancholy. "She has no place. So she says she will go home, now. She will not stop being sad, I think. It is sad that she is alone, now."

That put a dampener on things. The bar girls looked less certain about Peter and John and began speaking together rapidly in their own language while they cleaned the bar. Carl looked absently at his bitten fingers, while Chris tried to keep things going with tales of journalistic derring do, but the moment was lost. They all grew silent, wondering how they could each leave without being the first to go.

Carl was the first. He went to find Lydia, but nobody went with him and afterwards no-one wanted to ask what they'd talked about. He didn't come back until everyone else was asleep. By the time they were packing the van in the morning, hungover and trembling, Lydia was standing stiffly by Alexander's ancient VW. Alexander quietly opened the door for her, took her rucksack and placed it on the back seat, and then they were gone.

In the van, they all waited for Carl to speak, and when he didn't, they did it for him. Girls and tours, tours and girls, it never works. You're only as strong as your weakest link. She'll be OK. She'd survive a nuclear strike. Who needs a beer? Groans. Eventual capitulation. I'll have one. Sudden Celtic Frost followed by a sudden silence. Dougie offered to change the tape. After half an hour, it was as if nothing bad had happened.

The rest of the tour, Peter remembered only through a few sharp images. Chris Harris dropping lager bottles full of piss out of the back of the van as they travelled at high speed, watching them smash on the road like tiny rain drops. Dougie having a shit in a bit of scrub land only to find that it was right beside the train tracks. A commuter train was held up on the tracks for 15 minutes, and none of the passengers had anything better to do than wanly watch Dougie try to hide what he was doing. Learning to use a soldering iron. John's bass stolen in Hannover and then returned, oddly greasy, in Stuttgart. A fat promoter calling the woman he just slept with 'empty', refusing to let her eat before she went home.

They all swapped clothes. They all stank. They were all tanned and all dirty. They read nothing but road signs and menus. The faces, buildings, gigs blurred together. Sleeplessness made everything dreamlike; they felt as if they'd been on the road since birth, a cult-like family. Chris Harris took his leave, but promised to show them a good time when they hit France. Then Dougie left them.

He didn't like France. He couldn't score, and he didn't know where the venues were. The streets were too narrow, the whole place was full of collaborating Nazi scum and the girls were up their own arse. In Lyon he refused to help them unload the van, and sat in the venue getting hammered. They let him sleep it off in the dressing room but when they came off stage they found that he'd smashed all the mirrors, drunk the rider and disappeared. A panicked phone call to Deep Focus provided them with a series of louche interim drivers who preferred the radio to tapes and showed no interest in the games that had become the gristly thread holding them together. Without the games, the word-play, the sense of a force to push against and be cowed by – without Dougie – they were stunned, bereft. They arrived in Paris almost catatonic, with a plan to meet up with Chris for the last two gigs before going back home. Home! It was an ancient, alien place by now. Chris had big news for them, he said.

Chris was holed up in a vast barn of a place in the Bastille. Two enormous attics had been knocked together and fitted out like an adolescent's playground. Blow-up sex dolls lounged nonchalantly around the dinner table, arcade games lined the walls. A rank smell drifted out of the open toilet door, and the kitchen walls were covered in artfully defaced pornography. Peter, John and Carl, traipsing up the stairs exhausted, saw the massive TV, the bean bags, and immediately settled in to watch a dubbed episode of Knight Rider. Carl fell asleep with his head on Peter's shoulder, and Peter happily allowed it to go numb, rather than disturb him. The apartment was a French A&R man's model girlfriend's brother's flat, and Chris had the run of it, apparently indefinitely.

After his nap, Carl asked to use the phone, and spent an hour or so in a locked bedroom, muttering, sometimes giggling softly. John got stoned watching Columbo, and Peter took a bath, feeling bashful because Chris Harris sat on the toilet lid, smoking his shitty-smelling cigarettes and chatting to him the whole time. He was talking about The Industry, his hands forming quotation marks on the first and last syllables. The Industry, he explained, was full of sluts and vampires, it was filled to the brim with pretenders, company men and sycophants.

"In this world, Peter, there are precious few people with the wit and the grace to swim against the tide of shit and not choke to death or become a part of it. Chinaski – you guys – you've done it. You guys have it, and if I see it, others will too. It's axiomatic." He rubbed some ash into his trousers and gave a wolfish smile. "Where we lead, others will follow. Some of us are made to follow – most. You guys, others," – an elegant, dismissive wave at himself – "are meant to lead, in whatever capacity we can. That's what women don't understand, what she, what's her face, Lydia, didn't understand, is that we don't belong to them. We belong to ourselves. We don't have family, we don't need all that saccharine stuff. We're a lot more primitive, but, Peter, what comes from the primitive but all the good shit? The *roots* eh? All the fucking, all the music, rock and fucking roll, eh? It's the primitive that keeps us alive. I mean, what do you think of this place? What do you think of this flat?"

Peter said it was very nice. Chris looked at him with patient pity. "It's a shit hole Peter, just like anywhere else. The difference is, the *only* difference is, is that it doesn't think it is. It thinks," – again came the finger quotation marks – "it thinks that it's *unusual*, or intimidating, or cool or whatever. But. What it is. Is. Shit. It's all been designed so it doesn't look like it, but if you scratch and sniff it, it's shit."

Peter didn't say anything because he knew he'd be wrong. He really wanted to wash his balls, and he shifted miserably in the cooling water while Chris shook out a little coke onto a copy of The Face and rubbed it on his ulcerated gums. "And that's why I think you guys have it. Have. It. Because you seem blissfully unaware of artifice. You haven't been designed. It's all been organic."

Peter thought of Carl's lost years, being trained in Dom Marshall's lair in How To Be A Star. He thought about the different ways Carl treated different people. He thought about this sudden, hallucinatory success. It didn't seem organic, it seemed like it was a combination of talent, construction, and dizzying luck. He told Chris as much but was immediately dismissed.

"Oh I think you misunderstand me. You think you've constructed yourselves, we all do. You think you're in control of it, but I'm here to tell you you're not. Some people are born to lead. If they had any control over it, then they'd probably say no. It's a lot of hassle, leading. A lot. But. Some people have no choice."

Peter had heard something like this before...from whom? Something with the same creepy message at heart, but put in a different way.

"So we're here to save music?"

Chris was sitting glazed eyed and Peter had to repeat himself. Chris blinked. "What Oh no! God no. *Carl's* here to save music. You're just the rock on which to build his church. Oh, I like that! That's very neat." He chuckled and abruptly stood up. The Face fell onto the dirty floor. "There's no towels, but there is some brandy." When he left, he left the door open.

130

14

Chris had set up a whole itinerary of activities for them. Mostly photo shoots, and one impromptu gig at fashion school, where they would be met by someone from Rolling Stone. The band now existed in some hinterland where Deep Focus was a world away, in which Chris Harris appeared to have taken over their career.

There were parties in the flat, each one leaking into the next with barely any difference between them; even the people looked the same, said the same things, made the same vehement points in the same range of accents. During these parties, Carl was quiveringly alert. He knew how to laugh in the right places, how to softly insinuate, how to show just enough displeasure to force others into silence. He'd been much the same in school, but fascinating provincial adolescents is relatively simple. Here he was out of his natural element, and that's what made it so impressive. Peter felt pride, really, a glowing pride in Carl. One of our own! One of us, sitting at the centre of this whirlwind. On the sidelines, Peter saw the hundreds of unfolding narratives that the mere fact of Carl created and shut down, and felt nothing but admiration. Nobody could begrudge the attention Carl got, he was made for it. He made people hungry.

Carl was weighed up like gold. People watched him, and watched others watching him, guessing who he was watching. Sitting cross-legged on that table, girls draped over him (one of them's a model, a proper model!), one nervous, jittery knee moving up and down, up and down, while someone kisses the back of his neck. Charging up onto the roof, his guitar on the longest lead, determined to play during a lightning storm. As he washed his skinny frame in the shower without the curtain, he could be seen through the half frosted glass. His fingers twitched in the morning, sending his pills skittering across the floor. When bored, his heavy head drooped, but sometimes he would give that taut smile reserved for the favourite, the loved one, the carer, spreading wide across his face and so many thought about it privately as they tried to sleep. Carl, never alone, was snatched at by so many, assessed, pieces of him stored away, stitched together into something nearly whole.

Chris Harris was at his elbow at all times, whispering, nodding, to emphasise. He weeded out the strident, opinionated girls, the ones that were too tall, and hustled them off to Peter, who was ill at ease, and made them so, or John, who took it where he could. He allowed the smaller, dove-like creatures with little English and soft, compliant limbs to stick with Carl. They drifted about decoratively and were seamlessly replaced from one party to the next. But none of this stopped Carl from calling Lydia, like clockwork, every evening at 7, for that whole first week in Paris. He would disappear into the big bedroom, firmly shut the door, and conduct his maddeningly quiet conversations in privacy. After the phone call he would quietly unlatch the door and lie down on the bed, perfectly still with his eyes on the ceiling. One by one, Peter, Chris and John would tiptoe in, not allude to the phone call at all, and begin tempting him with fresh new parties. And so it went on. Until Carl got sick.

The two gigs in Paris went well, and they were given two more. The last, in a desanctified chapel in Pigalle, was filled with A&R men from major labels. Sullen students were paid to slink up the aisles with trays of sweetened vodka. Candles hovered on the choir stalls, along the worn stone steps of the pulpit, at the feet of Christ. The seated audience, unconsciously affected by the fact of being in a church, whispered and murmured together, and their cigarette smoke looked, but didn't smell, like incense. The band waited backstage in the vestry with a skittish Chris Harris.

Carl, subdued all day, had violet rings under his eyes, and his hands shook. Since morning, he'd been tonguing his bottom lip and over the hours an angry red crescent had formed, raw and painful to look at. He was tired. He was just tired, he said. The sound check was peculiar – all those echoes – and Carl, from some dimly remembered Catholic past, had trouble keeping his back to the Cross. There was no support band – this was a showcase, not a real gig – and the artifice made them all quail a little. And Carl's hands shook, his head bobbed and that red sore grew bigger.

Chris Harris wore ironic tweed and spoke perfect French. He arranged for food, which Carl didn't touch, and moved amongst the crowd with his face fixed in a smile and a mouth filled with ashy compliments. He advised Chinaski to come on late, to have a few beers, to relax. In retrospect Peter wondered if that didn't have something to do with what came later.

By 10 the vodka had become more plentiful, and the noise less reverent. The doors had been ostentatiously locked, and the wave of expectant applause that hit the band when they came on stage was overwhelming. For all it was an altar, and not a stage at all, it was still a bigger space than they were used to working in. Usually Carl had to watch that he didn't hit John with the arm of his guitar, and John had fallen into the drum kit more than once just by taking a step backwards, but here they had space to roam, and it was intimidating. The guitar monitors were hulking, satanic looking things, next to the broken effigy of the virgin, and the outline of the altar itself could still be seen through the black backdrop strung from the ceiling. Chinaski felt, and looked, as if they'd been dropped there by some particularly fiendish God, to confuse the natural order of things. Or at least that's what Chris Harris wrote in his review.

It all started normally. Peter found that he was able to ignore the surroundings after a while, and it became just another gig. The lack of movement from the audience was a bit off-putting – they stayed in their seats, signalling for more vodka – but the applause was appreciative, long, and apparently genuine. About halfway through, though, things changed.

Carl began moving strangely. It began with the odd flurries of violence he'd displayed before – smashing at the pedals, whipping the neck of his guitar viciously from side to side, sudden leaps in the air – but somewhere along the line the posturing became apparently genuine rage, almost ridiculous at first, unsexy, inelegant. One of his guitar strings broke, then another, but rather than breaking to restring, he carried on playing, flaying his fingertips and knuckles, thin blood staining and soaking his clothes. By the middle of the set he was gore-streaked and howling. Peter and John became, separately, anxious, and peered into the vestry for Chris Harris but couldn't see him. The lights, set low and blinding, isolated them from each other, so that they were forced to carry on playing in a bubble of glare and increasing worry. The monitors were shit, so it was difficult to hear how far from the path Carl had strayed – if he was even playing the same song as them anymore. The noise of his by now three-stringed guitar was hideous, and Peter strained his neck, desperate to catch John's eye, needing a sign. He stopped playing when he thought he ought to, according to the hints he was getting from the monitors, and he appeared to have got the timing right, because he heard the expected whine of feedback from Carl's guitar and felt relief. The applause rolled over them, and he discerned little breaks in the blinding light – figures standing up, moving about. There must have been a lot of them because the alternating dark/light dark/light had a strobe effect.

"Chris says to stop," shouted John.

"What? Why?"

"Just says to stop."

Peter stood up. Feedback was still whining and twining itself about the pews and rafters, and as he followed the noise, he came across Carl's smashed guitar abandoned in the central aisle, like a motorbike after a hellish accident. Tripping over the guitar lead, he was caught by a gaggle of A&R men in buttoned up coats, sporting huge smiles. One of them hauled him up by the elbow, while another clapped him on the back.

"Great gig! Great gig!" and Peter, dazed, smiled back. He had no fucking idea what had happened, and scanned the mass of satisfied faces, looking for clues. There was a trail of clothes, and now he noticed dark smears on the sides of the front pews, some no bigger than raindrops, some like sinister skid marks, all leading in the direction of the vestry. Drops of blood, little splatters in a shower, and a shoe print where someone had kicked the door open.

Peter was the last to arrive. There was so much blood. Carl was half naked and covered in it. It matted his hair and pooled in the hollow of his collar bones. John stood next to him, mute and confused, while Chris Harris dabbed at the superficial wounds, smiling and chatting, and Carl sat catatonically in an upright chair, his hands placidly on his knees, the blood caking around his knuckles, saying nothing at all.

"What happened?" Peter's voice was hoarse.

Chris looked up, grinned, "You just gave the show of your life is what happened. Seriously. If you wanted a major deal, I could open the door right now and get you one, like that –" he clicked his fingers, but they were too tacky with blood. He clapped instead, "Like that. That was the show of the fucking decade as far as I'm concerned." And he lit a cigarette, gave one to Carl. Peter crouched down in front of his friend.

"Carl, are you OK?" Nothing. "Carl, mate, are you OK? What the fuck happened?"

A shaky hand put the cigarette to his frozen lips, and Carl inhaled and exhaled through a smile that was made all the more ghastly by the blood that stained his teeth.

"He tore rock and roll a new one, that's what happened. In a few minutes we'll go to the after party and they'll be on you like the proverbial flies, just watch." Chris scrubbed at Carl's face with a scrap of toilet paper. "But not if you go out there looking like fucking Carrie. There's got to be somewhere to wash here – priests have to shower don't they? Look, have a wash in the basin at the back and take my shirt until we can get you changed. We can be fashionably late to our own party, I'm sure."

He fussed about Carl, pinching him to get him out of the chair, arranging a taxi, hustling him out of the chapel in the most public way possible. Carl's hunched figure in the button-down shirt was immediately swamped by the crowd, and Peter and John, separated from them, had to force their way out of the door, just in time to see Carl being pushed into a waiting car and Chris Harris issuing instructions to an expectant knot of people. Chris gave Peter a thumbs up.

"See you at the flat, we can regroup there!" He yelled, and then they sped off, and Peter and John were left on the Rue des Martyrs, the traffic blowing rubbish about their ankles.

On the way back, John gave Peter his version of what had happened. At some point Carl had got frustrated with his guitar, either that or he was doing it for effect. He hit it a few times, with no real force, against the altar rail, and a string broke. Then another. He carried on playing so brutally that he tore up his hands – that's where most of the blood had come from. It looked worse than it was, John thought. But things had started to get really weird once he began tearing at himself. He twisted and tore at the neck of his t-shirt until it hung off his shoulder, but then he carried on pulling at it and yanking at it until it fell off altogether. Then he took a walk down the aisle.

"He did what?"

"He jumped over the little fence thing, the bit with the cushions, and walked down the middle. And his fingers are all fucked up by now, you know, and he keeps on playing. And I kind of look at Chris, and he's laughing and going 'carry on, carry on' and I hear you carrying on, so I do too. And so Carl's at the end, and I don't know what he's doing because of the lights, but I hear people kind of laughing – not like laughing ha ha, like it's funny, but more a kind of 'what the fuck' kind of laugh, you know. So Chris says 'carry on', so I do. And then I see Carl come back up the aisle thing, and he's looking really fucked up, I mean brutal. Fucking scary, mad. So I think, oh fuck this, and I look at Chris, but by now Carl's kind of gone nuts on his guitar, proper fucking it over, and they all seem to love it. So I think, OK, alright then, he's just putting it on, OK. But then he looks bad, I mean really sick or something, and he goes to the room, and Chris gives it –" John drew his fingers across his throat, "so I go and get you. End of. But it was fucking weird, because I go back and I kind of expect Carl to be giving it all, you know 'oh what a laugh, oh that was massive' all that, but instead he's just sitting there like a big fucking doll and Chris is acting like it's all a joke. So. I dunno. Where are we going? Do you know the way?"

They were too afraid to take the Metro and not sure what their stop would be anyway. Since they'd been in Paris, they'd barely left the flat – the party had come to them. Now that they were left alone in the streets, they felt very young, very vulnerable. In the couple of months they'd been on tour, they hadn't really had any time to just walk about. There were never any worries about language, because there was always someone who spoke English at the venue. They never had to think about finding their way around because they always had Dougie, or Chris. Now, as they trudged along the increasingly cold streets, they felt like abandoned children. Neither wanted to admit this to the other, and it crossed both their minds that they didn't really know each other very well. Outside of the smut and the perfunctory, they'd never had a real conversation. And so they both leaped all over the one thing they had in common: Carl, the band. John wanted to know if Peter thought Chris Harris really had any sway with major labels.

"He talks it up, but does he have the contacts?"

"He knows a lot of people," Peter hedged.

"Yeah. Yeah. But, I mean –" John blushed a little, "I mean if he does, then why pick us?"

Privately, Peter had thought the same thing. Reading some of the things Chris wrote about them, he found it difficult to square the shimmering phrases with his own band. Peter didn't have any illusions about his drumming. Carl imitated whatever guitarist he was enamoured with that week, while John's bass was like road markings on a straight, empty road: apparently necessary, but ignoring them wouldn't make that much difference. Sometimes Peter felt as if they could be a great band, a really great band, particularly when they played live. 'Shattered' had some good things in it, very good things, but the influences showed. Carl's constant fiddling had made for an uneven record, a series of demonstrations of what they could do in various styles. So when Chris Harris wrote about the album's circular narrative, the animal thread of woe, running through the core of it, and meeting the authorial voice head on – whatever that meant – a little voice in him protested. What narrative? What grand plan? They'd gone into a studio and laid down over twenty tracks, some of them covers that ended up being reworked and disguised as original songs. These tracks had been cut up, overdubbed, tweaked, tuned and polished by a professional engineer, and brought into being while Peter was in the pub, while John was watching TV and smoking weed. They hadn't even paid for the studio time. They hadn't even had a say on what tracks made it onto the album. Ian had done it, with help from Carl and Mason. It had been a project with many managers, nobody had suffered for Art. But then he thought of Carl, living in the studio throughout the sessions, sleeping just long enough to dream an idea and then spend hours testing it out, driving Mason mad. He thought of all the ideas Carl been given of himself from Dom, from whatever Lydia told him, and now Chris. Maybe Carl did have a grand plan that everyone saw except his bandmates. Perhaps Chris was right.

John said, "Perhaps he wants to use us," and Peter shut that down right away.

"Maybe he sees the truth, and we're just too close to it?" Peter suggested. "And, I mean, it's not like we came out of nowhere. I mean, me and Carl have been practising for years. And you too. And we're good, so why not good enough for a major?"

"I just don't want it to be like, we're just the session guys, and it's all about Carl, you know? That's not what I – that's not –"

Peter took a deep breath, "It's not like that though, is it? Me and Carl – and you on the last two tracks – we wrote them. The songs. I mean it's on the sleeve that we did. All the money's split. The singer always gets the most attention, but that doesn't mean, you know, that it's all about him or we don't matter –" John kicked at some rubbish, "I don't think we have to worry. I mean we're not going to get fucked over. And Chris is on our side."

"He's on Carl's side," John muttered.

"But it's the same side!"

"We didn't get a lift back, did we?"

"No –" Peter wondered how to turn this one around, "but there wasn't room. I mean, we don't know what other people were in the car too. They might be meeting with someone, now. About a deal."

John's hurt eyes belied his twisted smile, "Then why aren't we there, if we're so important too? And isn't that our label's job?" And Peter tried, failed, to find an answer.

They walked in silence for a few more minutes, until, quite by chance, they saw their building on the next corner. John stopped Peter on the way in.

"All I'm saying is that we have to look out for ourselves in this. I don't know Carl that well, I mean, I like him. But, I know you a bit better, and all of this has been fucking –" he raised his hands in the air and made the sound of an explosion, "but, you know, after tonight, and Carl pulling that weird shit and Chris acting like he'd found the golden ticket, I'm a bit fucking freaked out. To be honest."

Peter held his shoulder. "Look mate, don't worry. Seriously. Don't worry. Carl can be in his own world a bit, but he's not flaky and he's not – he doesn't forget his friends. Look, it'll be OK. Let's go up, we'll talk, see what's happened."

Chris' voice bounced off the apartment's bare walls and high ceilings. The phone cord twitched and slid as he moved from room to room. When Peter and John came into the living room, he was in mid conversation.

"– Like, I don't know, like *Evil Dead* or something. I'm not even *kidding. The* single most insane thing I've ever seen. I'm *not.* No, sweet, I am *not* given to hyperbole. This day will go down –" he saw Peter and John, and enthusiastically shooed them to the sofa, "– it will go down as The Death of The New. Yes! The death of all this loathsome, shoe gazing, slacker shit nonsense. *Yes* I'm calling it that! Why *not?* It has an academic ring to it. Yes. *Yes!* I'm taking them to a party now. Oh, you can be such a terrible cunt. Yes, you! Terrible. Ok, ok, kisses kisses, bye, bye, bye."

He came towards them with hands outstretched, his red face hacked in two by a smile, and shook their shoulders. The album lay on the coffee table, and one fat line of cocaine had been carefully placed beneath beneath Peter's picture, another under John's. A snail trail of coke scurf remained under Carl's. Peter and John looked at each other over their 10 franc notes, eyebrows raised, questioning. You think? said John's face, and Peter answered by blinking and snorting.

Chris Harris loved to share. He loved to share drugs, drink, and tales of the unexpected. But most of all he loved to share good fortune, and tonight he was brimming with it. Tonight, they were told, had been their grand debut. He brought over shot glasses and tequila.

"And like Cinderella, I am taking you to have a ball. I have some serious big beasts on the hook, *panting* for you. There's a gathering an hour ago that we'll just be able to make an entrance at, and a few more later that may involve serious drinking. So –" he clinked glasses with Peter, "– up your arse," and he downed the tequila, gagged, and began laying out a few more lines. John licked his finger and dabbed up the remains of Carl's line, and that reminded Peter – where was Carl? He got up a little unsteadily to look.

"Oh, he's in the bedroom. Calling his little friend." Chris threw the words over his shoulder. "See if you can make him see any sense about that one. She's OK for wherever you're from, but she's cooked her goose now. Completely unsuitable. Could stand to lose a few pounds too. Tell him."

Peter knocked at the bedroom door. Carl was stretched out on the bed, looking at the ceiling as he always did after talking to Lydia. He'd washed his face, but a tidemark of blood still showed around his jaw, and there were long dried drips down his throat. The cuts on his fingers were nasty and deep looking, the skin ruddy and swollen around them. Peter sat down heavily on the bed, and Carl rolled his face towards him, put his hand out to be held. His lips parted in a weary, melting smile, and he began to say something. Peter leaned towards him.

Suddenly the hand became rigid and pulled Peter towards the bed. Fresh blood oozed as Carl's hands clenched and unclenched. The slippery blood allowed Peter to pull his hand away, and he instinctively scrambled off the bed, landing on the floor, wrapped in the eiderdown. Carl was shaking, jerking, his thin legs and chest rigid. Surges of horrible electricity ran through his body, pinning him down. His arms, held at an unnatural, painful angle, moved quickly, out and in, up and down, in a rapidly changing rhythm, like puppets' hands. His blonde head, mashed into the pillows, bobbed frantically, and his trapped-animal eyes rolled over in their worn looking sockets.

As soon as he realised what was happening, Peter got up and held on to Carl's shoulders, trying to stop the shaking, looking anxiously at his lolling tongue, hoping he didn't bite it. He bellowed over his shoulder for Chris and John, and after what seemed hours, Chris slunk in with a brandy glass and a lit cigarette that fell out of his mouth as soon as he saw what was happening.

"Holy fuck!"

John ran in behind him and pushed Peter out of the way. Rolling Carl over onto his left side, he put a pillow under his bucking head and pressed down on his shoulder, whispering to him. The bolts of energy lessened and grew weaker. John kept saying the same phrases in a low voice, "It's OK, it's nearly finished, it's OK, it's nearly ended. Nearly done now, nearly done," until the shuddering subsided, stopped, and room was calm in that uncanny way, as after an earthquake. John pulled the eiderdown off the floor and covered Carl, whispered something to him, and left the room, beckoning the others to follow.

"My little sister has it," he said once they were back in the living room. "She's only nine, so it's bad for her." His mouth was a line and his eyes were moist. "Best thing, if it's bad, is to leave them to sleep afterwards. It takes it out of them." He turned to Peter. "Why didn't you tell me?"

"He takes pills. And anyway, I didn't think it was that bad, I didn't think he had it that bad I mean."

John reached for a beer. He still looked sad. "He'll need to see a doctor, if the pills aren't working." Peter, dazed, nodded at John's superior knowledge.

"Well," Chris Harris looked unruffled, but he was pale and his hands were still shaking, "in that case, it might be best if he stayed here with me for a while longer. He probably shouldn't travel."

Peter looked at John.

"He could travel, there's no problem with that. I don't think," said John.

"No, no really," Chris sat down and pressed his fingertips together, "Really, if he's sick, then he should take a break. Relax. Recuperate. There's no point in going back home and joining the whirl again is there? God only knows what Deep Focus have planned, and it would be just like Carl to overdo it. No. No. It's best he stays here, calm and quiet, with me for the next week or so. I have this flat as long as I want it, so it's no problem. And they have doctors here too, after all. In case it happens again."

Peter felt, somehow, that he ought to put up a counter argument. He opened his mouth but no thoughts fell out of it, and when John questioned Chris, Peter found himself backing Chris up. Really, maybe this was the best thing. It would only be for week or so, and Carl wasn't likely to relax at home, not with Lydia clamouring for him. Chris was right. It was good of him to put his own schedule on hold, just for Carl. John still looked sceptical, but caved under their combined assurances. Yes, yes. Carl needed to stay. It was the right thing to do. They have doctors here, after all...

And so they'd come home without Carl, without Dougie, without the van, and without their gear. Apparently it was going to be picked up by someone – they didn't know who –and they'd get it back in a week. It was a sad end to such an odyssey. On the ferry they got disgustingly drunk to deal with the weirdness of it, and had to be poured into Ian's little Fiesta when they arrived. It felt like being picked up by your dad from a party. On the way back Peter was sick out of the window.

Three years later, Peter reflected that that was the last time they'd been a band. The last time they'd had some element of control, anyway. After that it was all mapped out, organised, and they each withdrew to their own corners, Carl most of all. The last time they'd all been together it was because Carl had summoned them to an emergency meeting. He'd been drinking all day and claimed to have heard that Nirvana were planning to bump them to third on the bill for the New York show. What would this do to them? What would this do to sales? The album was due out in a few weeks. He wanted to know, he demanded to know. What kind of a cunt would do something like that? Only Chris Harris was able to calm him down. It was a shoddy last memory to have of a friend.

When Peter left, Freida was still sitting on the floor, gazing at the photographs in the file. Ian crouched outside the door amongst his cigarette butts, and when Peter came out he jumped up and grasped his arm.

"I'm sorry Pete, you shouldn't have to deal with all of this. It was good of you to come. I'm sorry, I'm sorry that Fred's like this today – she's been like that since she heard." He glanced at the door and lowered his voice. "It's like Carl was, I don't know, her son or something. She hadn't seen him in months, but then, as soon as we got the call – Christ. I thought – I mean she just broke apart. Completely broke apart. She won't leave the office, even. Won't go upstairs to sleep, won't eat. What do you think? Should I, you know, should I get her to the doctors? Or something? What do you think?"

Peter wanted, desperately wanted, someone to ask how *he* was, take care of him. After all, he was the one who'd made most of the phone calls, and had to deal with the disbelief, the tears, again and again. But no. No. It was all about Carl, just like it had always been, and Peter was the caretaker, just as he always was. He closed his eyes and reached for Ian's soft shoulder, saying things he'd heard on TV about grief. Stages; needing time; bear with her; if there's anything I can do, and Ian's face relaxed into its grey folds, relieved.

Each time Peter made someone else feel better, it felt like he took on their pain. Each time he heard a voice on the other end of the phone stop choking, take a deep breath, and say calmly, 'thanks for letting me know', he felt the weight of tears and rage behind his own eyes and rising in his throat. This walk, this sentimental journey, had been meant to take him away from all that, but ending up at Deep Focus had brought him full circle, and it took all his will not to punch Ian in his grateful face.

He tried again with the pretty girl on the way out – suicidally flirtatious, almost aiming for rejection, which he got. She was polite. She was sorry he felt so bad. She really didn't want to go for a drink, and she thought he should go home. Yes, she'd heard of Chinaski. Had she liked them...? An arch smile. An apologetic shrug.

"To be honest? I thought you sold out? Once you signed to DCG, you really sold out. I mean, I didn't like you that much anyway, but that single, the one with that video? You know, the jumping one," she rolled her eyes, "it wasn't really...it was a bit *corporate*."

Corporate. What did corporate mean? Well produced? Polished? Fucking successful? What was wrong with that? For sure, when Peter had first heard the final mix of the second album he wasn't sure what to think. It sounded too smooth, like some Mötley Crüe record. But then Carl had made him realise that that was the subversive thing. Chinaski had made a Trojan horse of a record. It was catchy, it was radio friendly, it could march right into bedrooms across the country, under the noses of parents, and change their kids forever. It had that power. Carl was gleeful and it rubbed off on Peter, who learned to love the album and defend it fiercely. But then who was there to defend it against? Old indie stalwarts, jealous, backward-looking bastards. People who were afraid of success. What power did they have? What point did they have anymore? And if Chinaski's importance was doubted, he brought up the live experience: Carl comes alive on stage, he would intone in interviews, when he sensed criticism was imminent, we're really a live phenomenon. Except he couldn't say that now, could he?

Peter needed a drink after what that bitch had said to him, but didn't want to be in his flat, alone with the phone that could ring, so he went to The Bristolian, a large imposing pub at the hub of a series of spidery lanes. Chinaski had played their first few gigs here, four years before.

Inside it was so empty he could hear the rattle of his cigarette paper burning down, the faint wheeze as he inhaled. He almost recognised the girl serving behind the bar. She took one look at him and said, "I'll get you a beer, it's on us. We heard about Carl." Looking up he saw that the girl – Nikki, Nikki, that was her name – looked wonderfully sympathetic. Kind. Peter felt like crying in gratitude.

"How did you hear?" he managed.

She gestured to the end of the bar and a familiar figure in shorts and a leather jacket. "Dom told us."

"How did he know?"

"You know Dom. He always knows what's happening."

The last two years had not been kind to Dom. Always creased, his face now was crushed, vampiric. His cheekbones shelved under his eye sockets and his tattooed tears ran into the wrinkles on his cheeks. He'd lost some more teeth and his hands vibrated with palsied shakes. Peter had to lean in to hear what he was saying.

"The boy. The boy died then."

Peter nodded and drank, not knowing what to say. He should have called him somehow, found him, to tell him what had happened. He started to apologise, but Dom held up his hand, closed his eyes and leaked a few tears. Nikki immediately came over with two shots of whiskey, and Dom picked one up, pushing the other over to Peter. They touched glasses. Dom shuddered.

145

"Poor boy," he muttered.

They sat quietly together. Nikki brought another few drinks over, and Peter made a feeble show of getting out his wallet. Dom gave his vehement wave again and said something indistinct that made Nikki smile and nod and Peter understood that he didn't have to pay for anything. Huddling down, inches from the bar, Dom spoke in a choked mutter that was difficult to hear.

"That boy will leave a gap. Already left a gap, I've seen it. I'm feeling it. Talk to Nikki and what's his name, Landlord. Lawrence. They're all tears."

"I'm sorry, Dom."

"I've known him for years. Years. Since he was small."

More pints came with whiskey chasers, and Dom rolled fresh cigarettes and muttered, "...dying like that, in secret, no note, accident? I saw it coming, but not the time. You?"

"No. No-one did."

"Oh, someone must have. Someone always does. A boy like that. Loved like that. Someone will know. Ask his nan, they should do that."

How did Dom know all of this? How did he know where Carl was found? How did he know that there wasn't a note? You could spend years with Dom, just thinking he was a crazy old man, and then he'd say something downright spooky, like this.

"What do you think happened?" Peter was hesitant.

Dom was silent for so long that Peter thought he mustn't have heard. And then, that choked whisper, "I think he'd had enough. I think he saw what was coming."

"What was coming? What do you mean?"

"After you get what you want you don't want it," Dom sang.

"You mean the band? But we'd only just begun – I mean it's what he always dreamed of, always wanted. I know that, it's all he talked about."

Dom shoved out his bottom lip and raised his eyebrows. "People will want something from you."

"What will they want?"

146

"They'll want an explanation. Yes. People don't just die. They'll need a reason. You'd better be ready. I'm saying."

"I can't give them that."

"They'll take it boy, whether you have it to give or not. That's what he's set you up for. Better be ready."

Time passed. Every now and again the idea of going back home and making more phone calls crossed his mind, and he'd push it away with more beer. Why should he deal with it? Why couldn't Carl's family do it all? Or the label? Let Freida get it together to do it. Why him?

Soon more people arrived who'd heard about Carl, and they hedged around Peter and Dom in small groups, not knowing how to approach them. At first Peter ignored them and they went away; but as the night wore on, emboldened with beer, they pulled up chairs to join them. So much sadness. So many sorrys. A lot of free drinks. Peter sagged under the weight of it all. Some girl was talking bug-eyed and loudly about hiring the upstairs room.

"Like an Irish wake," she yelled. "Like a celebration!"

A celebration of what? thought Peter, maybe out loud.

"A celebration of the boy. That's what she means," whispered Dom at his side.

Over the next hour Peter was prompted, pummelled, into supporting this idea, until he felt himself getting carried away with it, as a way of discharging his duty to Carl. The idea spiralled around the now crowded pub, as Lawrence the landlord, Nikki and the various mourning drinkers jumped on the idea. It made them feel useful, a part of something. Only once did Peter wonder if this was a good thing, he knew that he was very drunk now. Maybe he should just go home. Maybe he shouldn't be with these people. But instead he heard himself shouting over the opening bars of 'Shattered': "People are too fucking scared of feelings! Don't you think? Really? People need to...just...FEEL? No?"

"You're a Pisces my friend," hissed Dom at his elbow.

And Peter was on the phone, trying to get hold of Chris Harris, Lawrence the Landlord was offering the top room free, Nikki was crying again, and Dom, nodding soberly, offered Peter a Tarot card. He took one, and it was Death.

"It never means Death. It means Rebirth," Dom said.

"OF COURSE!" laughed Peter.

The wake was to take place a week later. Peter woke up the next day suspecting he'd made a mistake, but by that time Lawrence had got flyers made up and there didn't seem a way out of it.

Chris Harris

Sean sat on the stiff leather sofa, trying not to slouch or drop his expensive new portfolio. His feet barely touched the floor and he had to push himself back up every few minutes with his toes. He only had a few hours before he had to catch his train back home and was getting worried about the time. How long had he been waiting now? Should he be pissed off? Was it a test to make him leave, or had they forgotten about him? Another involuntary slouch down the seat, and another toe spring back up. He sighed. The receptionist raised her eyebrows and smiled at him.

"It's lunchtime," she said and made a little drinking motion, "it might be a while." Half an hour later Chris Harris swung in through the glass doors, smelling of lager. He led Sean into his office and told him to sit down on a swivel chair at the desk.

Sean had a lot of respect for Chris. He enjoyed the little cynical shards amongst the whimsy in his writing, and he knew him too, vaguely. Sean had photographed him with Nirvana and Chinaski at Reading, when Carl had been in full media assault mode and everyone had been falling at his feet. There had been a few times when he got the idea that Chris hadn't really bought into the image that Carl was putting out – despite the effusive reviews he gave them. Backstage at Reading he'd seen him smirking at Carl's more fanciful outbursts, and once, when Carl likened himself to Jim Morrison (to the obvious distress of the rest of the band – how fucking lame was Jim Morrison?), Chris had nodded sagely before laughing in his face. Sean couldn't figure out if Carl really hadn't noticed, or had chosen not to.

Sean liked him because he found him puzzling, and Sean liked puzzles. The laugh in the face didn't join neatly with the alliterative, ecstatic reviews. His tweeds, brogues, ashy pockets and dirty ties were more suited to an academic in an out-of-the-way university than a rock journalist. But even then, the tweeds, brogues and the rest of it…something didn't ring true about that either. It was a costume, it wasn't real. Chris Harris stuck out like a teacher at a school disco, and he wore his odd costume with a sleepy irony in his voice, so low you had to strain to hear it. But Sean heard it, which was why he wanted Chris to see the pictures first.

Chris smiled tiredly, flicking through the portfolio, "What's the idea?"

"When I was still at college Carl asked me to follow him around for a few days and take pictures – sort of to document his day. He said it might be a good project for me."

"Was it?"

"Well…my tutors didn't like it, so it was kind of useless in that respect, but it was interesting. And it might be worth publishing now."

"Because he's dead?" Chris said, and Sean's heart lurched. He glanced at Chris, embarrassed, but he was calmly arranging the pictures on his desk and didn't look angry. Sean thought he'd risk honesty.

"Yes, because he's dead. Though I think they'd have sold anyway."

"But not for as much?"

"I don't know. It seems like a good time to do it though, with the album coming out soon."

"Friends were you?"

Sean felt reckless. "No. No. Well, at first. I quite liked him, but he was, or could be, a bit of a bullshitter. I kind of believed him at the beginning. But I was younger then," he laughed nervously and Chris looked at him with no expression at all. "I mean, I think he had this idea of what he wanted to be like, appear like, and getting me to do these photos was a part of that. So I was ambivalent about it. But I mean, it was all practice. Experience. You know. He knew about all the stars who had had like a personal photographer with them, documenting their lives – like John Lennon and David Bowie. He saw some of those Peterson photos – that guy who worked for Sub Pop – those scene photographs he did. And he wanted me to kind of do the same thing, but under his direction."

"He wanted control?"

"Yes."

Chris pulled down one side of his mouth and raised an eyebrow. "Talk me through them and we can get the text right. Start with this –" he handed over a photo of Carl asleep on a sofa with his arm around a girl.

"This, he wanted some kind of ironic, like homage, to that video for Sweet Child o' Mine, the one when they're all waking up with groupies at the start? Carl wanted that kind of thing. So he showed up with a girl and he pretended to be asleep."

"Cheese."

"I know."

"We'll use it though. Probably. What's this?"

"This is when German Joe came over to do tattoos. Carl met him somewhere – this big guy from Kreuzberg who said he'd worked with Neubaten and all those people. Test Department. He probably didn't though. Carl found him in a pub somewhere and introduced him to everyone, and he wanted some tattoos and this guy was a tattooist –"

"So everyone got the same tribal tattoo done with a dirty needle for free."

Sean felt stupid. "Yeah pretty much. I didn't though."

Chris looked at the tattoo pictures. There was only one of Carl, looking to the left of the frame, laughing at something a friend was saying, a lit cigarette and a cup of coffee steaming on the arm of his chair. He held a blood spattered tissue in his hand and the needle burrowed into the flesh of his bicep. German Joe's brutalist profile loomed at the top, furrowed in concentration.

"That's a useful one. The one with the girl I can use maybe. What's this?"

"Carl, I don't know if you know, but he left home when he was really young – like 15 or something. I think it's true. And he knew all these homeless guys from then, so we were walking through the centre and he spotted these guys who were always on the steps of the square. He knew a few of them, I think maybe they'd looked after him for a while when he was on the streets, so I took some photos. But Carl didn't like them, didn't want me to keep them. He didn't think they reflected well on him."

Chris pawed through the photos. Grizzled men with inadvertent dreadlocks. A younger skinhead with a swallow tattooed on his neck. A woman in her thirties who looked as if she'd blacked out a decade before and never found her way home again. A bald man in a leather jacket and shorts. Carl was mostly self consciously posing, but in a few appeared to have forgotten the camera and was speaking vehemently to the skinhead, sharing a beer with the man in shorts.

"We can take a few of them, quarter size with one bit of text. If I get the homelessness thing in, that'd work." Chris circled three photos and pushed them aside. "Next, we have, what's this? Oh, the band."

Drinking in The Bristolian. Peter sitting half in shadow, under orders not to move. Carl told to laugh, it made his cheekbones look good.

"No," said Chris.

"No," said Sean. "There are some better ones though – here."

Carl's face lit up from the juke box. Carl, Peter and John at the bar, the photo of their backs and the reactions of the people next to them; one old man wrinkles his nose, a woman smiles wryly. A table filled with beer, cigarettes and elbows. Lydia, with heavily pencilled eyebrows, her dyed hair in dreadlocks aiming a mock punch at Carl; Peter sitting beatifically at the back with his eyes closed; John glaring intently at something outside the frame.

"They're...OK. Got any live shots?"

"Yes, uh...hang on...here. Some of Reading, and some others." Sean looked up and handed Chris a sheaf of photos, "There's one of you here, and a few of Carl and Kurt Cobain, about the time Nirvana started working out the support for the US tour." Sean kept his voice steady, but he knew that this was the selling point. "This one's pretty cool."

Carl trying not to appear starstruck, sitting on a beer crate and smoking a cigarette while Kurt Cobain leans over to whisper in his ear. Another posed shot, Carl raising one eyebrow and clenching his jaw to make his cheekbones hollow, while Kurt Cobain grins maniacally.

Chris Harris puffed out his cheeks and let the air out slowly.

"Take the first definitely. It makes them look like friends. The second, it could be any fan with Kurt Cobain, doesn't do Carl any good."

Sean blinked. "Doesn't do Carl any good?"

"No, he looks like a hanger on here and that's not what we need."

"Well, Carl was a bit like that. He was genuinely speechless when he met that guy. He never stopped going on about it."

Chris Harris gave him that tired, ironic look. "Look, Carl died. A lot of people liked the band, and a lot of people thought that they were going to get better and do pretty great things. Some people thought that they were important."

"Did you?"

"That's not my point." Chris began pacing the small office, like a professor at a tutorial. "Carl died when he was, what, 23?"

"24, I think."

"24. OK. That's still good. At 24 you don't need to have been great, you just need the promise of being great in the future. If this had happened when he was, say, 27, then he'd have had time to disappoint, or impress more, but as it stands we only have what he did. And like I said, a lot of people thought that was good. But the potential is what sticks with people. The boy was potentially a new Kurt Cobain, and it's the potential that will sell an album, a double spread in a magazine, all that stuff."

"But it wasn't just Carl, there was the band too. I mean, that's what I wanted to get across with the pictures. There's loads more of the band, that Carl didn't really want me to take. But I think they're probably better than all this posing stuff that Carl did, it's more honest, and gives a better sense of the band as a working entity –"

Chris Harris spread his hands and showed his sleepy smile, "And who cares about that? Really? Do you think they'd be able to carry on without that guy? Here you've got a band that are not that good —"

"But you liked —"

"OK, but not too great in the grand scheme of things. Mildly derivative. The one thing they have going for them that might give them a head start over all the other bands out there peddling the same kind of stuff is a charismatic front-man. And they don't get more charismatic than a pretty boy who's dead at 23, or 24 or whatever. That image is gold. And if you fuck with that, it's at your own peril. Nobody wants a star who's like themselves."

Sean opened his mouth and shut it again. Chris sat down again with a sigh and lit a cigarette without offering one to Sean. He patted a pen against the pictures of the rest of the band and swept them into the wastebasket. The remaining photos he spread on the desk – Carl and the girl; the tattooist; three homeless pictures; Kurt Cobain; Carl biting the skin around his fingernails waiting to go on stage; Carl held up on the hands of the ecstatic crowd, the mike lead wrapped around his bicep.

"These are the ones I'll take."

* * *

Sean missed his train and spent the evening with Chris Harris, drinking the headliner's rider at a gig at the university. He woke up on Chris' sofa with a mouth like an ashtray and a promise of regular work. There was an event Chris was interested in covering, and Sean could be useful.

Post mortems

Four days after Carl died, at the same time that Peter was watching Freida cry; the same time as Lydia was stumbling to the toilet, and Sean was making an appointment with Chris Harris, the post mortem began.

Orderlies wheeled Carl's body into the hospital mortuary and the pathologist's assistant checked the name on the tag tied to one of the body bag handles, and noted the position of the body. He took some photographs, as well as nail and hair samples, before the orderlies heaved it out of the body bag, stripped, washed it and put it back onto the cart.

There had been a colleague's retirement party the night before, and both pathologist and his assistant were mildly hungover. They could have done without dealing with a body that was at least four days old, but it was too late to swap shifts, though they'd both tried.

They noted some identifying features: a tattoo on the top right bicep of an upper case C inside a circle. Another tattoo around the left bicep, of an intertwining pattern. Three non specific scars were seen on the chest, jaw and right buttock, and the top of the left thumb was minorly deformed. Each earlobe had been pierced twice. The pathologist took out his dictaphone:

"The body is a white male who appears to be the stated age of 24. The body is of 71 inches in height and thin. The head is normocephalic and covered with light brown hair of moderate length that has been chemically lightened. The eyes are blue. The teeth are in good repair. The neck is unremarkable. The abdomen is flat. The clothing, examined separately, consists of –" he gestured to his assistant, who held up the items with gloved hands, "– a black and red t-shirt with printed words on the front and back. There is a moderate amount of brown emesis on the left shoulder of the t-shirt. A pair of jeans with dried mud staining the back leg cuffs. A pair of blue boxer shorts. One black and white converse tennis shoe. A pair of white socks with grass stains on the soles. Additionally the body wears a necklace made of – what's that? What would you call that? Woven thread with a small plain silver ring hanging from it."

He sighed and turned off the dictaphone, and they both took a break before the cutting began and sat with their back to the body. The pathologist told his assistant that his daughter was a fan of this boy – he was in a band, apparently.

"She says she wants me to snip some hair, to give to her. Can you believe that? She was serious too."

When it was time to begin again, the assistant put a rubber brick under the back of the body, so that the neck and the arms fell backward and the chest pushed upwards. It was easier to cut open that way. The pathologist made a deep, Y-shaped incision from the tops of the shoulders to the bottom of the breastbone and swapped to shears to saw through the ribs and remove the chest plate. The assistant took each organ that was handed to him, weighed it, took some samples, and then placed it, dripping, into a bucket. The pathologist muttered softly into his dictaphone, and a heavy, sleepy lull descended on them both. They started to think about lunch.

Once the torso was emptied, they started on the head, putting the rubber brick under the neck this time. Pulling away the scalp from the skull, front and back, the assistant grunted and braced himself on a fixed doorstop he had brought from home especially for this purpose. The skull was sawn open, the spinal cord severed, the brain removed for examination, and only a series of cavities remained of the young man on the slab.

They took another break, turned their backs again and carried on their conversation.

"It's the not knowing them anymore. That's what gets to me," said the pathologist sadly. "You have them, they love you, and then suddenly, they've gone. She's always out, dressing in rags, like so many of them do now. Says she's a vegetarian now too." The assistant shook his head in sympathy. "And when she heard we were doing him," he pointed at the body behind him with his thumb, "she went mad about it. 'You can't do that! You can't cut him open!' Shut herself in her room, running up the phone bill to all hours. Real drama." He sighed heavily. "That's the main reason I tried to swap, didn't need the aggravation."

The assistant offered him a mint. "So did she calm down in the end?"

"Oh, yes, eventually. But it took a while. I said to her, don't you want to know how he died? and that did the trick. Think of his mother, I said." The assistant sniggered. "I said to her, young people die all the time. We do this all the time, and you don't care about them, and she says, but he's special. He shouldn't have died."

The assistant rolled his eyes, "Special!"

Then it was time to finish up.

When everything was done, everything weighed and washed, the assistant padded the empty chest cavity with cotton wool, put the sacks of organs back in, and sewed everything up.

Luckily, they'd finished in time to order the full English breakfast at the canteen.

* * *

DCG issued a statement:
"We are shocked and saddened at the sudden loss of such a gifted musician, artist and performer. Our hearts go out to Carl's family, friends and fans at this difficult time."

So did Deep Focus:

"Carl Howell was not only a charismatic and talented performer, he was a dear friend and a member of the Deep Focus family. Words can't express the loss we feel and the pain we share with his family and friends."

So did Chinaski:

"Carl was the soul of the band and we are struggling to come to terms with what has happened. We appreciate the respect of our fans and will make a fuller statement soon."

So did Carl's parents:

"We are deeply saddened by the death of our only son. Carl brought love and laughter into every heart, and we will miss him every hour of every day."

Chris Harris wrote a short piece in NME, and had it placed on the first page surrounded by a black border:

"Carl Howell, lead singer with Chinaski, died unexpectedly a few days ago. Just before the release of their glorious new album, 'Smelling Roses, Hearing Flies', an audacious shot across the bows at every other pretender out there. This young man, poised to take us kicking and screaming into a new musical frontier, leaves us all bereft, all weaker, all diminished. Perhaps, just perhaps, Carl Howell died for our sins."

The piece was lauded and vilified in equal measure; hated, lampooned, loved and defended in the letters pages for weeks to come. Graffiti appeared throughout the city, throughout the country, scratched into bus windows, etched onto benches, scrawled on walls and phone boxes:

'Carl Howell died for your sins'.

Then the album was released, two days before the memorial gig at The Bristolian.

NME

REVIEW OF CHINASKI'S 'SMELLING ROSES, HEARING FLIES'

And here we have it. Chinaski, the latest indie snack devoured by the majors, release their long awaited second album, and it's as close to perfect as we hoped.

For too long, alternative rock has been fearful to stray far from the rules written by Hüsker Dü, Minutemen, and, yes I said it, Nirvana.

Unlike most of the post-hardcore crowd, Chinaski have had the balls to climb out of the primordial Underground and take a chance on songs that risk poignancy, grace, charm. We saw this on their debut 'Alloyed', but the originality and the subtlety of that record was all but hidden behind the walls of muddy sound that so often marrs Deep Focus releases. Signing to DCG, in this case, has resulted in the band's blossoming. 'Shattered', the latest single, is a fine mix of menace and sweetness that manages to be authentic and radio friendly. The thrashy leanings of 'No Sense' and the smudgy dark rock of 'When We Try' nod to their metal-infused hardcore roots, but push past them, into the light. On 'Then The Trouble Started', Carl Howell's splintering vocals hint at an unimaginable pain, and there is something terrifying and liberating about witnessing that amount of balls-out drama. Never have I heard a record that oozes this much raw emotion. It's a fine line between authenticity and indulgence, but Chinaski never tip over to the dark side.

It will be interesting to see them supporting Nirvana later this year. While Nirvana show every sign of becoming the bloated rock gods they claim to despise, Chinaski are the sharp-witted guttersnipes waiting in the wings to steal their ill-guarded thunder.

(Since going to press it has been discovered that Chinaski's lead singer, Carl Howell, has died. Our sincere condolences go out to his family.)

Melody Maker

REVIEW OF CHINASKI'S 'SMELLING ROSES, HEARING FLIES

Chinaski return with their second album, this, their debut for DCG.

While 'Alloyed' did much to cement them a place in the indie foreground, this latest has the look and feel of something conceived in haste and born too soon. The band claims to consider long and hard what songs they record and how they record them, the stories of frontman Carl Howell's perfectionism are legion. That aside, in the last two years we have had their debut album, two singles, an EP, another single, and now this second album. On balance it might have been best to take a break and think things through a little more.

From the opening track we are on very familiar ground. 'Shattered' takes the same guitar melody as their first single 'Down', and couples it with a borrowed bassline from Bowie. 'No Sense' references The Melvins (and, by extension, Sabbath) and appropriates an entirely inappropriate Pixies style fade out. Only on 'Then the Trouble Started' and 'Walls to Window' do we get vintage Chinaski, the sound that was so refreshing two years ago, and even these are diluted by flowery guitar overdubs and studio trickery. The fuzzy, doomy quality of 'Alloyed' has been replaced by a clean, crisp, flat sound that positively reeks of good health. This is a shamelessly mainstream album, which I wouldn't have a problem with at all, if Chinaski hadn't been so forthright about their aims in signing to a major. In retrospect perhaps their defiant posturing about not changing their sound was a way of masking insecurity, an attempt to stave off the inevitable. Much will be made of this album, in the light of Carl Howell's untimely death, and I have no doubt it will do very well. But those of us who saw something interesting, even unique, in them before, will be sorely disappointed. Much as I admired Carl Howell as a singer and as a musician, I can't believe that he would be happy with this album. It's a frustrating end to what was in many ways a remarkable career.

The saddest thing is that now they won't have a chance to put right the wrong.

13th August 1993

On the day of the memorial gig at The Bristolian, a hard core of teenagers congregated at May Howell's front gate, bringing with them candles, flowers, ghetto blasters, guitars. At first the neighbours complained, but soon began giving interviews to the press instead. Some of the more enterprising charged the teenagers to use their toilets.

A photographer arrived with a journalist; they took pictures, gathered quotes. They said it was for NME – a pull out special about Carl – and so everyone was happy to pose, cry and philosophise for the camera.

After an hour or two the crowd had swelled, spilling over onto adjoining streets. The police moved them on, ushered them to the bus stops and told them to go back to town, and when they did, they followed a breadcrumb trail of flyers posted on walls, phone boxes, windows. Some of them tore the flyers down and passed them around amongst themselves. A crude black and white picture of Carl was printed on each one, and while the text differed between flyers, the message was the same: Memorial. Till late. Carl Howell. The Bristolian. Free with this flyer.

Over the last few days these scraps of paper had been kept and coveted in dozens of back bedrooms across the city. Those who had managed to get one, copied them for those who hadn't, and at first they were given out free to friends, but before long they were changing hands for money. By the morning of the 13th, teenagers had positioned themselves along the side streets leading to the pub, and were selling the fake flyers, now printed with 'not to be resold' to make them seem more official.

The Bristolian was locked and dark, it was still morning. People brandishing flyers waited around the doorway or perched on the sills of the large low windows waiting for it to open. Others congregated in the side streets and alleys. The noise grew. By noon, police were urging groups of teenagers to wait in the nearby park, or go home and come back later. Not many went home, and those that did were quickly replaced by more, eager to get into the pub and start mourning. Some fanned out across the city to the record shops or the City Hall steps to wait, but at least a hundred of them obeyed the police and went to the park.

It was a beautiful sunny day; there was a happy, expectant atmosphere. Rings of kids hovered around ghetto blasters and money was collected for beer and cigarettes. 'Smelling Roses' was played, rewound and played again as girls cried next to boys who were happy to comfort them. A slight boy in a Chinaski t-shirt, with a passing resemblance to Carl, brought out his guitar and began hesitantly picking out the melody of 'Shattered'. Girls and boys edged closer to him, nodding to themselves and each other, whispering the words, wiping away tears.

* * *

At two o'clock Peter was spotted walking through the park on his way to The Bristolian, eyes on the ground, headphones in his ears, blind to the unusual crowd. He remained unaware until he was surrounded by drunk, sunburned teenagers, staring at him in mute sympathy. A pretty girl who could only be 15 touched his arm: "We all loved him," she said. "We all loved him too."

He was given an opened warm beer and the small crowd waited respectfully until Peter had taken a sip and handed it back. "Will you be playing tonight?" someone asked.

Peter shrugged, "How?"

"We can play, if you want. Me and my band," piped the slight boy in the Chinaski t-shirt. We've been working on covers, we have the whole first album learned. We can play, I mean, if you want a tribute."

Peter shuddered but told him to show up at The Bristolian just so as not to hurt his feelings. He'd think of something to say to him then, some way of putting him off.

"But I don't think this will be that big a deal. I think we should all just have a few drinks and kind of say goodbye. But I don't think this should be an event."

"Bit late for that," said another boy cheerfully, indicating the crowd.

When Peter went on his way, the pretty girl ran after him and gave him a note. "This is for you, now," she said, shyly brushing his crotch. Edged around with dirty finger prints, black in the folds, smudged with lipstick, it was addressed to Carl. She must have carried it around for a long time, waiting, hoping to meet him. And now it was too late. Peter opened it up as he walked. An obscene note from a child to a dead man.

He took the long way to the pub so he wouldn't have to encounter anyone else and pulled his baseball cap further over his face while he knocked at the door. The bar staff moving about inside didn't look prepared for what was to come. He wondered if any of them had walked through the park and seen the number of people there. He wondered how many flyers Lawrence had printed, and how all those people were meant to fit in the pub. Looking over his shoulder, he saw a TV camera crew at the end of the street, interviewing teenagers.

The cool, dark bar smelled of stale beer and cigarettes. Someone was scrubbing at a stain on the carpet, coughing, and Lawrence was emerging from the cellar with a lit cigarette and a bad looking hangover.

"Are you ready for this?" asked Peter.

Lawrence, sick, squinted over the smoke, "How's it looking out there?"

"How many flyers did you print?"

"A hundred maybe?"

Peter shuffled his feet. "Look, I think this is a bad idea." Lawrence widened his red eyes.

"I mean," Peter mumbled, "I mean, this isn't what we thought. I don't think we thought this through. Something's happened that's weird. I mean it's insane out there. It all seems a bit..."

Lawrence poured himself a coke, hesitated, and added a shot of vodka. "Peter. It's happening." He softened a little seeing Peter's face. "It will be OK. Most of the people who show up today will be friends, you know? People want to say goodbye, well then they'll say goodbye. It's not going to get weird. Not being funny, but you're not a big enough band for it to get weird."

"There's TV cameras out there though."

"Oh," Lawrence finished his vodka and lit a cigarette, "I doubt it." He gagged as he inhaled. "Jesus God if I get through today it'll be a fucking miracle."

Later on, as Peter was setting up upstairs, Lawrence came in a few times, each time slightly drunker and slightly more unsettled.

"There's a lot of them."

"I told you."

"Yeah..." Lawrence was shifty, "I told some of them you were going to play. Kind of. Just to get them off my back."

* * *

As the day went on, Peter got more and more nervous. He stayed in the upstairs room, pretending to himself that he wasn't hiding. The noise from the bar downstairs edged up over the minutes and hours, and by four o'clock it was a bolus of sound, rolling out of the open windows and into the streets. The chatter, the music, merged with the sun drenched clamour in the park nearby, until the whole area hummed with a weird charge. Those unable to edge themselves into The Bristolian spilled over into pubs close by, bringing the infection of jittery excitement with them.

Their voices thrummed with it. Their bodies quivered with it. This was a happening of their own making. Some set up ghetto blasters in the street, hunkering down on their heels, perched on curbs, nodding to the music. Pint glasses towered up on pub windowsills and cigarette stubs clotted the drains.

By five o'clock the sun had grown hazy and the atmosphere began to change. Fractious girls cried easily, boisterous boys tipped over into aggression and more and more of them funnelled into the gaps in The Bristolian. Nikki was pushed aside when she asked for flyers in return for a handstamp. There was no bouncer on the door – that wasn't how things worked at pubs like these, but the usual compliance of the kids had disappeared. They wanted to come in. They wanted what they'd been promised. There were already rumours going around that something big was going to happen. Maybe...maybe Carl wasn't dead after all? Maybe he would be here, tonight.

* * *

Upstairs, the hastily booked band was nervous. If they had started playing earlier in the day they could have counted on the goodwill of the crowd, but now, after a hot afternoon of drinking and grieving, the audience were likely to turn nasty. The boy in a Chinaski t-shirt fumbled his chords, scared. They all were, and they were all so horribly conscious of Peter, silent and fretful in the corner.

By now the bar area was stifling, despite the opened windows and the propped open doors. But still, even more came. Something about the discomfort made it feel more worthy somehow, as if physical suffering in public beefed up the grief and made it more real. When two new figures appeared in the back door, there was a lull in the chatter as Carl's mum was excitedly pointed out. She was on the arm of a woman in her thirties, 'Who is that with her... who is that?' and people reverently edged closer to try to glimpse a family resemblance – his sister? His aunt? But too soon the woman tunnelled out of the crowd, leaving

Miriam sitting at a central table, ready to talk and soon surrounded.

Word got to Peter that Miriam had arrived and he began to panic. He'd only met her twice. Once when she'd arrived at school, drunk, to try to collect Carl and had to be escorted unwillingly to the headmaster's office, and once much later when she'd turned up after a gig and tried to take the door money. This was bad. Miriam had the sick gift of being able to tip any situation into hysteria, and here she wouldn't even have to work hard to do it. He sent down Lawrence to try to persuade her to go, but Lawrence came back convinced otherwise.

"It's her right, man. It's her *son*."

He didn't tell Peter that he'd told the bar staff to let her drink for free.

* * *

Dom Marshall, at the pub since early morning, worked quietly and diligently unloading equipment, taping down cables, hauling barrels, collecting glasses. Every now and then he'd duck down behind the bar and help himself to a glass of water – no booze today – and although his shakes seemed worse, his eyes were clearer than they'd been in months. Every time the album finished on the PA system, he'd change the tape to the EP. When the EP finished he'd put on the single, the Peel Sessions, the first album. The order never changed, and the crowd became so used to hearing the same songs over and over again that they barely noticed them anymore, but their gestures and steps were in time to the music; snatches of lyrics entered normal conversation. Over the hours Dom turned the music up so gradually that they were like lobsters unwittingly brought to boil in a pot. On his glass collecting circuits, he kept an ear out for the conversational trend. If a group wasn't talking about Carl the first time he stopped by them, he'd leave them alone. If they weren't the second time, he'd make sure to hum a part of the single – just enough to make sure that a seed was planted, that Carl wasn't being forgotten. He prodded the saddest looking girls with empathy and whispered angry tears to drunk boys.

He also kept an eye on Miriam. She'd brought some childhood photos of Carl, and had them arranged in date order on the table. The girls, unable to hear her over the din, nodded mistily whenever she tapped a new photo with her polished nail. Dom positioned himself behind her, impassive and watchful, sharply pinching a girl's arm when she tried to stuff one of the photos into her bag. She put it back on the table without anyone noticing.

"Have a heart girl," he hissed in her ear. "She might be a daft cunt, but she's his mum. Have a heart."

* * *

Someone told Peter that there was another news crew outside. Looking out of the window he saw someone who looked a lot like Chris Harris being interviewed, and there was Sean, too, roaming about taking pictures. He also saw Lydia, ill-looking and slow, on the edge of a spur of people spilling out of the side door. Oh Christ. Lydia and Miriam. Each bringing their own unique brand of melodrama to an already fraught situation. At least Lydia didn't seem to be coming in, that was something. Maybe she'd be content to stay outside. She did look unwell and uncertain, which boded well. She might even go home. And then he saw that Chris Harris had beckoned her over to the camera crew, introduced her, was putting his arm around her, had made her cry. Almost immediately a knot of people tightened around them, Chris' hand gripped her shoulder, and Lydia began to talk.

* * *

Lydia was sick. Closeted at her parents' for the last week, lying on the sofa watching TV and taking Mother's Valium, it was Freida who'd tracked her down to see if she'd seen the flyers and planned to go to the memorial. Not really in control of herself, she'd washed her lank hair, pulled on some clothes and arrived, zombie-like, at The Bristolian an

167

hour later. Now, amongst crowds, music, lights and cameras, she allowed herself to be propelled here and there, she spoke when she was told to, accepted hugs, drinks, sorrow. She told her story; the story that hadn't really been hers for years. The mourning girlfriend, the lover in shock.

* * *

Peter knew that the thing was now out of control. Lawrence had been anxiously prodding him to come downstairs for an hour – just to show his face, just to keep people happy – and he knew that he couldn't skulk upstairs any longer. The bands that Lawrence had hurriedly lined up to play were getting restless. The best thing, Peter thought, would be for anyone with a stamp on their hand to be allowed upstairs, the first band to start playing, and Peter to make his appearance in the bar with a good third of the crowd absent. That might give him enough breathing space to persuade Miriam to leave and then deal with whatever havoc Lydia was causing.

What he didn't know was that the rumour was gaining strength: Carl wasn't dead. Carl wasn't dead. He was alive. He was here, now, tonight.

* * *

Lawrence announced that those with stamps could go upstairs.

Upstairs, the boy in the Chinaski t-shirt finally had his chords down and nodded to the drummer to begin. Peter stayed at the side of the stage with his head down, waiting for the right time to head downstairs.

Upstairs, the first few notes were all but drowned out by cheers from the crowd. Downstairs, kids with heads full of heat and beer sat up straight-backed like meerkats. Those outside cocked their heads and paused mid-sentence. Some surged forwards through the doors, pushing the crowd at the bar closer to the stairs. Those near the stairs saw the surge, stood up and moved forward in turn. Another cheer was heard from the room upstairs.

"Listen, listen, it's them," someone shouted.

"It's Carl!" cried a girl.

And unsteadily, untidily, the crowd downstairs and outside began to flow upstairs and in, pulling the kids on the edges with them. They heaved onto sills and landed on crowded tables. Glasses scattered and rolled. They forced the toilet windows and clambered through, not noticing cuts and scrapes, humming and singing the song they assumed they were hearing. They trampled, shoved and panted past each other up the stairs, the first of them crashing into the room just as the vocal was about to start. A collective intake of breath, and a note sounded from dozens of throats as they lumbered towards the stage, towards a slight boy with hair in his eyes, a boy in a Chinaski t-shirt, singing a well-loved melody in an unfamiliar voice.

And then the surge stopped. It was a slightly different song. Not the same song at all. At All. And someone howled from the back, "Fuck you! Fuck you!" in a voice that broke and the disappointment travelled from mouth to mouth down the stairs becoming bitterness at the bottom. A chant began, "Fuck you! Fuck you!" Lawrence advanced as far up the stairs as he could manage, pushing people back against the wall as the band upstairs played bravely on. Clambering over legs and pushing aside flailing arms, he shoved his way to the front of the stage and climbed up, waving away the singer and signalling for Peter to pull the plug.

Lawrence began to talk, but it was tough to hear him. The chant grew louder and eventually fractured, becoming more general noise. The back of the room was still angry at the absence of Carl. The front had already transferred their frustration onto Lawrence, "Fuck you! Fuck you!" and there was the sudden sound of glass smashing, of furniture being thrown down. Dark waves of sullen faces pushed and pushed against the stage as more and more people scrambled in. The volume increased with the heat. Someone shouted, panicked, that they couldn't breathe. A few sank at the edges of the stage and were trampled before fighting themselves out. Lawrence shouted himself sweaty before Peter thought about plugging in the microphone again.

"It's not him! He's not here!" went the cry at the back of the room, heard in the bar below. There was a metallic crunch and Lawrence was heard amplified, shouting,

"Of course he's not here, twats. He's fucking dead. Now get off the fucking stairs or I kick you out. Move away from the stage. Move AWAY from the FUCKING STAGE or you're all barred."

An uneasy, unsettled murmuring edged out the shouts, and those at the bottom of the stairs drifted back into the bar. The crowd upstairs thinned out.

A girl said, "You said he was here?"

"Who did? Who fucking said that? I didn't. I never said that. No-one said that," shrieked Lawrence.

"Someone did. People did," the girl finished, confused. "Don't swear at us!"

More backed away, heads bowed, dazed. In the bar they slumped at tables and the floor, sitting in spilled beer. Up until this moment, most of them hadn't really understood that Carl was dead, and some hadn't felt especially upset until now, right now, when it was brutally confirmed. For most of them, it was their first taste of death – outside of family pets or silent grandparents – and it hit hard. And no-one was being nice to them about it. They weren't told that Carl was In a Better Place, or that he was looking down on them smiling. It wasn't a publicity stunt, or a way of finding out who his Real Fans were. He was just Fucking Dead. Someone young, like them, someone they felt as if they owned in some way, that they were kin to. It was terrifying.

These were normal kids, middle-class kids for the most part, who'd come in from the suburbs in their father's car, or from their university residences on the special bus service to the centre. They'd planned their day of mourning in the Student Union, in each other's comfortable living rooms. They'd run up their parents' phone bill discussing the day. They'd dressed with care, stocked up on booze, and prepared their emotions by listening again and again to the album (the new album. The first was a little too difficult). Poring over the lyrics, they *knew* Carl.

They knew him. They each knew him better than anyone else ever could. They each of them knew how and why he'd died. He'd killed himself because Fame Was Too Much To Handle. It was an accidental overdose. He hadn't killed himself at all. He had been worried about selling out. He'd had a heroin problem. He'd been murdered. He'd had powerful enemies. They'd learned these narratives from movies and TV. Now they found that the dead can't return to tell us what really happened, to tell us we're right; that there is no omniscient narrator; that there are no neat conclusions. Playing at mourning, they'd had a great day out, feeling like they were part of something big, some movement, and now, cruelly, they had found out that they weren't going to be rewarded for their constancy by the reappearance of Carl. Loss, an adult emotion, fell on the children in the bar, silencing them.

The album had come to an end and no-one moved to put anything else on the PA. There was no sound from upstairs except the forlorn twang of a guitar being tuned, and in the relative silence of the bar, the noise from outside was intrusive, almost insulting. The loudest sound inside was Miriam's voice, going through Carl's school days again, talking about holidays in the caravan, where they were posted, how many schools he'd been to, how adaptable he was, how it was that she hadn't seen him, how much he'd missed her...and on and on to her now mute companions.

Lydia, outside still, was sitting at the centre of a group of girls who sympathetically held her hands and wished she'd speak more about Carl. Sean positioned himself at a discreet distance, carefully framed the knot of girlish sympathy that had formed around her, and snapped away at Lydia, zooming into her face as someone said something to make her cry again. Then it was time to start on Miriam, still sitting pert at her table with her photographs arranged in front of her like a tarot spread, her gnarled fingers tapping Carl's Holy Communion photo, girls' droopy reverence. And then something happened.

In the quiet bar a voice was heard, louder even than Miriam's. It drowned out the guitar upstairs and made the crowds outside pause. It was a young voice, with a slight rasp to it. A voice with the overtones of the regional accent but with many other overtones as well, a voice that had travelled, a voice that made you listen. Few recognised it, but everyone knew who it was. Carl's voice.

People put their drinks down, opened their mouths and breathed loudly. The reverent girls turned from Miriam to the speakers. Lydia, close to the door, felt powerfully sick. And Sean carried on creeping and snapping, sometimes looking at Chris Harris for nodded instructions.

The voice on the tape was charming, boyish, old, self-deprecating, funny, wise, naive and heart-breaking. It was the voice of someone you had always wanted to know, someone you had always wanted to be like. The crowd inside and out found themselves smiling at his laugh, and also feeling angry, more and more bereft. Some shook and gulped down tears, while others let them flow unknowingly down their face, and nobody looked at each other. Nobody comforted each other. Everyone was alone with the voice and their own sorrow. Snap snap snap went the camera as Lydia wept, as hands tightened on hands, as Peter, pale and disturbed, finally came down the stairs. The whey-faced boy in the Chinaski t-shirt put down his guitar, and the ghetto blasters, finally, were turned off. Kids in the nearby pubs, aware that the street noise had stopped, went out to see why. The only people who moved were Sean and Chris Harris, quietly tiptoeing through the crowd, looking as if they were judging a game of musical statues.

Carl just about to get in the van. It had been a successful show. Yes, he was looking forward to the future, yes, it was incredible how much they'd achieved in such a short time. And yet, and yet, none of it seemed real enough to count on. He still couldn't sleep. He was still ill sometimes. He still wasn't sure it could last. He still felt, somehow, lost. Not real. And then he laughed nervously. Or heartily. Or sarcastically. Depending on who heard it. He still felt as if there wasn't enough time, as if he was running out of time. As if it was all going to end soon. The tape stopped there. There was a clunk as the record button was switched off and the hiss of the tape was startlingly loud. Sean glanced at Chris Harris who crinkled his eyes and gave him a thumbs up.

And now the applause started outside and rolled inwards. People stood up and aimed their applause and shouts at the speakers bracketed to the ceiling. Miriam sagged in her chair, blinking rapidly, looking suddenly 10 years older. Sean took a series of photos at the moment Lydia crossed the room to comfort her. Peter ruined a few of them as he ploughed through the crowd to get to Chris Harris.

"What was that?"

"What?" Chris widened his eyes.

"That tape? What the fuck are you doing? I mean, his mum's here."

Chris Harris glanced at Miriam and shrugged slightly, "She's heard him before."

"That's not...that wasn't right. That wasn't *right* of you."

Chris was amused in a tired way, "Who said I put it on?"

"It's your tape. You made it! I was there when you made it." Chris didn't answer. "I was *there*."

"You weren't the only one there. Maybe someone else taped it."

"Who? Who could have?" Peter realised dimly that he was allowing himself to get side-tracked, "Lydia? Did you put her up to it?"

"Oh, Peter. Christ. Does it matter?"

"Yes it fucking matters. Yes! I need to know who's messing with people here! You must have given it to whoever did it though, you must have told them to put it on!"

"Maybe," Chris was bored.

"You can't *do* that to people. You can't shock them like that, you –"

"Oh really? Really? Because what was this little party all about, Peter? Tell me that?"

"It was meant to be about Carl. But it got out of control, I mean, I wanted it to be more people who knew him, but then Lawrence printed up the flyers and stuff. But listen, that's not what I'm talking about here –"

"Oh fuck that," Chris was angry now and there was no trace of the languid gentlemen. His face was an ugly red, his lips pulled down in contempt, "Fuck you. This was some sentimental fucking kids' party that went wrong. With your stupid little local bands and your tiny venue and your – Christ! – short*sight*edness. What did you think would happen? All these little girls and boys whipped up into a frenzy and you give them some local college rock fucking *cover band* and hide upstairs? Be honest with yourself, for fucking once. If you wanted to give the guy a send off

174

you should have done it properly. If you wanted to keep it private you shouldn't have done it at all. As it stands you've got a genuine event on your hands here that you're just letting slip through your fingers, and do you want the focal point of that event to be a politely failed riot? I didn't. *They* didn't. They came here because of Carl, and that's what I've given them. Because you were too gutless to. So either you help me or cry into your fucking beer because I'm running the show now."

The crowd's applause had morphed into a happy drunken chant: "More! More! More!" and Chris Harris twirled his index finger at Dom who obediently turned over the tape. Carl again, playing acoustic versions of songs from the EP, stuff that Peter had hated. Carl had talked about releasing it – an attempt to go for the mainstream market and make Chinaski more generally palatable. These tinkly, winsome versions of hard, grisly songs had embarrassed Peter at the time. Now they reminded him of the difference between him and Carl that had sprung up in the last year or so. Once, semi-jokingly, he'd accused Carl of wanting to become Nick Drake, and Carl hadn't taken this as an insult.

He looked around at all the soft, pliable kids draped on the furniture and each other and felt incredibly out of place, out of step with the suddenly generated atmosphere. People began to go back to the bar, ordering quietly so as not to drown out the music, and everyone appeared calmer, relieved; as placidly cocooned as a middle aged motorist listening to drive time on the radio.

Chris Harris leaned in, "I've made some calls and arranged for some people to play." He mentioned two up-and-coming bands, regularly written up in the music press. "So you need to get those children of yours out of the gig area now. I'll put the word about so people know what's happening, and if you've got any sense you'd play as well."

"And how are we meant to do that?"

"Find someone else. Loads of these kids would like to do it. That's it – make an event of it. Get people from the crowd to fill in. Let them be Carl for a few minutes. They'll jump at it."

"No, Chris...it's not – there's no respect in that."

Chris was exasperated, "You want a gathering, but just not with many people. You want a tribute with no fuss."

"I– I don't know what I wanted really. My friend had just died. I wasn't thinking." Peter realised that it sounded like an apology. Why was he apologising to this jumped-up little prick anyway? Had he ever expressed any grief? Any shock, or anything? "You knew him too. Why aren't you – why isn't it affecting you? Why do you want to be at the centre of all of this anyway? If you cared about him at all you wouldn't want to turn this into a fucking circus." Peter was shaking and lightheaded, in the same way he was the few times he spoke out of turn to a teacher at school.

Chris Harris' expression was a confusing mixture of pity and derision. "Carl loved the circus, Peter. He loved it. You didn't know that?"

* * *

Chris Harris worked hard to turn failure into success, and it became, as he intended, a bona fide event. Now that the evening had been reconfigured to something more familiar, the carefully picked and hyped bands played their impromptu sets and the crowd calmed down and behaved like any other crowd at a gig. The conversation became more general. It was almost relieving to be able to talk about something else other than Carl. Sloughing off the weight of a hard afternoon's grief they felt stronger, like they'd survived something, passed an exam or grown two inches. A few girls carried on the weeping longer than necessary, but stopped once they realised that the boys' sympathy had dried up.

* * *

Counting her photographs, Miriam realised that one was missing. She emptied out her bag and clawed through the contents, but no, definitely, his First Communion picture was gone. She twisted her head about in raging panic, trying to catch sight of one of those little bitches who had been sitting with her, but they all looked the same, with their knotted hair and makeup free faces. Why didn't girls take a little more care of themselves nowadays? Ducking too quickly under the table to look on the floor she felt sick, dizzy. The photo wasn't there either. It had been taken. It must have been. Some moon-faced kid had her treasured photo! Someone had their sweaty pampered hands on her darling! She got up, staggered a little, lightheaded in the cigarette smoke, and knocked over a drink. A few people looked at her, but nobody thought about who she was anymore.

Through the haze a small, upright figure walked towards her. He wore a trilby hat and an old fashioned, too big jacket. Christ, these kids will wear anything. But, no. Miriam squinted. It wasn't a kid. It was Bob. Bob Howell, come to save her, come to help her.

"Oh Bob! I lost the photo! They took the photo, Bob. Bob! I don't know what I'm doing here."

Bob gripped the flesh above her elbow and firmly pulled her towards the door. Miriam staggered again and sagged against his shoulder.

"Bob, they had him talking. On the radio or something. Or a tape. They had him talking and it was more than I could stand."

The muscles in Bob's jaw tightened and he put his arm around Miriam. Despite the difference in their heights, Miriam seemed almost fragile, bolstered against the firm arm that half led, half carried her towards the door.

"I knew you'd come Bob. I knew you'd come."

Chris Harris appeared at Peter's side and dug his nicotine fingers into the soft meat of his shoulder. "You're needed upstairs."

"Why?"

"You've got to start playing, it's all arranged. Chinaski's last stand!" Chris Harris waved an imaginary flag.

"How?"

"Like we agreed. Let a bunch of them do the vocals. Pluck lucky fans from the audience and let them have their place in the sun. You've got a 30 minute set before last orders and an impromptu after party to take care of. Chop chop."

Peter motioned towards Lydia and leaned in to Chris, "I don't want her up there. Not after what she's done. I don't want her anywhere near it."

"Oh, her," Chris gazed at her blankly. "Oh, she's not going anywhere anymore is she?" He turned away. Grasping Peter's hands, his face became solemn. "It's important that you do this Peter. I know you weren't keen earlier on, but trust me, it's important. It's something that I know Carl would approve of, and it's going to be the cornerstone of an article I'm planning that will make sure Chinaski do well, even now. It will help you too, you personally."

Peter smiled, worried that it made him look heartless, replaced the smile with an earnest nod. Chris knew best.

* * *

Just after Miriam left, Dom sat next to Lydia.

"Time to go, girly," he said. "You look sick. Time to go."

"I am sick. I've been in hospital."

Dom nodded, as if he'd known all along, "Time to go. It'll make you worse, staying here."

Lydia nodded with her head down, but stayed where she was. She saw Chris Harris standing at the bottom of the stairs, laughing up at someone. "He's happy."

"Well," Dom lit a cigarette, "it's his night."

"It wasn't meant to be."

"Whose was it? The boy's? Nah. Nah. The boy's dead. It's all his now," nodding at Chris. "It's his. He'll do it all now."

"What do you mean do it all?"

"Make sure it all happens, girly, make sure it all happens. Make sure the boy isn't forgotten. He can do that, and we should help him along with it. There's no choice anyway. Stars are made, they're not begotten."

"Carl wouldn't want this."

Dom pushed out his crumpled cheeks and let the air out slowly, "Oh he would."

178

"No."

"Oh he would. It's in his chart."

"Oh, horoscopes..."

"I done his. I done yours too." Dom leaned in. His breath smelled of pennies. "I know what you did, just a bit ago. It's in your chart." When he touched her wrist, his fingers were cold. "You need to take care of yourself, 'cause you'll be around a long time. A long time. Don't worry. But the boy, I saw it coming. I saw it. Didn't know when but I knew what he wanted, he just didn't have time. Maybe he didn't even know it himself. But it'll happen anyway. It's all being taken care of."

Lydia gazed at him and murmured, "God you're creepy."

Dom pulled his mouth apart to show his teeth, chuckled and moved away. A little later a drink arrived at her table, a gift from Dom. It was whisky, which she didn't like, but she drank it anyway and it hit her hard, making it tougher to get up. But by the time she heard the band start to play, and the first excited fans aping Carl's idiosyncrasies, she had no trouble leaving. No trouble at all.

The Evening Chronicle

14th August 1993.

HUNDREDS MOURN LOCAL ROCK STAR

Hundreds of young people descended on the city centre yesterday to attend a memorial concert for Carl Howell, singer with rock band Chinaski. Teenagers gathered in the Queens Park area of the city before heading to the centre to the legendary Bristolian pub and music venue to celebrate the life, and mourn the unexpected death, of one of pop's most charismatic frontmen.

Fans sat in circles, swapping stories and spontaneously bursting into song. Says Judith Seaton, 20, "He was the voice of our generation. I followed them from the beginning, and Carl always had a smile for everyone. He really cared about his fans." Asked how she feels now, her face darkens – "I think all the talk about a drug overdose is terrible. I don't believe that, and none of the real fans do."

Howell's friends and family were also present, hugging fans and passing round pictures. Carl's mother, Miriam Howell, was especially touched – "Every mother thinks her son is special, but Carl really was. He had talent from being a baby." Ex-girlfriend Lydia Hunt also accepted condolences from the crowd.

Band mates Peter Hamilton and John Coleman were unavailable for comment, but NME journalist Chris Harris – one of the earliest fans of the band – had this to say:

"Millions of fans can't be wrong. I think that Chinaski will go down in history as being one of the most influential bands to come out of this country. It's tragic that Carl was taken from us so soon, but his spirit will live on."

The tribute concert, featuring local bands as well as international acts, went on until the early hours.

Howell, 24, was found dead at his grandmother's house in the Brigham area of the city. Reports suggest that he had been there for some time before the body was found. The results of the post mortem are expected in the next few days.

* * *

NME

18th August 1993.

IN MEMORIAM, BY CHRIS HARRIS

Last week a young man died who, let me nail my colours to the mast from the start, I saw as extraordinary. Two weeks after their album's release, Chinaski's singer – Carl Howell – was found dead. So far nobody knows how. For the life of me I can't see any way that Chinaski can continue. And once the album goes gold (as it will, as it must) I can't see how we will be able to continue without them.

Four days ago I found myself at an impromptu gathering of people who knew and loved Carl. I arrived, not with my hack hat on, but because I, too, found myself profoundly affected by his passing. Public mourning is not something we do well in this country, and all I was prepared for was a drink or two with the band and their closest friends in their local bar. Just a few drinks and a toast to What Might Have Been. What I saw instead was a heaving, glorious, cohesive mass of fans, friends and family, united in experience, united in a love of music and a belief in its restorative powers that I haven't seen since I hatched from the egg at NME towers. To be honest I'd lost hope of ever really

181

experiencing anything like that. Oh sure, we've all heard smug baby boomers banging on about the sixties, and to be honest I've gotten pretty damn sick of imagining all those messy flabby love ins with all those messy, flabby rock stars. But a real, genuine, happening? On these shores? Never. Until that night.

Kids poured in from far away towns, bands arrived, unannounced, to play (including my Singles Choice from last week, Gag). I was taken aback, I was genuinely stunned. This is the country where cynicism has planted its roots in our hearts so deeply that I didn't think we had it in us to be so unaffected about love, about grief and, crucially, about music.

If you began this column expecting my usual facetiousness, verbal crescendos and printed pyrotechnics, well, so much for that. Come along again next week and maybe one of my colleagues can satisfy you. Today I am plain and simple. Because the plain and simple truth is that something important died with Carl Howell, something maybe as vital as our musical future.

If you do anything this week, buy a Chinaski record. And play it, play it, play it to hear what might have been, and perhaps if their seeds are sown, what could be again.

* * *

The week after the gathering at The Bristolian, Chris was excited, gleeful. He'd been invited to be on the panel of a late night cultural discussion show, 'Near Dark'. It would be his first TV appearance. He told Peter that he was doing it for Carl.

"I despise the medium. I do. But I'll make headlines with this. Watch."

Peter told John and Ian. John told everyone at DiscKings, Ian told Freida, who told Lydia. No-one knew what Chris was going to do, but NME carried tantalising hints, the story spread, and opinions varied. A rumour went round that he had evidence that Carl had killed himself. Lawrence heard from an excitable teenager in The Bristolian that Carl had been murdered, and Chris had the proof. Freida told Lydia that whatever it was would be cathartic for both of them. Lydia, fortified with Mother's Valium, sat like a lump on the sofa, refusing to let her parents change the channel. Teenagers all over the country sat in their bedrooms and waited, setting the video to record history. They tied up phone lines discussing it, and made pacts to call each other as soon as it finished. Nobody questioned that something was going to happen; the only conjecture was around what would happen, and how impressive it would be.

* * *

On 'Near Dark', the great and the good, the notorious and the available-on-short-notice, gave their opinion on the week's cultural events live on air. Guests were picked for their potential to disagree with each other, and this potential was encouraged by a generous bar in the green room. In the show itself, they were corralled into a fake pub and pressed to drink more. It aired, live, at 11pm.

Topics on discussion this week included Buckingham Palace being open to the public, Raymond Carver's legacy assessed with the forthcoming release of Short Cuts, and an exhibition at the Saatchi called Icons Inc. Chris Harris took his place at the bar alongside a bishop noted for his leftist views, an acerbic art critic, and an ex-MP whose minor disgrace was gradually being erased through relentless TV appearances. Although the show was live, each segment was prefaced with a pre-recorded introduction – a montage of sequences to support the debate. Hearts all across the country sank to the strains of Purcell; Buckingham Palace was first.

The camera rarely strayed from the faces of the female presenter and the art critic. Occasionally the bishop made a syrupy intervention, and the ex-MP nodded into his drink. All that could be seen of Chris Harris was a corduroyed elbow and some yellowed fingers digging into the nuts on the bar. Next up was the Robert Altman section. Again, the art critic and the presenter held sway. The ex-MP allowed for the fact that it was very modern and very clever to weave together so many disparate stories, but was it Art? Or was it Truth? This time the bishop nodded into his ginger ale. Chris Harris said nothing and the camera didn't even register movement.

Fingers twitched closer to remote controls; trips were made to the kitchen; impatient sighs collided with each other down phone lines. Lydia's mother began to tell a story about her brother's tasteless conservatory. Freida started thinking about touching up her roots. Peter, sitting in John's freezing flat, wandered off to see what was wrong with the boiler.

On screen there was a brief disagreement about the merits of Raymond Carver's editor, but nobody's heart was really in it, and they went into a commercial break. In the studio, the guests were given toilet privileges and Chris headed towards the gents and came back refreshed and energetic. He'd taken off his jacket and was wearing a Chinaski t-shirt. A make-up girl leaned in to wipe his brow with a sponge.

"Got some big pores there, love. Let's fill 'em all in with goo."

The floor manager began the countdown. Chris poured a drink, took a deep breath and shoved himself into shot, jogging the bishop's elbow and tipping crisps on the floor.

Now the topic was Icons Inc. A series of photographs of Jim Morrison, JFK, and Marilyn Monroe accompanied footage of the presenter walking around the Saatchi gallery, peering at scratchy lithographs of famous corpses, arranged under a neon scrawl that flashed 'Immortal'.

"What is it that grants a certain type of person immortality?" she intoned. "Why is beauty, that most ephemeral of possessions, so venerated?"

Back in the studio, the panel sprawled on their stools. The bar was littered with glasses and the camera caught the tail end of an altercation between Chris Harris and the art critic. Chris was leaning into his neck, talking through a smile, while the critic was grimacing and shaking his head violently.

The presenter, a strained beauty of 42, asked the panel their opinion on the exhibition.

"Bollocks!" shouted Chris Harris.

There was a silence. The art critic swelled like a toad and the ex-MP gaped. The cameras rounded on Chris, who obliged by staring into the red light, smiling amiably. "Bollocks," he said again.

The ex-MP tittered nervously; the bishop coughed; the art critic went for the throat: "It can be accused of being, *jejeune*. Possibly undergraduate in its reasoning. It's very definitely not the strongest curated show I've seen this year, but it doesn't warrant the, uh, the profanity we've just heard."

Chris mouthed, "Profanity," into the red light.

The presenter jumped in to save the situation, "Some of the artists represented are, or have been accused of being, derivative. I suppose what I'm wondering is that is this *deliberate*? Can these images be seen as *self reflexive homages*, rather than *distinct pieces*, if you see what I mean?"

The art critic returned to his natural size and smiled indulgently, "I think what we have here, you're right, is a very *self conscious* mode of expression that carries with it the *idea* of truthful reflection – it insists on the Platonic ideal, of fame, of beauty. But the manner of presentation is...problematic. It's a *dissatisfying* show in many ways. One yearns for the borders to be erased, for the icons to become *one* with us – the *creators*, in a very real sense, of the image so carefully contrived."

The presenter nodded. The ex-MP looked blank and the bishop shoved more crisps at his mouth.

Chris Harris looked long and hard into the camera again, grinned, and shouted, "Bollocks!"

The bishop scattered crisps onto the studio floor, the ex MP smirked, while the art critic and the presenter shouted. Chris leaned both elbows on the bar, laughing.

Across the country, teenagers gasped across phone lines. Parents were brusquely told to shut up, and the volume of hundreds of TVs was turned up to the max. John called Peter in from the kitchen. Freida stood still with the henna drying on her fingers like clay. Lydia, for once, ignored her mother's disapproval and carried on watching, rapt.

"I really think –" began the presenter.

"– really no need for –" huffed the art critic.

"Are we recording this?" John asked Peter.

"– having the balls to come out and say it –" Chris was saying as a camera dipped in and out of focus, "...no relevance at all. None of them had the sense to die early."

The presenter smirked, "Wasn't Jim Morrison 27?"

"No-one can be that fat at 27."

The bishop tittered and nodded into his goiter.

"And so youth is the only barometer for iconography? Is that what you're saying? Because that's specious in the extreme." The art critic jabbed his finger in Chris' face.

Chris slowly and deliberately got hold of the fingers and placed them firmly back on the critic's lap, "You will keep your fucking hands to yourself," he hissed, too low for the microphone to catch.

All across the country people asked, "What did he say? What did he say?" The art critic turned white, then red. Chris Harris dropped the smile, leaned back and began: "It's not the mere fact of youth. It's talent, it's having balls, it's being arrogant enough to be different in situations that make being different dangerous. In fact, and I stand by this, the earlier you die, the purer you are. Jim Morrison, bloated and balding and dying in the bath. John Lennon, spouting peace and the simple life and at the same time holed up in a millionaire's pad shooting smack. If he'd been shot earlier, he may still have been relevant. The real value lies in not disappointing your audience. You owe them your best. James Dean did it right. Syd Barrett had the sense to go mad and get far away from the public gaze. They owe it to us, because we are the fame makers, and we have the right to take fame away. What an exhibition like this does is rob us of that right. All these tired faces of people we're told we should respect and emulate, dying under the pressure. If they had any respect for themselves they would have killed themselves while they still had integrity, not expect us to do it for them."

"I don't like this," muttered Lydia to herself.

"What the fuck is he saying?" asked John.

"Oh this is reprehensible," cried the bishop.

"It is what it is," said Chris, and shrugged.

"And what about Carl Howard? Hmmm? The singer who just died? You were his champion, no? Are you still?" The art critic looked venomous, victorious.

"Oh that's low," murmured Freida, as Lydia froze, as Peter nervously lit a cigarette.

There was a pause, long enough for the presenter to begin to interject, but Chris cut her off. Bug-eyed, suddenly lurching off his stool, he pressed his face close to the art critic.

"His name was Carl *Howell*. Not Carl Howard. Jesus you're old." And then, to camera "Yes! Yes! If he had to die, then it was probably the right time to die. Maybe a year too early. People have already killed themselves in response to his death – did you know that? Now that's dedication. That's the kind of veneration that sterile dilettantes like you will never understand!"

"Leaving aside the tastelessness of your remark, are you really saying that immortality rests on something as simple as dying young? Doesn't a legacy rest on a body of work?" The art critic struggled to keep his voice steady.

Chris smiled, but his hands shook. "It rests on good bone structure, a loyal fan base and the kind of charisma that can't be exposed to age."

The presenter smirked, "And how old are you, Mr Harris?"

Chris smirked back, "A fuck of a lot younger than you."

There was the sound of splintered glass; the camera lurched to the left and the ex-MP came into view, beer stains on his trousers, advancing on Chris, insisting he apologise. Chris stood his ground, laughing, eventually mock cowering behind a bar stool, as the floor manager grabbed the ex-MP by his meaty elbow and led him backstage. The presenter was making an ad hoc apology to the wrong camera, while Chris advanced slowly to the right one, making sure his t-shirt was in full view the whole time, humming Ride of the Valkyries.

"– Oh this is a bloody shambles –" shouted the bishop as the screen went black.

As soon as the red light blinked off, Chris Harris stopped humming, buttoned his jacket and strode off to the green room.

"Might have picked up your viewing figures there," he threw over his shoulder.

The floor manager was struggling to keep up with him and leaned forward to grab his arm and slow him down, "You fucked up my show you wanker!"

"Oh no. I goosed it up a little, that's all. I put a few volts through it. You're fucking welcome." Chris shook him off, passed the presenter on the way, taking time to squeeze the slightly crêpey flesh above her elbow, "Bloody good work, there. Well controlled."

He made straight for the pay phones in the entrance hall. "Sean? I have a proposal for you. Fuck the article, how'd you like to do a book?"

As Chris had predicted, the show made the headlines. The same shot of him walking towards the camera in his Chinaski t-shirt and calling John Lennon a smackhead played on TV again and again, and Chinaski fans felt victorious. Chris Harris had stood up for Carl, for all of them! And on TV too! In some dim way the confusion and derision of their parents had been refuted – look, he's on the telly, and he's old too, maybe 30, or even older! And even he gets it, he understands what's been taken from us, what we've lost. You had John Lennon, who we all secretly knew was a dick, but we have Carl Howell! And he'll never get old, never disappoint us! Very few tried to remember what exactly Chris had said about Carl, they just remembered that he was defending him, standing up for him. More than a few kids wrote down their own version of it in their diaries that night. More than a few argued passionately and relentlessly with their parents over breakfast the next day. No, he wasn't drunk! No it wasn't cynical! No it wasn't just attention seeking! No. No! He had been the only honest person there. Chris Harris was a fucking hero, and yes I'll say fucking if I want! No I don't want any more cereal! Headphones jammed in ears, bags angrily swung, doors slammed and parental eyebrows raised all across the country.

The Chinaski logo was carved into benches, carefully drawn on school bags in preparation for the next term, daubed on bus stops. Sales of the album spiked and the single climbed higher and higher in the charts. Newspapers tried in vain to find out the names of the people who had killed themselves. Someone always knew someone who knew someone who knew them, but actual facts were out of reach. It was just known, that's all. It was just known that that girl in Yorkshire, or Leicester or maybe Liverpool had hung herself. That that boy in London, or Manchester, or Brighton had ODd. Two girls had a suicide pact and one clung to life in intensive care in Sheffield, or Derby. Peter had been taken to hospital with life threatening injuries. So had Carl's ex. And everyone knew that Carl had been killed. Everyone knew that Carl had killed himself. Everyone knew that Carl had a disease that took him before his time.

* * *

It was no surprise that, when the post mortem report came out the next day, it satisfied no-one. There were no injuries indicating violence. There was no note pointing to suicide. There wasn't enough Valproate in his system to kill him, although given the length of time the body had gone undiscovered, this couldn't be said for sure. There were trace elements of cocaine in his hair but none in his stomach, and the rest of his stomach contents gave sketchy information, bar the fact that Carl was not – despite his claims to the contrary – a vegetarian. Nobody seemed to know how long he'd been at his grandmother's house, if he arrived with anyone, if he ever left. Carl had died, apparently suddenly, peacefully, and for no reason at all. And so there would be an inquest.

Peter woke up to a phone call from their manager asking for his reaction to give to the press. The first thing he thought of doing was asking what Chris thought, but he knew that that would seem weird, so he begged off, saying he'd call back when he'd woken up and had time to think. Then he lit a cigarette and called Chris, who was engaged. He tried again with the same result. Frustrated almost to tears he forced himself to make some coffee before trying again, but now the phone rang into empty space. Chris didn't have an answering machine.

Peter was panicked. He had no idea what to say, he had no idea what his feelings were. Carl, the fact of Carl as a real person, had become increasingly out of his reach and hazy. It seemed months, years ago now, that he'd heard Bob's strained voice, giving him the news. An ocean of events had happened since, and Carl had been left on an island while Peter was carried out by the current.

He thought about calling his parents but knew he wouldn't be able to explain why he felt like he needed help expressing grief; they'd think him cold, freakish. He and John had an unspoken pact not to discuss Carl at all. He called Chris again, got no answer. Finally, he called back the manager and told him to say whatever he thought was appropriate. Leave it to him. It's his job.

Later, he saw the papers. Chris Harris and Carl shared the headlines:

POP JOURNO SICK SLUR.

Chris Harris of music magazine NME shocked fans in a sick outburst yesterday, branding singer Carl Howell of teenage faves Chinaski a 'sad figure'.

Tragic Howell died aged just 24, apparently of natural causes. When called for a statement, Chris Harris – real name Charles Transcombe-Harris – laid into his former friend:

"I think it's a great pity that he didn't kill himself," heartless Harris said, "it's better to go out with a bang than a whimper. It's a sad figure who doesn't choose the manner of their death, and how they'll be remembered."

SICK

Harris, who just hours before shocked the nation with his four letter outburst on Near Dark, has angered friends and fans. Says Chinaski fan Wendy Jenks:

"I think it's sick. We will have to wait for the results of the inquest before we understand exactly how and why Carl died. In the meantime we should think about his family and how they feel at a time like this."

Harris has been unavailable to comment since, but NME have provided us with this statement:

"Chris Harris is a colourful member of our team, and as such occasionally courts controversy. He is, and always will be a champion of Chinaski and Carl Howell and eagerly looks forward to the full facts of this tragedy being uncovered. He insists that the comments attributed to him have been taken out of context."

* * *

The weather broke on the day of the funeral. It had been uncommonly hot, sultry and close all week, but now the clouds darkened and the coppery smell of rain was in the air. By mid morning the first enormous drops fell onto the sizzling pavements, driving up at angles against the sides of buildings and spattering onto windows, suddenly loud.

At Miriam's house, quick witted women made sandwiches and phone calls, while Miriam sat on her bed upstairs, like a big broken doll. Kathleen jammed shoes onto her unresisting feet, keeping up a monologue, a behavioural mantra: "...We will have grace and dignity. Grace and dignity. We will take it in stages, hmmm? We'll go slowly to the door –" Miriam whimpered and shook her head. "– OK we will open our eyes. We will stand up," and when Miriam blinked slowly, "Oh Miriam, Miriam, lovely, I can't do this on my own!" and she started again, "We will have dignity. We will walk to the door. We will thank people for coming..."

Downstairs Bob sat neatly on the settee with his hat held tightly on his lap, his shined shoes square on the floor. He was so still you couldn't tell if he was alive or dead. Once or twice, when Miriam shouted upstairs, he raised his eyes, looked to the staircase, but didn't move.

By eleven o'clock people started arriving. Kathleen's two daughters were on door duty, and they led each new arrival through to the living room where Bob would get up, his knees creaking, shake their hands, accept condolences, and then sit down again without saying a word. Kathleen, neat and trim in black, trotted down the stairs now and again to welcome people, supervise the food preparations and whisper to Bob, and soon the house was full of relatives, real and imagined. Freida and Ian arrived and hovered by the door, not seeing anyone they knew but Bob, who didn't look at them. Peter arrived in his father's suit, accidentally walking in with Lydia, who looked like a cancer victim with her newly shaved head and sudden gauntness.

From early morning, fans had started to congregate outside, mostly girls, mostly silent and respectful, waiting for the funeral cars. Huddling together under umbrellas, some held flowers, others cameras. One or two had homemade signs in their bags. When the hearse was spotted moving slowly down the street, and they saw the coffin in the back with 'SON' picked out in white carnations, they began to mutter and wail. That sound was the first thing that let the people in the house know that the time had come. Upstairs, Kathleen twitched the net curtains, sighed, and turned to Miriam.

"Time to go, lovely."

Downstairs, Bob bolted up from the settee and put his hat on with a trembling hand. Everyone in the room took their cue from him and stood up in turn, all conversation stopping, making the noise from outside seem louder. They could hear Kathleen's light step on the stairs, accompanied by Miriam's unwilling, dragging footsteps, and when the door opened, Bob moved forward, without looking at her, and offered his arm. They made their way to the waiting car, Kathleen leaning in with an umbrella. The sound of the rain and the crowd almost masked her hissed instructions, "...Grace and dignity..." as Miriam saw the coffin, the crowd, the unctuous undertaker and her face fell apart.

The rest of the guests dashed untidily to their cars to avoid the rain, but Peter and Lydia were kept back by Kathleen's daughters.

"You're both coming in one of the cars with us. Mum says."

Peter and Lydia looked at each other. They both had the same thought – how can I stop this person making me feel even worse? – and they both took a ready poured whiskey from one of the trays in the kitchen.

"How are you Peter?" Lydia said finally and Peter found that he couldn't talk, that he was crying. And he felt immensely relieved that something had unfrozen in him enough to make him feel something; something more appropriate than dread anyway. He said the words in his head, 'Carl's dead. Carl died. I'm at his funeral', and he found that this helped the tears continue. And now Lydia was crying too, in the same ugly way as Miriam. She tried to catch hold of him, hug him, but Peter managed to move away without looking like he'd done it deliberately. How horrible! How horrible, he thought, that I can do that now. Looking at Lydia coming apart in front of him, he thought sadly, she feels what I ought to. How horrible! She feels what they feel outside. Why? Why her and not me? Is she for real? Am I the only honest person here? But then he remembered forcing the tears to carry on. No. No. I'm the cold one. He pulled her close to catch whatever it was she felt, so he wouldn't have to go through the funeral being such a freak. Lydia slobbered on his shirt, smearing mascara and didn't stop crying until Kathleen came back and pulled them apart, "Grace and dignity! This can't be a bloody mess!"

They were hustled into a car with Kathleen, her daughters, and a large woman with a smear of salad cream on one black cuff. "Carl's Aunty Cora," said Kathleen. Aunty Cora grunted and stared heavily out of the window at the crowd, at the cameras.

"He did well for himself. Famous." She nodded approvingly at a crying girl holding a sign saying 'We LOVE YOU Carl!'.

Kathleen cranked a window and blew smoke out of the gap. "I just hope they don't make a nuisance of themselves. It took me two hours to get Miriam out of bed and into her girdle. Any scene will kill her."

Aunty Cora shifted and peered at Lydia. "I met you. Before. Somewhere."

"You met her at my party, Cora."

"Yes. Yes. Nice of you to show up. More than any of the others have. Sluts."

Kathleen's teenagers smirked and kicked ankles while Lydia choked into tears again. Kathleen fixed Cora with her fearsome glare.

"Keep it nice, Cora, or I'll dump your fat carcass out that door."

Cora cackled, nudged the nearest teenager, "She's a one, your mum!"

"I am. Yes. And we will have no nastiness, nothing like that. Nothing

194

nasty about the boy." She flicked the cigarette butt out of the window and immediately lit another, brushing ash off her dress with great dignity.

The rain came down in great grey sheets. Landmarks passed in muddy daubs. Conversation stalled and they all smoked distractedly. Peter saw Lydia furtively take some kind of pill and close her eyes tight, taking deep breaths.

Eventually they entered what looked like a tunnel, and came to a sudden halt. Sickly light came in from the outside, and when Kathleen pushed the door open it banged into something soft but unyielding. She eased out of the tiny gap and almost immediately sat back down again, shocked.

"There's hundreds of them!" and she opened the door again, forcing it wider, making someone stumble and fall, and pushed herself out.

Her daughters twisted over each other to follow her and one of them ducked back in excitedly, saying, "There's cameras!" and then scrambled out, after her sister.

Bodies pressed around the queue of cars. Fans, the press, the curious, and the stricken lined the path to the church and all but blocked the door. The driver sounded the horn, and Peter saw six pairs of boots jump away from the open door before the car lurched forward again, the door flapping open.

"It's Peter! Peter!" shouted shrill and unfamiliar voices, and someone put a camera in his face, the flash temporarily blinding him, and the papers the next day carried a picture of Lydia open mouthed, shocked alongside a squinting serious Peter. He slammed the door, feeling adrenaline rise in his chest, hearing his voice shake.

"This is going to be tough."

Lydia sat as if pinned in the corner, her mouth still open. There was a great tussling and grunting next to Peter as Cora heaved herself sideways, dragging her dress out from under his thighs and straightening her tent-like raincoat.

"Can't get any further," said their driver.

Cora painfully shimmied her way to the edge of the seat, pushing on

195

Peter's shoulder for support as she got up to open the door. It slammed into a teenager who staggered sideways into the mud. Cora pushed the door even further open and gestured to Lydia and Peter with one baggy arm. Ducking under flailing hands, cameras and signs, they all jogged towards the church. Up ahead, Peter could see what looked like a small demonstration – banners, intense faces. At his elbow he felt, rather than saw Lydia's dread and willed himself to turn around and comfort her. She sagged against his shoulder and they walked together into the church. Kathleen had reserved them seats at the front, right in front of the coffin, while she sat with Miriam, on the family side of the aisle.

Strange how small a coffin always looks. There it was, on its ghastly gurney, all cheap wood and brass, covered with rain drenched flowers, and nobody wanted to look at it and nobody could look at anything else. People fidgeted, they didn't know how to act. The truly grief stricken tried to behave normally, while others wondered how best to display a grief they didn't feel enough for comfort. Peter looked behind him and saw Freida staring fixedly at her knees and taking deep, deliberate breaths. Ian sat beside her with an awkward smile, inches of space between them. Lydia, her eyes closed tightly, was shaking against Peter's side. Dom, way off to the edge in borrowed trousers and his leather jacket, stood frozen, staring at the coffin, his lips twitching. And who was that? The man crying at the back? Dougie? Dougie! Greyer. Thinner. The only clear sounds were Miriam's chokes and Kathleen's hissed "...Dignity...grace..." and these mixed with the sound of the crowd outside in the rain.

When Chris Harris strode into the church, wearing the same outfit he'd worn on 'Near Dark', he took his place with the family, shaking Bob's hand and hugging Miriam, as if he knew them, as if he belonged with them.

The whole service passed in a tragi-comic montage. The priest eulogised about a young man he'd never met. The organist began all the hymns in such a high register that they had to be sung in an uncomfortable falsetto. Rain dripped from the flowers onto the altar cushions, and then onto the floor, forming a puddle that Kathleen nearly slipped on when it was time for her to do her reading. When Cora's walking stick clattered into the aisle, Kathleen paused long enough to cause embarrassed giggles. At one point the back door blew open and conversation from the crowd drifted in. The congregation heard: "...might have been murder...". They heard snatches of sung lyrics and the kind of angry gaiety teenagers share when they're waiting for something, some event, something defining. When Peter looked back on it, that's what he remembered. The outside stuff, the local colour. At the time, he groped towards feeling for his friend in the box and tried desperately to summon up the magic phrases that had helped him to cry earlier – 'My friend is dead. My best friend is dead, and he's there, in that coffin,' – but it didn't work twice. There was too much to think about. Was there any point in carrying on with the band? Any band? Should he talk to John about it? Did he even want to work with John anymore? How long do inquests take? Was there any point in having one, just to find out that Carl took too many epilepsy pills? Did anyone seriously think Carl would kill himself? Had he killed himself? All these thoughts pulled him back into critical distance, back to lonely, cold observation. Carl's death was old news now, it didn't pack the same punch anymore.

And then it was time to go. The coffin was carried joltingly back towards the door, followed by the priest, and an awkward gap of comprehension. Was this like a wedding, where the family peeled off first and followed the happy couple? Or could you go when you wanted? People looked at each other, at Miriam and Bob, waiting for direction. Kathleen stood up decisively, but quickly sat down again. Eventually Chris Harris stood, lent his arm to Miriam, and made his way down the aisle, and the relief was palpable. People rattled their handbags and pockets for cigarettes, let out their coughs, whispers and sniffles, and spread out in an untidy tide through the doors, Chris leading the way with Miriam, Bob following behind, eyes on the floor.

Outside the rain had stopped. A camera swung towards Miriam and a suited stranger leaned in, trying to make himself heard over the crowd. Chris dug his fingers into Miriam's elbow and steered her towards the waiting cars; their sudden quick pace made the rest of the funeral guests trot and puff to keep up. The crowd of kids was smaller than it had seemed at the start, maybe just thirty or so, and they were arranged in a tight doughnut around a homemade sign: 'Justice For Carl'.

Keeping his head down, hoping not to be recognised, Peter heard a girl being interviewed: "We don't believe it was suicide, or natural causes or anything. We want an inquiry, we think it was murder." Her friend wore a homemade t-shirt that said 'Carl Howell died for your sins'.

"What does that mean, your t-shirt?" asked the interviewer.

The girl was shy, inarticulate, "It's just a thing, it's just, you know, a saying."

"So it means nothing?"

She hesitated, a silly smile on her lips, and looked at her stronger, vehement friend for support.

"We believe it was murder," shrieked the friend.

"Do you know anyone or have you heard of anyone who's killed themselves over Carl Howell?"

"Oh yes, yes, loads. And it's only the tip of the iceberg."

"But do you know anyone, by name perhaps."

The vehement girl hesitated, hating to give ground. "No. No. But it's common knowledge."

"He was so important, he was so important," whispered the quiet friend.

Peter felt Lydia quailing beside him, and he gripped her hand to stop her from making a fool of herself, thinking don't let them see me, don't make a fucking sound. He half dragged, half carried her towards the cars, where Kathleen was waiting with her sullen daughters, tapping her foot and smoking.

They began the long drive in silence. The girls stared out of the windows, bored. Kathleen's foot kept up its tattoo and she smoked constantly and nervously. They'd lost Cora somewhere along the line. Lydia asked where she was and Kathleen replied, "Oh, she won't set foot in a crem'. Doesn't hold with it. Says it's against nature."

"We're going to the crematorium?" Lydia was shocked. She'd allowed herself to imagine the funeral only in terms of her grieving alone by a graveside, visiting it every week, protecting Carl somehow. But cremation! It seemed so utilitarian, so brutally final. She imagined the furnace, the smoking chimney. She thought of flesh dripping, hair crinkling and toenails blackening into soot. Feeling trapped and sick, she looked wildly at Peter, who chose not to notice. Kathleen leaned forward and placed her thin hand on Lydia's knee.

"It's all the same thing. It's all very respectful, really. It's –" she struggled to find the right word, "– it's *clean*, cremation," and she nodded emphatically and Lydia found herself nodding with her, although she didn't agree, couldn't think and took another of Mother's Valium, not caring if anyone saw her.

* * *

It was a long, straight drive to the outskirts of the city. They passed the pub on the estate where Kathleen had had her birthday party. They passed May Howell's flat, the flowers by the door bedraggled now and bent under the pressure of the rain. There was a small group of Chinaski fans waiting outside, and when they saw the funeral cars they stood still, looking almost comically solemn. One broke ranks and waved, and Lydia, unthinking, waved back. They passed an industrial estate made up of low murky buildings linked by impossibly pretty names: Pleasant Row; Honeypot Lane. Eventually, at the crest of a hill, lime-tinged sunlight filtered through the low clouds, and the car made a sudden left down an unmarked track towards the crematorium, hidden tastefully from the road.

The service passed mercifully quickly for Lydia. That third Valium lent everything a dreamlike quality and kept her safe from the sharp edges of other people's emotions. She could sit neatly and breathe slowly, but had to remember to close her mouth and keep her eyes open. She was able to stand when she saw others stand. She noted, in a detached way, Miriam sobbing, great strings of snot hanging from her nose. She was able to watch Chris Harris making his – what would you call it? A speech? No. A...a...sermon. No. A statement, or something. A talk about Carl anyway, that she felt seemed too long but nevertheless seemed to fly by. She took none of it in. The coffin, upstage, began to move, while Chris was talking, and she assumed she was seeing things, but, when Miriam cried out and had to be taken away, Lydia noticed the electric hum of the velveteen curtains circling the coffin, hiding it from view as it trundled backwards. The curtains met and the whirring noise stopped with a snap and David Bowie came over the PA system sudden and loud. The distracted looking undertaker led them all out to a gravelled area to 'view the flowers', and this they all obediently did until they were told what else to do. The flowers were propped up against a painted breezeblock wall. 'SON' in white, but no card. A lily arrangement from DCG. A plain wreath from 'All at Deep Focus'. A cross of white with the card left unsigned, but covered with dense handwriting. Lyrics, or poetry maybe. A teddy bear carrying a toy guitar.

Everyone shivered in the damp air, hoping that someone would make a break for a car soon, not sure if they should speak or not, not sure how normal they should be. Bob stood apart and tearful. There was something about him that demanded and received distance, respect, reserve. Miriam on the other hand appealed for intervention; and, given the state she'd been in during the service, her absence was unsettling. Kathleen strode off to find her, pointing her daughters towards the car, while Lydia stayed near the flowers, furtively plucking one white carnation to take home with her. Her fingers closed protectively over the velvet petals and she kept her head down, moving unsteadily towards the car, and bumping into Dom on the way.

Dom was standing with a woman Lydia almost recognised, a woman with greying hair and faded tattoos on her hands.

"There she is," said Dom, smiling. Lydia smiled uncertainly back. "There she is. Here she is. That's the girl," he nodded to his companion. "She was always alright."

Lydia felt a warm rush of gratitude that someone was being nice to her. She didn't dare speak in case she didn't make any sense, so instead she just smiled and nodded at the woman with the hand tattoos. The woman gave her a beautiful, happy smile full of brown, worn teeth.

"Angie," she said. "I'm Carl's half sister."

"His half sister?"

"Oh yes," chuckled Dom. "This family's full of secrets, things they don't tell you. Tell her Ange."

But Angie smiled and shook her head. A great warmth emanated from her, and Lydia found herself swaying towards her.

"You're. You. Were. His sister?"

Angie nodded, beamed, "I wasn't around much though."

"I didn't know he had a sister."

"There's always things you'll never know. Best that way." She took Lydia's arm and led her to the car. "You need a rest my love. You've been through it, Dom says. You're a good person, I can feel it and you need to take care of yourself."

Lydia, dazed, allowed herself to be settled into the car. Angie leaned over her to tuck her coat in around her legs like she was an invalid.

"He must have loved you!" she whispered. Angie smiled gently again.

"I don't think so. I loved him though. That's what counts, isn't it?"

When Kathleen came bustling back to the car, Angie slipped away like a ghost.

Lydia dozed during the drive back to Miriam's house, warm under her coat, and by the time she arrived, Freida and Ian were leaving. Freida pulled on her arm, telling her that it would be best just to go home – Miriam was in a funny mood. It might be a bit upsetting – but Lydia, bolstered by Valium, felt fine. Felt good actually, really felt the worst was behind her, could really face the future better now, but thanks so much, so much. And she wandered into the house alone.

"I don't understand these people," said Freida on the way home, "I don't understand how Miriam could be absolutely beside herself one minute, joking the next."

Ian was more forgiving. "Maybe it's a way of blowing off steam, or maybe she's just embarrassed about how she was at the funeral and now wants to make up for it, make it a party. I don't know. I think we need to be careful not to judge. I mean, we have no idea what it's like to lose a son."

They drove back in silence, each alone with their own pain.

Miriam had made a remarkable recovery since coming home, and was holding hilarious court in the living room. She'd changed from her formal funeral dress into her normal black leggings and jumper combo and was sitting back on the settee, flanked by several other middle aged women, all holding drinks and cigarettes. The funeral party had split into two. One half, made up mostly of women, stayed in the living room with Miriam, drinking, laughing and listening to Miriam's stories. The other half, mostly men, hung about the kitchen, also drinking but in relative quiet, while Bob stood at the sink methodically washing glass after glass. He still had his hat on, but he'd rolled up his shirt sleeves neatly. Chris Harris sat at the table topping up drinks, nodding occasionally at whatever it was that Dom was whispering to him. Angie squatted on her heels in the corner, rolling cigarettes. She waved at everyone who came through the door and grinned cheerfully. Peter took a seat beside Chris and accepted a drink. The men solemnly clinked glasses. There was the sound of laughter from the living room, and furniture being moved.

"Dancing," said Angie from the corner. Everyone looked at Bob's back, saw him stiffen, and rewash a glass, shaking his head.

"Everyone will remember this in their own way," smiled Angie.

Elvis came on in the next room and Miriam's voice drifted in with the smoke "...caught in a trap..."

Angie stood up and whispered something to Bob, who nodded, and she trotted next door. The men in the kitchen heard voices raised over the music, and then the music was turned down. They heard an indignant, "...what I want in my own house!" indistinct murmurings from Angie, and Kathleen saying, "No, no, she's right though."

At length the music came back on, but not Elvis now, and not loud either. Angie came back into the kitchen and sat down in the corner again.

In the living room, Lydia sprawled on an upright chair, watching

Miriam spilling her drink, kicking off her shoes and massaging her bunions. Lydia felt distant, as if she was separated from everyone by frosted glass. The general hilarity didn't offend her, didn't even really touch her. The funeral itself seemed very long ago, and this, here, now, had nothing to do with that at all. She even clapped along when Miriam began singing. That was fine. Angie coming in to stop the music, that was fine too. She gazed at Angie's beaming face and felt great love for her, great love for everyone in the room. And when she left, and Miriam was being gently scolded by Kathleen, she said to everyone and no-one, "I really didn't know that he had a sister, Carl I mean. She's very nice. She's lovely."

Miriam turned tearful and hurt eyes on her, while Cora pursed her lips and stared at the floor. Kathleen coughed and hurriedly filled the glasses again. A little later she took Lydia aside, "We don't talk about that. Best not to. She's Bob's daughter. And she's mad anyway, that Angie. Tried to kill herself once. Joined some Jesus cult. Best not to talk about it, especially in front of Miriam. They never got on."

Lydia blinked confusedly and said slowly, "Why did she try to kill herself?"

"Why do any of them?" Kathleen shrugged, "Maybe it runs in families, eh?"

"But Carl didn't kill himself," Lydia managed. Her mouth was dry. Kathleen drew the corners of her mouth down and didn't reply. "He really didn't!" she said again, and must have said it loudly, because more looks were directed her way. Kathleen shoved another drink at her.

"We know, yes, yes, we know. Best be quiet though. Best leave it."

Over the next hour the volume in the living room crept higher and higher. The men in the kitchen leaned closer to each other, raised their voices and relied more on gesture and booze. Shrieks and snatches of singing reached them from the living room, where the music was loud. Angie didn't intervene this time. In between tracks they heard Lydia say, "This is the weirdest funeral."

Bob had finished the washing up some time ago, but had stayed at the sink with his back to the men gathered around the table. Now he rolled down his shirt sleeves, put on his suit jacket, kept his eyes on the floor, and walked to the living room. Squawks of female hilarity greeted his arrival.

Miriam said, "Come and have a boogie!"

And then the men in the kitchen heard the noise of the stereo being overturned and the dull slap of records hitting laminate flooring. The women all let out the same low gasp –as if they'd been collectively punched in the stomach. Miriam said, "What did you do?" Kathleen said, "Bob... Bob...really, come on," and someone shrieked, "Wanker! Wanker!"

The men in the kitchen looked at each other and a few moved uneasily towards the living room.

"Wanker!" It was Miriam. Lydia laughed senselessly and too long, and Peter, hearing it, shivered in irritation. He said, "Someone should get her out of here."

Dom, at his elbow, replied, "She's got a right. We've all got a right. But I knew it'd end up like this. Didn't I Ange? I said so."

"He did," Angie was solemn as a child. "He said so."

"Best get your dad."

Angie nodded, disappeared into the living room and came back with a silent but shaking Bob. Someone had thrown a drink at him. It had soaked his hat. Angie was cooing to him, holding his arm tight and matching her steps to his. They both left the house without saying anything to anybody. Miriam shouted "wanker!" again and the music came back on in the living room, but nobody sang along and nobody laughed any more.

The men in the kitchen began to shrug on their coats. Kathleen collected glasses and plates and shouted at her girls to push the hoover around. Only Miriam and Lydia stayed where they were, Miriam maintaining a mutinous and aggrieved silence, while Lydia was simply unaware that the atmosphere had changed. Eventually Kathleen told Peter to take her home.

"I don't know where she lives," he lied.

"And I don't care. She's a young girl in a state and if you were any sort of a gentleman you'd look out for her. Take her to yours. Or her mum's," and she stood over Peter with her hands on her hips until he agreed to leave with Lydia.

He had to pull her up out of the chair and her legs gave way. She giggled foolishly, apologised, and Peter, seething, dragged her out through the kitchen, past Kathleen and her scornful daughters, into the street.

"You're being nice to me," Lydia said, too loud near his ear. Her head was lolling. Peter gripped her harder, pulling her towards the main road. Maybe there was a taxi rank, or a bus stop. Just dump the bitch somewhere.

"Do you have any money?" he asked her.

She fumbled in her bag and gave him a fistful of change. "I'm glad you're being nice to me. Carl would have wanted you to be nice to me."

Peter said 'Jesus' under his breath and tried to get her to speed up, but her legs seemed boneless. She'd lost a shoe somewhere and her big toe was bleeding. "Jesus," he said again.

Up ahead he saw a mini cab office. "Where are you staying? Where are you living at the moment?" She blinked at him slowly, not understanding. "Where do you want to go?"

She blinked again, and began to cry, "I want to see Carl."

"Oh fuck off Lydia. Really. Fuck OFF. Where do you want to go?" but she kept on crying and Peter felt like hitting her, shaking her out of this stupid act. It had to be an act. Nobody could change that much, lose all their gumption, turn into a rag doll, in a matter of weeks. "Is this all the money you've got? Will it get you to your parents' house?" He thought she might have nodded. "OK, get in this cab."

She banged her head on the way in. She couldn't work out how to fasten the seat belt, so he leaned in and did it for her. Her breath smelt of vomit and her skin was grey. The taxi driver eyed her warily in his mirror.

"Go to your parents', tell him the address. Go to sleep," Peter told her and he slammed the door and walked quickly away without looking back. How dare she make it all about her! It was fucking typical. Even on the day of Carl's funeral, it all had to be about poor lonely Lydia. Well, she could fuck off, he didn't have to have anything to do with her anymore. He'd done his duty and got her safely home, and that was the end of it.

He strode quickly down the street but ducked into a newsagent's when he saw a group of teenagers in Chinaski t-shirts heading his way. He felt stupid, hiding. Carl wouldn't have hidden. Carl would have lived his life, gone where he wanted, regardless of fans, regardless of anyone. But then he remembered, Carl hadn't been living his life, at the end, at all, had he? Carl had been holed up at his grandmother's house, hiding behind net curtains. Peter didn't even know how long he'd been there or why he'd gone there in the first place, but it can't have been a happy decision. Something must have driven him there and kept him from leaving, and no-one now knew what it was. No-one knew his mind.

He wandered out of the shop and took his time lighting a cigarette. He'd seen a pub that didn't look too bad from the window of the funeral car and decided to try to find it. Even if fans were in there, he'd go. Maybe it would be good if some were, it meant he'd have something to do, some role to play, just to get him through the next few hours so he could feel like a normal person.

But there were no fans in the pub, just a taciturn barman and a couple of silenced TV screens. Peter ordered his drink and slouched over towards the corner near the window when a hand snagged his trouser leg on the way, making him spill some beer on the floor. Dom Marshall sat with Chris Harris, both perched on high stools, both smiling mysteriously.

"Sit," Chris told him, and Peter did sit. He was drunker than he thought and misjudged the height of the stool, banging his shin painfully on a metal leg.

Dom slid down and handed a plastic bag to Chris, "It's there. All in there. All you'll need. I trust you." Chris jiggled the bag and nodded. "There's the books there too," Dom went on, "And the charts. You'll need them. To do it right." He hesitated, smiled, with tears in his eyes. "Do it right. Promise?"

206

Chris said nothing but stared at him until he left. Then he said, "Jesus," and shook his head.

"How was that for you, Peter?"

Peter looked confused, gestured at his leg.

"No, no, not that. The thing. The funeral. How was that for you?"

"It was – not as bad as it could have been."

Chris pulled a face. "Not bad enough. Not enough of an event, no? All too civilised. No blood on the walls."

"That's good though."

"Oh, no my friend, it isn't. They had me going about the suicides, all those little girls. I got quite excited, but it's not so is it?"

Peter nearly said 'Sir?'. Instead he said, "Huh?"

"What I mean is, Carl's going to be forgotten quickly, unless something happens to keep him in the headlines. And a suicide or two would have come in handy. If he'd killed himself even. Or heroin. No heroin?"

"No heroin. I mean, I think. Wouldn't they have found it in his system?" Peter was faintly appalled at how matter of fact he was sounding. He didn't feel ready yet to expose his lack of feeling to anyone, even Chris. He must have looked vulnerable, though, because Chris backed off, changed tack.

"Ah. Yes. Sorry. It's crass of me to talk about this now. I'm sorry." He paused. "But, you have to admit that there ought to be more of a story here. Young people don't just *die*. For no *reason*. I mean, it's ludicrous. It oughtn't to be."

"I suppose it happens all the time."

Chris made a sour face, "To the ordinary, maybe. To victims. Or the terminally unlucky. But not to Carl. It doesn't fit."

"What's in the bag?"

"Ah," Chris rattled it, "potentially gold, perhaps just shit." He tipped out the contents onto the table. Cassettes spilled out onto the floor, a couple of notebooks landed in the ashtray, all marked with a date, all clustered around six years ago. Next to each date, in halting capitals, was written 'Carl Howl speaks'.

"What's this about?"

"A book deal. A book. And, if you want to be a part of it, here's your chance."

"I –"

"Look, Peter, I don't know what your plan is, but by my calculations, you have about one more year of mileage in this before you either get a proper job or join another band. Less for the latter. Carl died with a lot of interest attached to him. A lot. Most of which I've generated, and that interest has got to go somewhere."

"You're going to write a book about Carl?" Peter knew he sounded stupid.

Chris smiled. "I'm going to write *the* book about Carl. And I'll need your help. Probably."

"And there's a lot of money in it for you?" Peter tried to sound angry, offended, but just came off as tired.

"There'll be some. If it creates and maintains an interest in Carl, and by extension the band, there'll be some in it for you as well. It'll keep you in the public imagination for long enough that you can make your next move in relative comfort – by which I mean that if you wanted to start another band, and I assume you do, you wouldn't have much work to do. Just ride the wave."

Peter tried one last time to be upset, "You're a cynical bastard."

Chris smiled and spread his hands, "I am what I am. I am an opportunist, but then don't we all have to be, Peter? Carl sure as holy hell was. He didn't drift, he made himself. Built himself. And now all his hard work has got to be kicked over simply because it's tasteless to celebrate him? Well, that's bullshit. I know that and so do you. Or you ought to."

Peter realised dimly that he was being manipulated, that Chris had no great opinion of his intelligence, his talent, his loyalty. But at the same time, he was being offered that irresistible role of trusted sidekick that he had enjoyed so much with Carl. Peter felt the parameters of his self image harden and lock around him in a protective shield. He felt the relief of someone else doing the thinking for him. But still he hedged.

"Where did all those tapes come from?"

"Dom. He made them years ago apparently. Bit creepy. Recorded conversations. Want to listen with me?"

Peter shuddered and shook his head. Chris blew some ash off one of the notebooks and opened it, widened his eyes, and handed it to Peter.

The same painstaking block capitals crowded together on the lines. Something about Will. Something else about Freedom to Lead. Astrological symbols arranged around bisected circles. An exclamation point. 'Leo/Cancer! Gemini Moon!'. Chris fished another book out of the ashtray and cocked an eyebrow.

"Fucking hell," he muttered and shook his head at Peter. "You don't want to see this."

"What is it?"

"Madness."

"Let me see."

It was a diary, or it was written in a diary at least. Some pages had normal enough reminders written down – sign on 11am, give Tess £5, 27 bus to Fairfax Ave. Others were covered with spidery graphs, improvised flow charts mapping a trajectory from birth to death, obscurity to fame; a plan, a forecast. There were surprisingly deft pencil sketches of a young Carl with his eyes closed, perhaps asleep. And here was an envelope carefully sellotaped onto one page containing six polaroids of Carl naked in a sleeping bag. He looked asleep in these too, and very pale, very young. This would have been when he stopped going to school, Peter thought. Or maybe before. How old would he be? 14? 15? There was a note in Carl's handwriting, half missing but the other half firmly fixed into the centre of a whole page with sellotape. "–ing famous means never having to sa–"; this last obscured by a coffee stain and a smiley face drawn with a marker pen. On the last page Dom had stapled in a postcard from Paris. Again Peter recognised Carl's handwriting, but he'd only written the address, there was no message, the card was blank. Turning it over again he spotted a tiny stick figure drawn in biro tumbling off the Eiffel Tower.

Chris glanced at the naked Polaroids, grimaced, and put them back in the envelope. "Well, thanks for the crazy, Dom." He shut the book

209

up and lit a cigarette. "I have a pretty good chance of making this book thing happen, and it would be better to do it with your help. I'm off to the States next week, but before then or after, or maybe even during if I can get you over there, I'll need to interview you, get it all down. You know. And soon. Are you in?" And Peter nodded. "Good! Good. I mean, there's no point in all that –" he waved irritably at the window, and Peter understood that he meant grief, the funeral, "– if I can really make something out of this. Really do the best thing for Carl, well. That's the plan." He was getting up, collecting the tapes, putting on his corduroy jacket, stubbing out his cigarette, on to other things. Peter wanted to stay with him, but didn't want to ask.

He couldn't get those Polaroid pictures out of his mind. He'd never asked Carl if he'd been, well, if he'd been *alright* during those lost two years. Had he been safe? You heard of bad things happening to runaways, and Carl had been a runaway really, hadn't he? Most parents try to find their kids, raise the alarm, but not Carl's. Everyone had let him go, his parents, even Peter. And Carl had been so young! Too young to be alone, no matter how in control he'd seemed.

Peter stayed in the pub for a few more hours, hoping that some Chinaski fans would come in, give him something else to think about, but none did. When he left, unsteadily, he ended up getting lost in the nearby estate, but was too drunk to feel scared, and he woke up the next morning with no memory of getting home.

* * *

For the next few weeks Peter expected Chris to contact him. He got excited about being flown to America, and he waited in for the post every day and checked his answer machine, but there was nothing. Eventually he began, in a desultory way, to work on some songs with John. They would meet ostensibly to rehearse, but spend most of the time remembering Carl and talking about what the memories meant, although John did most of the talking. In the intervening months, he'd taken Carl's death increasingly seriously. It was, he explained, a delayed reaction.

"When I heard from you, I didn't feel much. I mean, I felt so tired after the album, the promotion, all that, that I kind of didn't have room, you know? To mourn? I didn't even go to the funeral," John shook his head, teared up. He must have been reading self help books, because all his talk nowadays was couched in these terms. 'Space', 'room to breathe', 'the inner me'. "And now that there's been a break, I can kind of see what it means to me. He was like a brother to me –" Peter rolled his eyes behind his hand. "– we were such a –" don't say family, don't say family, thought Peter. "– a *unit*. You know? A team. Almost like *family*. I mean that's how I feel, that kind of loss. You know?"

John wanted them to support one another. He suggested tributes, a farewell ceremony involving writing down questions for Carl and burning them while holding hands. It was too much. It was too late.

They wrote nothing and they played nothing. Peter was reminded that John had never contributed much anyway; he and Carl had done most of it. Chinaski had been their band, his and Carl's. When John stopped showing up to rehearsals Peter was relieved, and when he told him that he was going to India to get his head sorted out, Peter gave him his full support, offered to store some of his stuff in his flat and got happily drunk with him at the airport. Since seeing him off, he'd barely thought of him.

And still there was no word from Chris about the book. Carl receded from the front pages of the papers. Autumn and winter drifted by, and by February Peter began to think about setting up another band.

And then he was summoned to the inquest.

The day of the inquest fell on the fourth consecutive day of rain. The grey sky leaked drizzle, and people had stopped looking each other in the eye, stopped smiling unless they were indoors. Peter had been asked to read a prepared statement on Carl's state of mind the last time he'd seen him, and he had more or less decided when that was. With the help of his lawyer and for the sake of argument, he'd decided that it was the last week in July, just after the video had aired for the first time. Carl had been a little anxious about the tour, Peter was to say, keyed up, but not overly so. No they hadn't spoken for long. Yes, Carl had had a drink, but he wasn't drunk.

Peter found these drill sessions initially alarming, despite his lawyer's reassurance, "It's just in case someone decides to question you, has an agenda," and it was meant to sound soothing but felt just the opposite. Peter was hazy on why there even was an inquest anyway. In the intervening months there had been a steady but not increasing mutter of discontent amongst some fans, talk of conspiracy, of cover-up. Peter, having these crazies following him in the street, sending him letters, forcing him to change his phone number, felt like he knew them by now, and he knew that they wouldn't let go of this unless it was starved of media oxygen. An inquest would only muddy the water even further – any nut job who wanted to would be able to have a say, badgering people about half remembered conversations, petty grievances, dates and times. But his lawyer said no. No. It won't be like that. It will come out as an open verdict,"...although..."

"Although what?" asked Peter.

"Well. Wouldn't suicide be more likely? He'd been taking that medication for years and knew not to mix it with alcohol but what does he do but take a handful and wash it down with vodka? Seems...unlikely."

Peter felt weary. He knew he was being asked for an informed opinion, and he wished he could give one. But the truth was that he simply didn't remember how Carl was, how he was behaving at that time. He rarely saw him. There was also the tiring idea that if his friend had killed himself, he had done it in the full knowledge that his doing so would confuse everyone, and that seemed in character, even if self harm didn't.

"I can't see it. Carl had too much to live for." Peter said what was expected from him. Young people, people like Carl, beautiful people, loved people, they don't kill themselves. Not without leaving a note. "He would have left a note," Peter told his lawyer firmly. He kept that in the front of his mind, whenever he sensed that Carl was hovering around the edges of a conversation, when he saw the question form on people's faces, when he woke up in the night. He would have left a note. Surely.

And this is what he was thinking as he strode up to the steps of the court, earphones in, hat pulled low. That's what he thought as he dashed past the crowd outside, skirted a sodden sleeping bag and shouldered past a cameraman. That's what he thought as he felt someone grasp his arm and jerk out the earphone. Then he heard Dom say, "Why no note? Answer me that? Ask them that."

"Hi Dom," Peter smiled, still walking, but Dom held onto him with surprising strength.

"Why no note? Eh? Not enough pills in his system to kill him. So got to be suicide, right?" Dom's eyes were dim and he smelled. "Murder! That's right, I said it. Now you say it, now. To them."

Peter tried to free himself, but his arm wasn't going anywhere. "Come on Dom, really? I mean, you said it yourself that it was written in the stars that he was going to go, you told me so."

"Didn't say when or how though, did I? Nothing about that, couldn't tell it. But I've been down the library. Researching –"

"How about Chris Harris' book, the one you're helping him with?

Perhaps he'd like to hear all this, and he can, you know, put it in the book. Get it out there."

But Dom wasn't so far gone that he'd fall for that. He chuckled, leaned close and spoke low in his ear, "That's a cover-up, that book, and you know it. If it happens, which I doubt. No. No. I've got my own book. Here." Peter felt paper being shoved into his pocket. "Read that and then tell me you still believe the shit they're saying."

The clock struck and even though he didn't have to be in court for another half an hour, he gently told Dom that he had to go, he was going to be late. As he walked up the steps he heard Dom saying, "You're on the side of the angels! You'll stand up for the boy!"

Peter hung around the smoking area inside the building, avoiding the doors, keeping out of Dom's sight. He tried to make some sense of the papers he'd given him. It was a thin book – a pamphlet really, badly photocopied and stapled together by a shaky hand. Inky photos of Carl had been reproduced at the bottom of each page, like dirty thumb prints, and above, a series of bullet points:

- *Where was the lucky coin he kept on him at all times?*

What lucky coin? thought Peter. Carl didn't have a lucky coin. No-one has a lucky coin. He sighed.

- *Why hasn't his grandmother been interviewed? Why has she been kept out of sight?*

Because she's a mad old lady and you can't rely on anything she's likely to say? Peter had met her once or twice and she'd been gaga then. God knows what she'd be like now.

- *Why were there grass stains on his clothes?*

Ok, that might be a bit weird. But not worth building a whole conspiracy about.

- *The autopsy report mentions scars and bruising. How did he get bruised? Who was he running from when he got covered in grass stains? Did they hurt him and ask his grandmother to cover up the crime?*

Yes, thought Peter. That's what happened. He was chased through suburban undergrowth by someone intent on beating him up and forcing him to

214

swallow his own medication. That same murderer then persuaded an old woman to leave her own relative rotting in her flat, and then deliberately leave a tap on in the bathroom, in order to make the neighbours call the landlord, who called the plumber, who discovered the body. Easy. Perhaps the plumber was in on it too. And the neighbours. Peter flicked ahead but there was no mention of this, just more astrology charts, portentous quotes from the Book of Revelation and a handwritten poem Dom claimed Carl had dictated to him. It was all madness. It was all depressing. But still he put it carefully in his pocket when he was finished. It didn't seem right somehow to leave such heartfelt stuff on a bench, where anyone could read it, laugh at it and throw it away.

The court was running late. He kicked his heels against the bottom of the bench, smoked too many cigarettes, walked around before worrying about getting lost and missing being called in. It was deathly quiet inside; the heavy doors kept most of the noise out. Very occasionally, the wind would blow some chant his way: the kids outside were working themselves up. There must be a TV camera there now.

After waiting for nearly an hour, he heard the unsteady click of heels on the tiles, accompanied by a familiar voice and mantra, "...Grace and dignity...grace and dignity," and Miriam appeared around the corner, leaning heavily on Kathleen. At first it seemed that she was overcome with grief, unable to stand under it, but he soon saw that she was incredibly drunk. Her ankles buckled painfully and Kathleen was struggling to keep her upright. Peter offered his arm and together they pulled her onto a bench, arranging her limbs to prevent her from falling off.

"What a day, what a day!" Kathleen said brightly, kicking off her shoes.

"Did she go in like that?" Peter asked.

"Her? Oh no. They wouldn't let her in like that. Though to be fair she wasn't *like* that when we arrived. She'd had a few, but she wasn't, you know, like this." She brushed some hair away from Miriam's cheek. "Here, budge up. I've got her feet in my way." She took off her jacket, folded it up and placed Miriam's head tenderly on it. "Poor cow. I can't blame her really. No mother should have to go through this, even if, you know, they weren't such a great mother." Kathleen shivered and accepted Peter's offered coat, "Learned some manners I see? Well, I don't mind if I do, just to take the chill off. No, she'd had a few just to be able to get here. I said to her, why do you even need to go? But of course she'd have to. I would, if it was one of my girls. But she must have brought a bottle with her, kept nipping to the loo, and by the time it all started, well. Look at the state of her. They were very good, said they'd give me half an hour to sober her up, but I'm not a miracle worker – thank you," she took one of Peter's cigarettes and accepted a light, "I'm not a miracle worker, I said to him, the judge. And he laughed, well, not laughed, they can't laugh, I mean smiled. Understanding. Yes." She craned her neck and nodded at the door. "There was quite a party out there when we arrived, did you see that?"

"I tried to ignore it. I saw some signs."

"Well, they were all shouting and pushing when we arrived. One of them grabbed her, Miriam, and was saying all this rubbish, all this 'fight for your son, justice, blah blah' and Miriam got scared, spooked. Thought they'd turn on her. And I said to her, 'Miriam' I said, 'Miriam, you might not have been the best mother in the world, but you can hold your head up and say that you tried. And if he killed himself, well, that's nothing to do with you, no matter what people are saying'. But, you know, you can only help some people as much as they want to be helped." She slipped on her shoes and ground out the cigarette onto the floor with one pointed toe.

Peter heard his name called, got up awkwardly and gestured for his coat.

"Can I take a few more of your ciggies while I'm waiting for her to come round?" Kathleen asked and without waiting for a reply she fished into the pockets, coming up with Dom's pamphlet. "What's this? Oh. Oh this, yes, we got one too. Well I did, Miriam chucked hers. Quite interesting. He has a point."

"I think it's bullshit."

"Well," she handed him his coat with one brisk movement, "Time will tell. I'll take the rest of the packet, eh? There's only seven or eight left, and

God knows I could be waiting a long time." Miriam, as if in response, let out a loud snore and tried to turn over on the bench. "Steady, steady, don't break your neck. Grace and dignity." Kathleen shoved her further towards the top of the bench, left a hovering hand over her hip to make sure she didn't fall off, and, sighing, lit another cigarette. Peter realised she'd taken his lighter too, but didn't have the courage to ask for it back.

Inside the court it was all beige walls, screwed down chairs and strip lighting. He'd been told by his solicitor that anyone could show up but he didn't see anyone he recognised. It was very quiet as he read out his prepared statement. He heard his last words echo, and glanced around again. Surely there must be someone here – Lydia? Chris was still abroad, but had they asked him for a statement? In any case, what statement could be made? How many times could a court hear the same empty sentences: 'I hadn't seen him for a while', 'He often disappeared for a few days', 'We weren't really close anymore', 'I don't know how he felt'. In any case, Peter made his statement, was asked a few perfunctory questions – the same questions he'd been practising with his solicitor – gave answers that demanded no further questions, and was told he could leave. A pager went off and the coroner glared.

As he was shrugging on his coat outside the court, the owner of the pager knocked into him, apologised, and broke into a run as his pager went off again. Peter looked for Kathleen to retrieve his cigarettes, but there was only a little pile of ash on the floor to mark where she'd been. Far off down the corridor he could hear a loud conversation, an argument? No, one-sided, on the phone.

"And when? Fuck. No, no, I'm still at the Chinaski thing. I know, totally. I agree. This is massive. Is Chris there? Shall I do it this end then? I mean I'm here anyway. OK. OK. No, I can be there in an hour if I try, I might be able to get some local colour stuff here too, though – statements. Yeah. OK. OK."

Peter dawdled by the door, looking for any lost cigarettes that might still be in his pocket. The man with the pager came towards him, and as Peter asked him for a cigarette, he said, "Peter? The drummer?"

"Yes."

"Press. I saw you in there. Heard the news? Can I get a statement?"

"No. Take what I said in there."

"No, not on that. Did you not hear? I would've thought you'd hear before us – Kurt Cobain's dead. Shot." He waited, expecting a big reaction, didn't get it, and so continued, "Shot himself in the head. Brutal. You knew him right?"

"Well. I *met* him."

"Lucky for me I'm here, I've got someone who actually knew the guy! OK, can you give me a reaction, on the spot, from the gut, you know."

"Not really, I mean, it's –"

The journalist was exasperated, peevish, "It's pretty big fucking news. Puts all this –" he gestured towards the courts, "– into perspective. Blowing your head off beats ODing on epilepsy pills any day."

Peter winced. "Don't get nasty about it."

The journalist scowled at him and threw open the doors, a few cameras took his photo, thinking he might be someone important.

"Kurt Cobain just died!" he announced to the small crowd, and Peter heard a flurry of excitement, some gasps, some wails. The cameras turned to the Chinaski fans, stunned and crying. "It's obviously a shock, but can you give me your reaction?"

A frail looking girl gasped out the words, "He was so important. Nirvana were like our Beatles, he was like our John Lennon. I can't believe it!"

Peter stepped outside into the sudden noise of photographers, the sudden bursts of lights. His cigarette was burning unevenly and smoke drifted into his left eye, making it water suddenly. As he winced and rubbed it there was a flurry of camera shutters, quick, loud, like beating wings, and on the third page of the eight-page special on Kurt Cobain's death in Melody Maker the next day, there he was, fixed for all time with a caption – 'Friend Peter Hamilton wipes away tears after hearing the news'.

Attracted by the activity, more people soon collected around the door of the court. The girls in Dom's little prayer circle ditched their Justice for

Carl banners and turned instead, tearfully, to the cameras. They hugged each other, vying to describe their grief. Dom tried to shout over them with his own cracked chant – something about murder, something about Carl – but he wasn't powerful enough. On the evening news you could just see his ragged profile over one girl's shoulder, holding a sign turned away from the camera. A few people watching thought he looked a little old to be a Nirvana fan. But then, Kurt Cobain touched so many lives, was such an icon, would be so missed. It was a sad day.

Later that night, after issuing an official statement via DCG, after taking a phone call from John in India ("Weird, weird shit. It's even made the news over here. It's like Kennedy was shot or something. I haven't paid for a drink all night."), Peter looked at the nearly empty vodka bottle in front of him and thought, 'I'm free'. Perhaps he could start another band now, something more – oh fuck it just say it – something more friendly, more amenable, more...more *him*. Chinaski had been Carl's band, always. But Peter could put that behind him, he could play guitar now too. Why not? What was to stop him?

That night he dreamed that he was walking up the stairs to Freida and Ian's office at Deep Focus, but when he opened the door it was pitch black and freezing. He groped for the light switch, felt frost on his fingertips, could see his breath billowing. It wasn't Freida's office, but Peter's own rehearsal room, the one in his parents' basement, and everything was covered in that fine frost. Peter saw that the window was open, the wind was howling through the gap and tried to shut it, but, struggling, finally realised that the sash had been broken and the pulley system cut. In his dream he fell asleep, waking up shaking on the old broken sofa, facing his first drum kit. It was dark now, except for an anglepoise light in the corner, and underneath the light was Carl. Carl with his back to the room, hunched, his head at an unnatural angle, grass stains on his socks. And Peter felt dread as he found himself moving towards him, he heard the sound of his own pumping blood and he knew, with a dreadful certainty, that once that pounding stopped, Carl would turn to look at him. He tried to shout, but, as so often happens in dreams, no sound escaped his lips. The pounding got louder and louder. He was close enough now to touch Carl's frozen shoulder, to feel for a pulse, but the thought of touching him was horrifying. Carl's head twitched suddenly, drops of dark blood splattered onto the floor beside him and Peter screamed, screamed, screamed himself awake.

The Evening Chronicle

Friday 8 April 1994.

HOWELL INQUEST RECORDS OPEN VERDICT

Carl Howell, singer with the band Chinaski, died of an overdose of epilepsy and anti-depressant medication, combined with excessive alcohol consumption, an inquest has heard. Howell, 24, was over three times over the drink drive limit and had taken more than five times the recommended dosage of Epilim and Prozac.

The inquest, which took place today, has recorded the singer's death as an open verdict.

Howell was found at his grandmother's flat in August last year by neighbours. He had been dead for more than three days.

The court returned an open verdict after hearing that the family had had no concerns over his mental state, no suicide note was found and there were no suspicious circumstances.

His father told Bridgeton Coronor's Court: "He was a talented boy who came from a loving family. He showed no sign of distress or depression the last times I saw him. How and why this happened is a complete mystery to me."

His mother had to be escorted from the court after becoming distressed.

The court heard that Howell was in the habit of disappearing for days at a time. When asked if he had been concerned, his band mate, Peter Hamilton, said: "This wasn't the first time he'd gone off without telling anybody. I just assumed that it was just like all the other times, and that he needed some time on his own. Nobody expected this."

Howell had been recently prescribed Prozac, to help him combat anxiety and depression, the court heard. His doctor, Dr Ben Biskind, told the court that Mr Howell was aware that mixing either his anti-depressants or his epilepsy medication with alcohol was unwise. "We had a talk about it, and he assured me that he didn't drink anyway because of the Epilim. I had no reason to doubt him."

Howell's grandmother, May, was the last person known to have seen him alive, but she was unable to attend the hearing or give a statement for health reasons.

The court was briefly suspended when a fan burst in on proceedings. A 48-year-old male was arrested and later released without charge.

24

A year or so later, Peter ran into Sean at a party. By now, Sean was in demand as a photographer, and had just come back from documenting Lollapalooza. The portraits of Courtney Love he'd taken to accompany Chris Harris' recent exclusive interview had been well received, getting him fashion commissions and a Vanity Fair spread that Chris was planning to do on the OJ Simpson case. Sean was Chris' preferred photographer nowadays, and they thrived together.

Peter's new band was also attracting the right kind of attention – TV spots on some of the less frivolous music shows, talk of a Mercury nomination. Interviewers still sometimes asked him about Carl, but it was becoming rarer.

It was one of those parties where everyone knows half of the people in the room, so there isn't much motivation to mingle. They hedged about each other for an hour or so, exchanging a nod, but probably neither of them would have bothered to talk to the other had they not found themselves in the same dull, braying group for longer than was comfortable.

Peter congratulated Sean on the Courtney Love portraits. Sean told a series of amusing, but obviously well-used stories about the difficulties of working with her, but when he'd finished, he looked unhappy, edgy, and there was an awkward pause. Peter thought about calling it quits and going to the bar, but Sean spoke suddenly,

"I'm sorry about the book. The Chinaski book? I'm sorry about that. It just – things, events just seemed to take over. The Nirvana thing, you know. And all the rest of it. Chris has been so busy. Really." A look of irritation crossed his face, "But I don't have to make excuses for Chris. We were all depending on him to make it happen, and it's not my fault if it hasn't. I am sorry though. It might be too late now. I mean, you have other stuff going on, we're really busy – I mean. I mean, we've probably missed the boat on it, you know what I mean?" He looked miserably at his boots. He looked so miserable that Peter felt like being magnanimous. In truth he'd practically forgotten about the book idea. Sean was right, they had all had a lot of other things to think about, the book had fallen by the wayside, and perhaps that was a good thing in the long run – stopped them being tethered to the past. On the other hand – well, Sean didn't know that Peter had written the idea off, had forgotten about it. And if Sean didn't know, then Chris wouldn't either. Peter felt a strong need to make Sean, and by extension, Chris, feel guilty.

"I'm not going to lie, I'm disappointed about that," he began, "I thought he, Carl I mean, was owed that," and he let it lie at Sean's feet to see what he'd do with it. The silence grew. It was long enough for Peter to nearly finish his drink, long enough to regret starting this game in the first place. Eventually Sean said quietly,

"I don't blame you. But...events," he made a vague gesture. "The more I see of this stuff, fame and all that stuff, the more I think that Carl would have hated it anyway. And then I thought, if he'd have ended up hating it, what's the point in doing a book to make him more famous. I mean, that's even more disrespectful when you think about it."

"That's pretty convoluted."

Sean passed his hand through his hair, "Yeah. Maybe I'm just trying to let myself off the hook. I don't know. If I'd pushed it more with Chris, maybe it would have happened. But I'm not even too sure of that, really. I work for Chris, if I'm honest, not really with him, I mean I don't have much sway over him, you know. It's all..."

"You just do as you're told?"

Sean looked hurt, then resigned. "Maybe. Yes. But then, we all do, don't we? We all do what Chris tells us, when we're with him. You guys did. Carl did. And maybe that's it, why the book would be...dishonest in some way. You see, Carl did what Chris wanted for a while, and it all worked out well, but honestly, could you see Carl doing that forever? Bowing down? And Chris gets bored of the same people after a while, you know that. He doesn't like to play the same game for too long. Doing the book would have been Chris' deal, not yours or Carl's. It was all about him making a star, I think he even came up with the idea before, before Carl – you know – died. But looking at it now, I really don't think Carl could have handled getting more famous. And. Oh I don't know. Look, if you want him to do the book I'll do my best to make it happen, honestly. I will," he rubbed his head again. He's losing his hair, Peter realised, he looks older. "But, it is too late now to capitalise on – you know –"

"His death?"

Sean winced, and that was answer enough. Peter felt suddenly very tired. It always made him tired to think about Carl. The orderly files of his mind would shuffle themselves together, events magnifying, merging, and some disappearing completely. His internal narrative became muddled – was he a good guy? Had he grieved enough? At all? Had Carl used him, taken him for a fool? Was there still a debt owed? Or were they finally square?

Sean was looking at him and Peter wanted out of the conversation. "Mate, don't worry. It's too late. You're right. No use pretending it's not. Tell Chris I said so, not that, you know, he'll be worried or anything."

"Oh, Christ! Chris won't be worried," Sean laughed, relieved.

* * *

Pitchfork 2012.

EXCLUSIVE INTERVIEW WITH LEGENDARY JOURNALIST CHRIS HARRIS

Chris Harris is the epitome of the 90s rock writer. Lean and nicotine stained, the companion of rock luminaries like Kurt Cobain, Eddie Vedder and Peri Farrell, Harris was one of the

biggest stars of NME before he decamped to the United States
in 1994 to forge a freelance career as Profiler Du Jour. His
interviews with such disparate figures as Barbara Streisand,
George W Bush and OJ Simpson have attracted praise and
censure in equal measure. He has been tipped for the Pulitzer
and, infamously, threatened with deportation live on Fox News
by Carl Rove.

It's easy to get sidetracked by the peculiarities of Harris' history
– as well as the playful way he has of inflating or debunking
the various myths surrounding him. Born Charles Christopher
Transcombe-Harris, he is the son of a stockbroker and is the
younger brother of Bernard Transcombe-Harris, conservative
MP for Yeovil East. He kicked against his comfortable bourgeois
roots from the start, expelled from Merchant Taylors' School – he
claims – for setting fire to the sports hall and being briefly jailed
for shoplifting. Arriving at the now defunct Sounds magazine
in 1985, he lied about his previous experience as a journalist
and faked a letter of recommendation from Chrissie Hynde.
Unfortunately his editor knew Ms Hynde personally and was
quickly able to see through the ruse. Harris' obvious desperation
to get into music journalism impressed him, however, and he was
taken on as an intern. Stories of Harris' exploits at Sounds are
legion and eventually he was sacked for filling the office with
helium during an editorial meeting – though some claim that he
was actually let go for tardiness and an increasingly serious drug
problem. Harris was immediately taken on by NME, and began
a career of nurturing up-and-coming bands, like Nirvana, Pearl
Jam and Oasis. At root, he is a tenacious and dedicated writer,
currently preparing a book detailing his life (so far) as chronicler
of what he terms as 'the Outsiders Inside'. I caught up with him
on a crackly phone line from his home in New York, to talk about
his notorious past.

You started as a rock journalist. What drew you to that?
Oh I think sibling rivalry. My elder brother was the Good One.
I had to carve some space for myself, and the only thing to do

was go bad. And as luck would have it, I was very good at being
bad. And, you know, being bad and rock and roll go hand in hand.
Also at school I was a chorister and I think in a strange way
that's where my appreciation of music and hierarchy comes from.
There is something beautiful in the collective working together,
don't you think? To produce a sacred sound?

You said recently that you see yourself more as an archivist
than as a journalist.

I see my job as capturing the essence of the subject. It might look
like a common or garden bug, until you see it preserved in amber.
There are a lot of things that capture your imagination and you
think, 'Oh, God, I really have to pin that down for posterity'. Of
course in the long run, you find yourself running down a lot of
blind alleys, chasing rainbows, but there are some genuine points
of light there, that I think I've saved for you ungrateful ingrates.

In the early days you made your name first with a British
band called Chinaski, and then later with Nirvana. Peter
Hamilton, Chinaski's drummer, has of course gone on to
greater things as the guitarist in the multi award winning
group Silencer. What was it that attracted you to Chinaski in
the first place?

It's funny because Peter asked me this himself a few months
ago when Silencer were over here. I feel like being a little more
honest with you than I was with him. I think it was for two
reasons. Chinaski were quite good, is the first. And the second
was that, frankly, at the time, I fancied the idea of managing a
band – seeing it through to being huge. It was pretty obvious that
they were never really going to be huge, but they got pretty big.

Thanks to you.

Yes. Well, it was a bit of an experiment, and it taught me a lot. Not
least that I loved journalism more than micromanaging teenagers.
But I might even have stuck with it if the singer hadn't died. But,
of course, after that, the whole thing was shot. And then I fell in
with Nirvana and experienced what a really huge band was like
from the inside, and it was like living in a tank – very unwieldy,

227

very claustrophobic and an easy target. And that experience put me off music management, not necessarily covering music, but being the boss, being responsible.

I'm glad you're being honest! What did you tell Peter Hamilton?

(Laughs) Well, I probably said something a little less bald. Something about us all being young and idealistic. I imagine I said something like that.

Nowadays, when you cover music, you cover the mainstream, even interviewing Barbara Streisand for Vanity Fair. What's changed?

My priorities darling. If it's good, if it's quality, then it stands the test of time. Hence U2, Coldplay, REM. And Barbara Streisand.

And all the rest is...?

Well – maybe not as valuable. If, say, Chinaski had been as valuable, they would have stood the test of time, whether the singer died or not. Just look at Nirvana – they still shift a tremendous amount of units every year, they're an industry in themselves twenty years later. A band like Silencer, too, who appeal to a huge amount of people across the board, from an industry point of view, they're the gift that keeps on giving. They're not exclusive, they're not inaccessible, they're just good. And that's why they've done so well, because they have a very inclusive sound. I'm a big believer in meritocracy.

And that's why you live in America now?

Why else? America is where the dreams haven't died. They might be on life support, but they're clinging on. Like me!

August. Years later.

Over the years, Peter had come to hate award ceremonies. They were always the same: all the glitter and excitement kept carefully in camera range while the TV audiences never see the scuffed gaffer tape holding down the cables, the swaying sets, the camera rigs. They never see the queues for the toilets, the crumpled styrofoam cups in the pock marked green rooms, the scattering of cigarette butts on the red carpet, the drunks being led out through fire exits. When he was younger, and Silencer were first getting big, it's true that he'd enjoyed them, because it had all been new. Even the seediness of them had a glamour to it. Now though, with six albums under his belt and a greatest hits compilation to promote, he'd had enough. Everywhere he looked he saw the same jaded eyes in the same faces. He'd seen the same fashions come and go, each more post-modern and ironic than the next. His interviews had become indistinguishable from one another; the same questions in the same hotel rooms with the same flowers and the anxious PA, the inflated room service tab, the bad mirrors that he swore made him look older than he was. He was tired. It made him tired.

He was seated just left of the main apron, a little too close to the speakers that played havoc with his tinnitus. A drunk was sitting in front of him, looking for all the world as if someone had stuffed a vagrant into a Tom Ford suit. The drunk listed to the side, and shouted things in a hearty but cracked voice, attracting glances and disapproval. During the Best Video With A Message award, he had to be shushed; and later, during the Best Emerging Artist preamble, Peter saw him stumbling down the aisle on the arm of a teenage usher. Peter had already been on stage to give out the award for Best Single, had already mimed to a medley of hits designed to drum up enthusiasm for the compilation. By the time the man was escorted out, Peter was anxious to leave, have a few drinks, go somewhere quiet. God he was old. Was he old? He ducked out early for a cigarette.

The designated smoking area was mercifully empty. There was only one other person there, the same man he'd seen leave earlier, but a few cigarettes in the fresh air seemed to have sobered him up. Not many of us smokers left, Peter thought, and he gazed at the man's back, rippling with coughs now. Peter himself had tried everything – hypnotherapy, nicotine patches, those fake plastic cigarettes that were meant to give you the same feeling but without all the nicotine, but nothing had worked. He couldn't shake the habit, and if anything it was getting worse. If he woke up in the night now, he'd reach for a cigarette without even turning on the light. He remembered, long ago, Carl Howell bragging that he was such an addict that he had to smoke in the shower. Carl had started Peter smoking in the first place, teaching him how to inhale, thumping him on the back when he coughed. Carl had bought him a packet of Marlboro Reds on his 16th birthday – wrapped up in shiny paper and tied with a dainty, ironic bow. It's funny the things you remember, little things. He remembered too that he'd kept the box and the ribbon after he'd smoked all the cigarettes, hidden it away as a precious thing. Anything from Carl seemed precious when he was that age, seemed like it might become a relic. Christ, that was nearly thirty years ago. Lately he was thinking a lot about the old days, the beginning. The other day in some green room or another he'd found himself humming a Chinaski song. 'Alloyed', he'd noticed, had turned up in some Top 50 albums of the 90s list on Pitchfork. It was number 46. Everything comes round, everything reappears. Even things you thought you'd forgotten, surpassed.

When the event finally ended and the smoking area began to fill up. Peter found himself pushed up towards the fire exit, next to the coughing man. A waiter came through, and the coughing man swiped two glasses of champagne from the tray without even looking – like he'd just sensed the alcohol near him, and struck like a parched animal. Peter managed to get one too, just as the waiter was moving away, but someone jogged his elbow and the drink slopped over onto his hand, soaking his lighter. Shit. It would dry out, but not for a while, and now he'd have to *ask* someone for a light and they might want to *talk* to him. The crowd pushed him further into the coughing man, not coughing now, but talking loudly on his phone, braying almost. Almost familiar, that laugh. Peter tapped him on the shoulder and asked for a light. If the man was busy on the phone then he wouldn't want to talk to Peter even if he knew who he was. Which he surely wouldn't, he was too old. Some industry investor maybe, or an aged producer.

The man flapped an arm irritably at Peter, without looking at him. "Some *cunt* keeps *hitting* me. I'm serious!" And Peter, taking offence, poked his head over the man's shoulder, mouthing 'light?' to show him that he wasn't a cunt. He was, in fact, quite famous. And then he saw the man's face, and it was Chris Harris.

When had they last seen each other? Christ – five years? No, more like ten. More? Peter studied him, trying to peel off the years: his hair had receded more, but not by much; he was still reasonably lean. It was only the face, really, that was different. His eyelids dragged down, meeting the rivulets of lines running down his cheeks, sinking into folds at the neck. How old would he be now? 55? More? Peter waited for recognition to dawn on his face, but it didn't happen, he just looked vague and annoyed. A tinny voice came out of his phone and Chris kept his dim eyes on Peter while switching ears.

"I don't know where they are, and I couldn't give a shit. Frankly. I've been with those vapid bitches for a fucking *lifetime* and I'm taking a break." Chris absently handed Peter his lighter, swapped ears again, "They didn't have credibility when they were *young*. And *thin*. And now – no. I might tomorrow, but if I have to hear anything more about their dietary requirements or their fucking C-sections, I'll shoot one of them. The fattest one. I'll shoot her. You know I will."

Peter handed the lighter back, Chris took it and seemed to see him for the first time, "There's someone here from my deep and dark past. I might call tomorrow. Might. Depends on whether I survive the night." He put the phone in his pocket and stared at Peter, beginning to smile.

"Peter."

"Yup."

"Christ on a drip! When did I see you last? All Tomorrow's Parties in that dreadful holiday camp?"

Peter shook his head, "That wasn't me."

"Oh, I think it was, no?" Chris cocked his head. "Or someone else, perhaps."

They smoked in silence. Peter felt embarrassed, but was too hemmed in to leave comfortably. Chris had his eyes closed. His phone rang again but he didn't answer it.

Peter coughed. "How come you're here?"

Chris opened his eyes and swayed forward, "Some story I couldn't get out of." He mentioned the name of a popular girl group, now reformed. "They wanted the Mythmaker, asked for me. I owed a few favours and agreed. But it's meant *living* with these people. Practically. For *two days*."

Peter remembered the girl band's winsome appearance at the ceremony. They were hawking a greatest hits too. "Everyone's reforming now," he offered by way of conversation.

Chris shuddered dramatically and lit another cigarette. "Horrible, horrible trend. *You're* not I hope?"

"Well, we haven't split up."

Chris opened his eyes, blinked. "Peter."

"Yes."

"Chinaski?"

"Well. Not for a long time."

"God, that band. Been thinking about them. You. That boy. Lately. Strange. Are you off to the after party? There's two. One for the faces and one for *hoi polloi*. Guess who's running the last one? Guess. You'll never guess."

Peter smiled foolishly, feeling the years roll away from him. Chris had always made him feel like a slow witted child. "I can't guess."

"Guess!"

"I can't."

"Lydia! That lumpy girl! The one with the thing about Carl Howell, remember?"

"Of course I remember."

Chris wasn't listening, "Well, I remember her. I knew it was her as soon as I saw her. She did the pre-show drinks, with some company called Easy Tiger Events. Can you imagine? She was even wearing a t-shirt with a tiger *on* it for chrissake. *Winking*. I really think we should go. Both of us. Show our faces. Be fun."

"I don't know –"

"Well I do. I know. It'll be fun." Chris opened his suit jacket and took out a tin labelled 'COCAINE' – "This might make a man out of you."

* * *

They didn't go to the second after party right away. First they made an appearance at the main party and drained it of Jägermeister. Photos in the next day's papers would make much of Legendary Rock Journo Harris partying with Old Pal Peter, showing the youngsters how to do it. It was around midnight when they made their way to Lydia's party, in a warehouse only a few streets away.

As Chris had predicted, there were no real famous people here, just drunk journalists, industry types and D-listers. But it was crowded, loud and anonymous enough for Peter, who by now was feeling his drinks and the lines of devastatingly pure cocaine that Chris had pressed on him earlier. Peter had forgotten about being old, being tired, being jaded. He felt happy again, like Chris' best friend. Chris, too, looked younger now, with the same swaggering vigour that had always impressed him. Together, they were the best, the funniest people in the room – in any room.

The party had a 90s theme. Boxy, muted TVs propped up in corners played MTV Unplugged. Thin, bored looking boys with piercings and dreadlocks drifted around with cooler boxes of beers. Most of the girls had their hair tied up in little knots, wore platform boots and silver mini dresses. Bar staff in Nirvana t-shirts gave out temporary tribal tattoos and glow sticks with the first drink. Scatter cushions spilled out of four transit vans parked in the corners, and TVs were placed in these, too, playing back-to-back recordings of Top of the Pops and Snub TV.

Peter and Chris gaped and giggled, snagged some beers and groped their way to a van.

Once inside, Chris chopped out some lines on a record sleeve.

"Why are there records here?" yelled Peter, dabbing up the residue, "I mean, who would have records in a van? It's stupid. How would you play them? What are they doing here? You had *tapes* in a van. And they're not even the right kind of records, look, Aerosmith...fucking LL Cool J. It's just, what's the word? Anachronistic? No? No. It's just *wrong*. Who would tour in a fucking van, with records, *these* records? It's *stupid*."

"If you're searching for internal logic in this situation –" Chris finished his line, sniffed and swallowed with a shudder – "you're in for a world of hurt." He lurched out of the van and grabbed a passing waiter by his dreadlock wig, "We really ought to have some more booze here. Vodka wouldn't hurt. And the Lady Lydia, bring her!"

The waiter straightened his wig sullenly. "I don't know who Lydia is. She on the bar?"

"The boss. The architect of this confusion. Her." Chris jabbed his business card at him. It said 'Cunt At Large' in embossed gold lettering.

When the waiter came back with a bottle of Stolichnaya and four mini cans of sprite, Chris pulled the van doors shut.

It was dark now, and quieter. Weak light came from the silent TV, showing a hits compilation from 1993. There was Whitney Houston, Soul Asylum, Cypress Hill. And, suddenly, there was Peter, young again, chubby and serious at his drum kit. There was John, the sides of his head newly shaved. And there was Carl, shining in the collective gaze of a paid audience of extras, all beginning to jump and heave forwards to touch him. Carl was a blur, his hair hung across his eyes, his arms flailed at his guitar, his chapped lips touched the microphone, a glint of teeth. The camera followed the vertiginous lurching of the crowd, moving forward to touch and envelop him, and the stage itself made surreal undulations towards their outstretched hands.

The near touch, and then the sudden retreat, like lovers pulled apart. Peter watched his younger self, feeling his eyes water, his throat tighten. Everything on the screen seemed so painfully pure. They were all so young, and so desperate not to look young, all of them, even Carl. Those wide eyes. That slash of a mouth. Those thin limbs, all burnt to ashes only months later. Such tragedy written large in a small frame. Peter heard his own ragged breath, and took a swig of vodka. He heard Chris chopping out another couple of lines. Subtitles giving information on the video kept popping up on the screen: 'Filmed in only one day in a condemned warehouse, the video for Shattered won several awards', then, 'The drummer broke two ribs during the making of the video for Shattered, when he fell off a trampoline'.

Well that's not true, Peter thought, but must have said it aloud, because Chris shuffled up next to him, saw what he was watching, and gave a cracked chuckle – halfway between contempt and indulgence.

"Fatty." He poked Peter in the ribs. "You were such a fatty in those days."

"I was chubby."

"You *were* chubby. Christ, I haven't seen this in years. Can we turn it up? No? Ah. Well. And. There he is."

Carl in brightly lit close up, pools of shadow in the dips of his collarbones, and that bruised mouth stretched open, those blue eyes squeezed shut.

"Christ. It's like seeing a ghost, isn't it?" Chris murmured as the mute Carl whirled and thrashed; the crowd leaned and yearned, while the two middle aged men watched, sitting heavy and still as stone, separated by decades; a lifetime. The last subtitle came up near the end of the video: 'Tragically, vocalist Carl Howell killed himself only months later. Peter Hamilton, the drummer in Chinaski, later formed the supergroup Silencer'. The screen faded to black and then a perky Janet Jackson appeared: 'That's the Way Love Goes was one of the biggest hits of...'

Peter and Chris turned away.

"They shouldn't have said he killed himself," Peter mumbled.

"He was..." – Chris gestured helplessly – "He was – *arresting*. Wasn't he? You know what I mean? Don't you? But frustrating. Slippery." And, as Peter nodded, "I find myself thinking about him sometimes now. Almost often. Strange. You?"

"Not really. It sounds terrible, but I don't. I should, I suppose." Peter drank with his eyes closed. The coke that up until now had had him feeling light, ageless and effervescent seemed to have turned on him, and he felt small stirrings of panic, almost of grief. What would Carl have been like now, if he'd lived? Would time have bulked him up, would age have suited him? Peter tried to imagine what a middle aged Carl would look like, but all that went through his mind was an image of Peter Pan, unstuck in time, with a mouth full of baby teeth and a memory wiped clean. He shuddered, looked over at Chris and was relieved to see that he was chopping out two more small lines on a record sleeve. In a while, he'd be able to think more clearly, or not think at all.

"I had a dream about him the other night," said Chris, passing the record to Peter.

"You said you had a dream?" Peter prompted a minute or so later.

"What? Oh yes. Yes. A dream. Disturbing."

"What happened?"

"I was going somewhere to give a talk, and I was late, forgot my notes,

236

got lost, fairly generic dream really. All that was missing was the nudity. So I nipped into the toilet for a breather, get myself together and sat down and I heard these *noises* from the stall next to me."

"Noises? Like –"

"No, no – not the kind of noises one would expect from a toilet. I mean like –" Chris creased his face looking for the right phrase," – a madman, crying. So I foolishly get up and knock on the door, you know, 'Are you OK in there?' You'd never do it in real life, but in a dream…and then the lock turns and the door is pushed open and suddenly it's incredibly light, fluorescent…"

"And?"

"And Carl is sitting there, but, you know, how they found him. And I realise that there's no way he could have made those sounds because he's dead. I mean, he's obviously dead. But then he does start again, starts making the sounds, talking."

"What did he say?"

"I couldn't make it out. I didn't *want* to. All I felt is that I had to get away from him before I began to understand, or, God forbid, he began to move. Ah. God, it was gruesome, Peter, I tell you. I woke up and was too afraid to go to the toilet alone." He laughed weakly, "I had to sleep with the light on. Like a child."

After a short silence, both men made a sudden rush towards the back doors of the van, pushing past each other into the light.

"Scared!" Peter laughed nervously, but Chris didn't join in. His hands shook.

They stood together, awkwardly paralysed with cocaine, on the edge of the dancefloor, frightened and bewildered, hoping to feel better. All around them faces flashed by and phrases reached their ears from the gloom. They felt blood rushing through their narrowed arteries, the heavy pounding of their hearts, and they were both on the verge of panic, when the dreadlock-wigged waiter swung by and rescued them with his normality.

"You still want the manager? He's over there." The boy pointed through the crowd at a table tucked away beside the bar.

Chris rallied: "Lydia's had a sex change?"

The boy gazed at him without interest, "His name's James. He's over there, I'll take you. You can't smoke," as Chris pulled out his lighter.

They threaded through the crowd and arrived at the table. A slim, modish man of about Peter's age looked up from his phone, smiled at them with his mouth only and asked them to sit down.

"I'm James. Catherine's business partner. Drink?"

"Christ, yes," said Chris, all bonhomie again, "Anything. Vodka?"

"Peter?"

"Vodka's fine," Peter thought he said. He seemed to be understood, so that was OK. The next challenge was sitting down neatly. Where was Lydia? He wanted to ask, but had trouble forming the words. Wait for a drink, have a drink, that might help you out. Drink. Nod at the right times. Ride it out. Peter edged around the table, clinging to it like wreckage, nearly missing the seat. Now, to speak properly, "How's Lydia?"

"Sex change!" said Chris again.

James smiled tensely, "She's very well. But she's called Catherine now. She'll be along in a moment or two. I'm glad to have the chance to meet you first, actually. When I saw the card, I assumed it must be the Chris Harris she used to know, but I didn't know that Peter would be with you. Double fun."

What did that mean? Double fun? What did he mean by that? James, or whatever his name is, what does he mean by that? Where was Lydia anyway? She must want to see them – she's probably been dining out on once knowing Peter. She was that type. Where was she? The drink arrived and Peter found he was able to pick it up without spilling it, and swallow without making a mess. All good. Nothing to see here. He saw Chris taking out his 'COCAINE' tin and hoped to Christ he wasn't going to chop out any more lines. What was he made of? How was he even still alive for fuck's sake? Jesus, he is, he is! Out comes his card, out comes the rolled up twenty. Down comes James' hand on Chris' twitching fingers.

"Can't have that here, friend. If you must, then be discreet. It's not the 90s anymore."

Chris gestured at the dreadlocked waiting staff, the transit vans and the TVs, and raised an eyebrow.

"Yes but this is an *event*. It's *supposed* to be kitsch. Catherine and I realised a few years ago that the new retro would be the 90s. So we bought all of this stuff – the clothes, and the old TVs and we keep them in storage to use at events like this. It's becoming surprisingly popular and we're ahead of the game. But we don't have to act like we're still *there*, surely?" There was an awkward silence. James, smiling, stared at Chris. Chris, eyes narrowed, sneer on his lips, stayed frozen for a while, and then put his tin back in his pocket.

"Catherine will be happy to see you," James went on, "but I can't have her upset." He looked significantly at them. "I can't have her... *teased*. And none of that," he touched his nose.

Peter found his voice: "She's ill?"

"No...not ill. She's very well actually. But she finds reminders of Carl Howell difficult. Especially around this time of year, with it being the anniversary of his death, it's hard for her. It might be for you too, so I'm sure I can count on you to understand and be kind." There was steel in his voice, behind the smile.

Even Chris looked chastened, but he wasn't going to go down without a fight, "It's been twenty years though, surely –"

"Yes, like I said, she's fine. She's very well. But some people don't get over things as easily as others. *You* must know that," – he smiled at Peter – "he can be mentioned, discussed even, but I can't have any *unkindness*, even as a joke. If that happens, I'll have to ask you to leave. And, here she is!" James stood up to greet her.

Lydia, elegant and lean, approached the table cautiously. Her brown hair fell in smooth layers past her shoulders, her teeth were perfectly straight. She looked nothing like the person Peter remembered.

"Jesus, Lydia, you look great!"

"Had some work done, have we?" smirked Chris.

Lydia twinkled, "How are we all?" James caught her eye and smiled as she relaxed into a chair. He went off to find a waiter.

Chris grimaced, "Who's the fag?"

Lydia ignored him, and turned to Peter instead: "How's it going? Did you win anything tonight?"

"He won the Rock Dinosaur category. Pure pedigree."

Now Lydia grimaced at Chris, "Surely you were up for the same thing?"

Chris raised his eyebrows, paused. Then tried a different tack. "And how is this? The business?"

"It's fine. Good. I mean, who doesn't like a party?"

Chris gazed at a group of drunk journalists goosing a passing waitress. "Who indeed?"

Lydia coughed, "And Peter. How are you? I haven't seen you in a long while."

Peter was still having trouble controlling his jaw. "Not since Carl's funeral," he juddered, and Lydia looked down again at her clasped hands and sucked her cheeks. Now Peter was talking, he found it difficult to stop, like a man falling down a hillside. Words tumbled over each other as he tried to make himself understood, grinding his teeth, asking questions.

"– and what happened to that guy –that old guy? The one who – Carl – lived with. You know the one – the one with the tattoos and the shorts. The bald one."

"Dom?" Lydia looked surprised.

"Dom, yes, him. Dom. What happened to him? Do you know?"

Lydia stared at him. "He was killed. It was all over the news about ten years ago. You didn't see it? Some teenagers broke into his flat, or they were there anyway, maybe he'd invited them in. They robbed him, tortured him. It was terrible, it took him a few days to die. It was all over the news."

"Jesus, that was him?" Chris whistled. "Jesus, I remember that."

"I've not been in the country much. Don't keep up with the news much," Peter shook out.

"Christ, Peter, you look like you're falling apart. Have a drink, get yourself together," said Chris, irritated, and Peter ducked his head and got up clumsily.

"...Head out for a smoke..."

Lydia and Chris watched him cannon off tables towards the exit. There was a pause. Chris took a healthy hit of his drink. Lydia sipped water and frowned at her knees.

"You changed your name. Why change your name?"

Lydia shrugged. "I didn't change it. Lydia is just my middle name and I went by that for a while, that's all. Then I –"

"Grew up?"

"I suppose so. Or I needed a change. And how about you, Chris – did you grow up, did you change?"

Chris rolled his eyes, "Oh I'm permanently changing, sweetheart."

Lydia laughed at him. The thought passed through her mind that she finally had the guts to laugh at Chris Harris. Maybe tonight would be OK after all. Maybe *she* was OK after all. When James came back and gave her a concerned look, she smiled at him. It was OK, her look said, really. But stay with me.

James carried a bottle of Moët and four glasses. "We'll wait for Peter, but I'm sure a toast is in order."

"I was talking to your *partner*," said Chris, ignoring him. "All this recreating the past, it's impossible to get it right and why would you even *want* to?"

"I was explaining to Chris that the 90s is proving to be a popular theme for parties at the moment," said James. "But I really don't think we're trying to recreate the past. It's more of a...homage, I'd say."

"Fucking paltry decade anyway. It didn't produce anything of value."

Lydia laughed at him again. "You don't put too much value on yourself, do you?"

Again she felt that wave of triumph, as Chris scowled, fruitlessly searching his mind for a put down. He was just a man. A drunk at that. He really wasn't anything to be so scared of.

Peter weaved through the crowd, looking a little better. He sat down heavily, snagged a passing waiter's combats, and asked for a beer. "Thank God dreads haven't come back. Jesus."

"Do you remember when you had dreads, Peter?" asked Lydia, sweetly.

"I didn't!"

"You did. Remember? You went to see The Levellers and came back with dreadlocks. They looked terrible. You don't remember? Before the European tour? They looked so natty that Carl said he'd throw you out of the band if you kept them."

"Fuck off."

"You did! I'm not surprised you don't *want* to remember, but it's true." Lydia turned to James. "They were all misshapen and lumpy, and someone had told him to put beeswax on them to calm them down and harden them up, but he put too much on and he just *stunk* of it. Horrible." Lydia was laughing now. Even James chuckled. Peter fought back. "Ok, how about when you came to Reading with us, and you had that fight with that bouncer who wouldn't let you into the VIP tent, and he had to come and get me. Remember? He thought you were a man because you had that shaved head, but you were claiming to be Carl's girlfriend."

Lydia shook her head, suddenly serious. "That wasn't me."

Peter smiled patronisingly. "Oh, I think I'd remember."

She shook her head again. "No. It wasn't. I didn't go to Reading. I wasn't invited."

"No, she's right there, Peter. She couldn't have been there. Not then. She was on the European tour," said Chris.

"I *know*." Spit flew out of Peter's mouth. "I *know* she was. She nearly killed me with that door, remember?"

"I'm pretty sure Carl opened the door, actually. I mean, it was an accident, but it was Carl who did it. I just got blamed," said Lydia.

Chris rubbed his hands together and cackled, "Oh! It's all coming out now!" Peter scowled at him. "Still," said Chris, "I'm sorry to hear about Carl's dad dying like that."

"What?" Peter stared at him.

"Beaten to death, or whatever happened. What she just said." It took a minute for everyone to realise that Chris was talking about Dom.

"He wasn't his dad!" said Peter.

"Well, who was he then?"

Peter wrinkled his brow. "An uncle? Wasn't he married to Miriam?"

"Miriam was his mum," said Lydia.

"Dom's mum? No, too young."

"No, Miriam was *Carl's* mum."

"Oh God, it was all so complex, that family. Who can remember all that?" sighed Chris.

"I can," Lydia said quietly.

There was a pause. James cleared his throat and opened the champagne. All four of them made the noises that you're supposed to make when a bottle of champagne is opened, and Chris raised a toast, "To old friends and glorified acquaintances!"

After a few more drinks, Lydia, Chris and Peter huddled together, almost comfortable now.

"It's been a while since we did this, eh?" said Peter.

"It's been 20 years," said Lydia.

Chris screamed in mock pain. "Twenty years! No-one should be as old as me!"

"Do you still see John?" Lydia asked Peter.

"No. No. I think he runs a pub in Thailand. Someone told me."

"I have to say, Lydia, or Catherine, or whatever you're called, you look pretty fucking good. I mean it. Very – svelte. Very. I wouldn't have recognised you." Chris winked at her.

"Well. Thanks. I mean, we've all changed. I suppose. But, thanks. And you look...good."

"I *do*, don't I? And I don't do a fucking stroke of exercise. Listen, want to ask, what's the deal with you two? James? What's the story there?"

Lydia smiled at Chris tiredly. "Whatever story you want to make, Chris."

"No, really. He's not the type I'd have imagined you yoked to. No offence, James. But, Lydia always seemed to go for – a different sort. Hair. Tragic backstory. All that."

"We're not married," said James. "Why would you think we're married?"

"She's wearing a ring. Isn't she? Lydia, let me look – are you wearing a ring?" Lydia drew circles on the tabletop, keeping her hands far away from Chris'. But yes. Yes, there was a silver ring on the fourth finger of her left hand.

"I'm going to have to ask you to leave this, Chris," James was grimly smiling, but Lydia suddenly looked up, looked straight at Chris' face.

"James is the kindest friend I've ever had. He's – helped me. Things were very difficult for a while. Very difficult. And he played a great part in putting me back together. But this isn't a ring from him. I'm surprised you, or Peter, haven't recognised it." She put her hand close to his face, and both he and Peter peered at the ring.

"It's Carl's! I remember it now!" cried Peter. "But he wore it around his neck."

Lydia spoke with difficulty but great dignity, "After the funeral, after a few days, Angie gave it to me. You remember Angie? His half sister? She somehow tracked me down. She said –" and here her voice did break a little, "– she said that it would be my unbroken link. She said it would always remind me of how much I was loved. So now I have both – I have the one that Carl gave me – I wear that around my neck – and I have this."

Chris arched an eyebrow, opened his mouth to say something caustic, but met James' eyes. James shook his head slowly and Chris shut his mouth and let Lydia carry on.

"So, after a while, I gave up on music, management, all that. I was too thin skinned. And, music – it's a young person's game, isn't it? I had to reassess. I got stronger, learned what was right for me. James helped me start the business and it's going well. Like I said, who doesn't like a party?

"Hear fucking hear," said Peter, solemnly.

* * *

An hour and three bottles later, Chris, Peter and Lydia were all dancing to Chinaski. Lydia sang along with tears running down her face. Chris, all elbows and knees, bumped into the table, the bar, anyone passing. Peter air drummed, his eyes shut, his mouth open. The bar staff looked at them with amused contempt.

"Haven't heard this in years – it's good! It's good!" shouted Chris, while Peter nodded and drummed, Lydia smiled through the tears and sang along with what she thought she was hearing, and they all kept on dancing, not noticing that the music had changed some time ago.

August 12th 1993

The flat is cold. The flat is too cold. He's opened up the windows and propped the doors open. Says he needs fresh air. Yesterday or today he stood for ever such a long time in the lounge, watching the TV with the sound turned down. He doesn't want it up. He watches all those music shows, all that rubbish. And the news, he watches that too, but everything else he turns the sound down. I ask him, I think I ask him, why he doesn't turn it up, but he won't tell me. Leave him be I think, leave him alone if he wants to be like that. But I can't leave him alone. Love the boy. Come out into the garden I say, come and feed the cats. It's a lovely day. But he says, it's raining. Look. And I do look, but he's wrong, it isn't raining. But I don't say that. I let him close the curtains. It's cold now, he says. He's shut all the windows and all the doors. He's taken the phone somewhere, but I don't mind that. What's he done with the sunshine though? What's he done with that?

At night we eat off trays in front of the telly. Just like when you were little, I say. Just like before, when you were small. You'd come here and we'd play – you remember – in that fort your grandad built – out of – what was it? – boxes. And tin foil. Remember that. But he says there was no fort. He says what grandad. He says these things to pain me, I know. But I don't say so, because that would make him angry. Upset. And I love the boy. Love the boy.

He sleeps in the room and I sleep on my chair. I like company of an evening, I like the telly. We eat off our knees and laugh, laugh at the games they play. Do you remember grandad and the games we played? I ask him and he does, he does, and we laugh. I like the company. I tell him that. You stay as long as you like, I say. As long as you like. You're my darling I say. And I stroke his hair and he calms down. Like a boy. Like a little boy.

What should I do? He's crying. He asks me, what should I do? And I say, as the good Lord dictates. But he doesn't believe that, doesn't understand that. I feel comfort and try to share it. But he doesn't see that. And he's angry. And he shouts. And I feel fear. He says tell me what to do, and I put my hands out to him. I say do what you must. And then he calms down. I'm right. I'm always right. I must be right because he's calmed down. And he says thank you. Just like I taught him. Remember your please and thank yous.

I say what are you doing here, lying down on a nice day like today. I say you should be out flying a kite on a nice sunny day, not a wisp of wind, not a cloud in the sky. You should be out kite flying with your friends, climbing trees. Kissing the girls. You should be out. But he just stares at me from the bed. All sprawled out, all long and lovely. Looking at me, still. I say don't give me your evils, I say you need to perk up. Lovely day, out there. Play with your friends. But he looks at me and says nothing. Nothing. All that mess on the bed, he's been writing his odd notes. I clear them up. Rip them up. It's still my house, I say. You can't leave your rubbish anywhere you want to, I say. I pray for him all night, never stopped praying for him. I love the boy. Always have.

ACKNOWLEDGEMENTS

Siân Hislop
Jeremy Willett
Charlotte Mann
Lynda Kelly
Anne Naisbitt
Joanna Bernacka
All at Cillian Press

MEET THE AUTHOR

WWW.FRANCESVICK.CO.UK

WWW.FACEBOOK.COM/FRANCESVICKAUTHOR

TWITTER: @FRANVICKSAYS

Cillian Press|

www.cillianpress.co.uk

Lightning Source UK Ltd.
Milton Keynes UK
UKOW03f1357071014

239734UK00002B/29/P